THE
FOSTER
BROTHERS

A novel

by

EDWARD FRANKLAND

THE JOHN DAY COMPANY

NEW YORK

CONTENTS

[iii]

INTRODUCTION

by ARNOLD J. TOYNBEE

WHAT IS IT that we are looking for in other people's lives when we find ourselves wanting to read about them in histories or biographies or novels? If other people's experiences are to hold our attention, they must excite our curiosity; and, for that, they must be different enough from our own experiences to be interesting, but not so different as to be incomprehensible.

The art of writing about human affairs lies in bringing out this likeness-in-difference that binds us all together; and it is always a difficult feat, even when the writer takes his subject from the comparatively familiar contemporary world in which he and his readers are living their own lives. It is more difficult for him to introduce his readers to the life of some other age with which the writer has made himself familiar. But, if he can succeed in carrying his readers with him into this foreign world and in communicating to them his own sympathetic understanding of its, at first sight, strange inhabitants, he will be giving his readers a precious chance of widening their knowledge of life, for he will be helping them to find fellow human beings in characters that may be baffling at first sight.

The foster brothers' world is one in which the modern reader might find it particularly hard to make himself at home without the aid of a skillful and experienced guide to introduce him to it; for the world in which Arnvid and Gunnar suffer their losses and win their gains is the world of the "Heroic Age"; and this world is startlingly different, "in real life," from the mirage conjured up by its romantic name. The Heroic Age has made its name by the poetry or saga in which it has given its own account of its experiences, and this is the only access to it that is open to us. We cannot meet the men and women of the Heroic Age in the flesh; we can meet them only in their literature or in the reconstructions of their life that have been made from their literature by modern novelists and historians. But the *Iliad* and the *Mahabharata* need relentless interpretation, for they are such dazzling works of art that they may trick us into imagining that their heroes and their authors must have been as noble as this poetry is. The modern spectator, as he gazes at these heroic poems in openmouthed admiration, needs the aid of a deft and ruthless picture cleaner who will peel off, for him, the deceptive film of glamour and will so reveal the life of the Heroic Age as it really was. This life then turns out to be both more sordid and less foreign than it looks at first sight.

In the glimpse of life in the Scandinavian Heroic Age that is presented to us in *The Foster Brothers,* we find ourselves in a world of suddenly emancipated adolescents. All the characters are demoralized by being flung into a sophisticated grown-up society for which their own upbringing has not effectively prepared them, and in this unfortunate situation the criminals are likely to score the successes, while the more estimable characters are likely to be tragic failures because they will be helplessly torn in two between conflicting standards of conduct which they cannot reconcile.

In illustrating these two alternative destinies, Edward Frankland's characters in this novel run true to historic type. Turned loose in an England in which the traditions of Scandinavian barbarism are being broken up by the pagan invaders' encounter with Christianity, his Gunnar thrives on seizing opportunities for lucrative crime with an ability that is untrammeled by scruples; and this unattractive "success story" is, of course, one of the characteristic *motifs* of the Heroic Age. Clovis, the baptized Merovingian; Robert Guiscard, the "Christian" Norman conqueror of Apulia and Sicily; and Bohemund, the Norman "crusading" purloiner of Antioch, are historic examples of the Heroic-Age *arriviste,* while Stilicho, "King" Arthur, and Harold Godwinson are historic examples of the tragic hero, betrayed by an inner conflict, who is portrayed in Gunnar's foster brother and rival, Arnvid. As for Astrid, she is a typical woman of the Heroic Age in both the coldness of her feelings and the looseness of her sexual life.

Here we have our fellow men and women of the Heroic Age painted for us in their true colors. But, granting that this picture does arouse our curiosity, why, one might ask, should one go to find it in work of fiction? Why not go to some historian's reconstruction of life in the Heroic Age from the original literature that the Heroic Age has bequeathed to us? The answer lies in the nature of historical records, for these often fail to tell us directly just the things that we most want to know—especially the most intimate things about personal relations and experiences. That is why the people of the Heroic Age, who were infant prodigies as well as juvenile delinquents, chose to immortalize themselves, not in blue books or white papers, but in epics and sagas in which historical facts have been transmuted into fiction, as Vandal smiths used to melt down Roman coins and forge the gold into torques and bracelets for the embellishment of disreputable barbarian warriors.

After all, a so-called "work of fiction" turns out, on analysis, to be really an alloy of facts of two kinds combined in unequal proportions. Ninety per cent of it consists of facts taken from the social setting in which the story is placed, whether this happens to be Westmorland in the eleventh century of the Christian Era or Kansas City in the twentieth century. A novel is classified as "fiction" in virtue of the residual ten per cent of it. But what, in truth, are these "imaginary" characters who play their "fictitious" parts against a background of authentic "real life"? They are not incomprehensible robots or Martians; they are human beings alive with a human nature that the novelist has been able to lend to them because it is common to all human beings, including the author himself and his readers.

Edward Frankland, like every good novelist, is a close observer of the human nature around him; and that, no doubt, is one of the reasons why, in *The Foster Brothers,* he has chosen to place his characters in the setting of the Heroic Age in eleventh-century Westmorland, as well as in other parts of Britain. The author's own home is in Westmorland, in a dale between the fells; the dalesmen among whom he lives are of Norse descent; and in Ravenstonedale, if anywhere today, a saga lover with a novelist's eye can still see "saga types" caught in "saga situations." The writer of *The Foster Brothers* has made a work of art out of his personal experience and insight; and the writer of this introduction, being, by trade, not a novelist but an historian, is very conscious of his cousin's power of bringing the past back to life in an historical novel. In his freedom to recreate the landscape of a past age, and to people it with intimate personal life, the author has resources which are not at the historian's command; and we need all the resources that can be offered to us if we are to enter imaginatively into the lives of other men and women in other times and places. This is always worth doing, because our common humanity involves us in the lives of all our fellow human beings who have ever lived. The Roman playwright Terence makes one of his characters say: "As a human being, I am a party to every jot of human experience." This is surely a saying which we should all take to heart.

THE FOSTER BROTHERS

Breidi Fjord

ICELAND

From Iceland and Orkney

Kirkwall

DUBLIN

The Humber

LONDON

STRATHCLYDE

SCOTLAND

GALLOWAY

IRELAND

CUMBERLAND

WESTMORLAND

Ambleside   Hep Pendragon Castle
         Yoredale
HOUGUN   Masham

Man

NORTHUMBRIA

Lancaster   York

The Humber

Dublin

Anglesey

GWYNEDD

Chester

Derby   THE   Nottingham
        DANELAW

Powys   River
        Severn

OFFAS
DYKE

Kinver
   Chaddesley

MERCIA

Worcester

Tewkesbury

WALES

London

Bristol

WESSEX

Watchet   Wilton
Brendon Selwood Sarum

DEVON   Sherborne

Exeter

Wight

SUSSEX

CORNWALL

Penwith

Start Point

Torbrand's voyage

0   25   50   100
SCALE OF MILES

Chapter 1

ORKNEY

ON A DAY IN THE EARLY SUMMER of the year 1002 a ship was battling its way out of the ever-widening expanse of Breidi Fjord in western Iceland, head on to a cold and gusty wind. To starboard the green shores and rolling hills grew more and more remote, but on the port bow the land rose like a dark wall over the flying spray and towered up suddenly into an ice-capped mountain. Sixteen pairs of oars drove the long ship forward through the choppy waves, but once around the ness the square sail would be hoisted and the wind would carry her across the ocean toward Orkney and England.

Sigfrith, the master of the ship, stood on the steersman's platform in the tall stern, handling the rudder pole; a gaunt figure poised aloof and impassive high above his crew. His face was puckered and weatherbeaten, his pale blue eyes gazed shrewdly yet with seeming unconcern at the perilous coast, near enough for him to hear the roar of breakers against the cliffs. A sealskin cap was thrust down over his

bushy corn-colored hair and a cloak flapped about him like
the wings of a monstrous bird. Sigfrith reckoned himself to
be a peaceful trader, though he and his men were well-
prepared to fight if need be against viking marauders and
there were times, when he touched on some seldom visited
land, that plunder seemed to offer better chances than honest trade. As usual when he left Iceland he carried with him
a cargo of raw wool and sealskins, the property of his friend
Geirfin and other neighbors on Breidi Fjord for sale to merchants in Norway or England, or sometimes as far overseas
as the German harbors, or Rouen, where the land had been
won in the past by Northmen and their duke preserved
friendly feelings for his kinsfolk in Norway and Iceland.

On this voyage, however, he was obliging Geirfin with an
even more important service. He was carrying with him Geirfin's son, Gunnar, and his foster son, Arnvid, two young men
bent on seeking fame and wealth in England—like so many
others now that the land was distracted by war, a seething
cauldron out of which resolute folk could extract gold and
goods without too much difficulty. Year after year King
Sweyn of Denmark arrived with his ships and went harrying
where he would. Sometimes the English leaders fought him,
sometimes they deserted their armies and left the land defenseless. From time to time King Ethelred purchased the
withdrawal of the Danish army with a vast sum in gold and
silver. No wonder adventurers flocked to England like wasps
to a pot of honey. Sigfrith's glance traveled over the ship.
There was Gunnar just below him, leaning nonchalantly
against the platform. He had taken a share of the rowing and
now stood with folded arms, looking at nothing in particular,
very much the experienced man of the world for whom

travel is no novelty. He had, indeed, already made one trip overseas; he had sailed to Norway and he had been received as a guest in the hall of Earl Erik Hakonsson. After that Gunnar had got a passage to Denmark and joined a small company of Danish vikings in an enterprise against England. They landed here and there, killed, burned, plundered, but they did not collect as much booty as they had hoped, for Danes had been there before and peasants and landowners were only just beginning to make ends meet. Eventually they rowed boldly up the Thames to London and spent the winter feasting with Danish merchants in Southwark, a community that had been more or less peaceably established there for over a century. Gunnar had not returned a wealthy man to his native Iceland, but he had gained prestige and sharpened his appetite for further adventure. He was a handsome young fellow, thick-set and immensely strong, pure Norse in his ancestry, though Geirfin's father had not been reckoned a man of much note when he sailed from Norway to take up land in Iceland.

It was different with his foster brother, Arnvid, a few years younger, dark-haired, slim, and with a face almost girlish in its beauty. There he stood at the prow, obviously tense with excitement at being on a seagoing ship, yet trying hard to wear Gunnar's mask of cool indifference. Sigfrith thought that Gunnar would go far if he were reasonably lucky, but he was doubtful about Arnvid. True, his grandfather, Leif, had been of high birth and had for a few years made himself king of Westmorland, a small realm that some said was in England and others in Scotland. In the end he had fallen fighting beside King Erik Bloodaxe. Arnvid's mother, however, was a Welsh servant girl, a captive brought by vikings to Iceland and sold to a man called Harek. Welsh blood—it was seldom reckoned much of an asset in northern lands. What was it folk said about the Welshmen? More than men in the first attack, less than women in the second, hot as fire and weak as water, tough in words and brittle in deeds, fond of song and fond of lies, false to strangers and false to each other. Well, Arnvid was maybe not cast altogether in that mold, yet Sigfrith suspected that there was a strain of weakness in him, veiled by pride and obstinacy. The fact was that Arnvid had always matched himself against Gunnar. Close friends though they were, they bickered continually, Gunnar with careless good nature, Arnvid most often with a bitter jealousy. Granted that Gunnar was the stronger and the better swimmer, Arnvid could boast that he was fleeter of foot, more skillful on skis, and a better horseman. There was not much to choose between them when they practiced hand play with blunted weapons; Gunnar could deal a heavier blow, but Arnvid excelled in deftness and agility when, as more often than not, he yielded to a fit of ill temper. It was natural that he should become restless when Gunnar came back from overseas, mature, experienced, and a sudden source of interest to all the neighbors. Geirfin had seen nothing for it but to agree that Arnvid also should try his luck in foreign lands. He had always been called lucky ever since he shot over a crag, going on skis, and instead of being dashed to pieces caught fast in a birch tree and hung head downward till Gunnar came to rescue him. He was after all the grandson of a king, and there was a chance that he too might be chosen as king if he showed himself in this Westmorland, wherever it was. So Geirfin had put the matter to Sigfrith.

"I have reared four hawks," he said, "but now two of them are beginning to pine. Will you help me to set them free?"

"I have nothing against that," the trader answered. "If I guess your meaning, it is common report hereabouts that two of your sons will not settle in Iceland."

"Just so. Hauk and Helgi are content at home, but Gunnar and Arnvid long to be overseas."

"And where would you have me let them go free?"

"I have heard there is a town called York in the north part of England," said Geirfin. "There most of the leading folk are Danes. In time they may side with King Sweyn and he will reward them with power and privileges. My two youngsters might be lucky if they could throw in their lot with the man who will in the end win all England."

"York," said Sigfrith. "Yes, I have a good friend there called Audun. He may well buy the wool and skins and take Gunnar and Arnvid as guests in his hall. No doubt they will be able to repay him with some service such as defending his goods or killing an enemy."

So it had been arranged, but a day before the ship was due to put out, Arnvid had taken a sudden decision. He would ride over to Harek's farm and say farewell to his mother, whom he had never set eyes on since, as a week-old child, he had been taken to be brought up in Geirfin's house. It was an extraordinarily foolhardy thing to do; everyone said that, and even those who thought it in some measure praiseworthy said that Arnvid was not the man who could take such a risk without either loss of life or honor. No one forgot that Arnvid's father, Torolf, had got into a blood feud with Harek, who failed to kill him, but got him outlawed at the law court. Geirfin had been Torolf's best friend in Iceland, and Geirfin it was who had undertaken to foster Torolf's newly born son. That fostering had cost him dear, for Harek carried on the feud with Geirfin and there had been a long series of provocations and reprisals between the two farms and not a few servants had lost their lives. Harek and his son Grim would certainly kill Arnvid if they got the chance.

It happened much as Geirfin and Sigfrith had expected. Grim, by a bit of luck, was away shepherding, but Harek heard that Arnvid was there and came up with his bow from the swamp where he was shooting ducks. He was as famous as an archer as Grim was as a swordsman. Arnvid saw him coming, but anxious to betray no fear of his enemy, delayed to mount and ride. It was the old Welshwoman, his mother, who saved him by persuading a dull-witted farm servant to put on Arnvid's yellow cloak and try out his mettlesome horse. Harek let fly an arrow at long range and brought down his servant, transfixed between hip and ribs. He gave a shout of triumph as the man in the yellow cloak fell from the saddle. Arnvid galloped away on the servant's horse and his own horse raced after him. He was well on the way home over the mountain before Harek found out his mistake. He had the laugh on Harek, of course, but folk thought he had not much to boast of beyond his usual measure of luck. . . .

Sigfrith shook his head. Arnvid, for all the luck that went with him, was not the man he would care to have long in his company. Even the hardy Gunnar might have cause to regret being hand in glove with Arnvid. Sigfrith remembered Geirfin's advice that they should not keep together, for two men that did not see eye to eye were weaker than one. He had said to them: "You are both rash and headstrong. You, Gunnar, will take anything that comes to hand if for the mo-

ment it seems good, and you, Arnvid, will have nothing unless it be all that you desire."

Gunnar had answered: "You are a wise man, Father, but
maybe you cannot know the strength of the bond that holds
foster children together. It may well be stronger than that
between blood brothers."

Geirfin said: "If you saw both Helgi and Arnvid in peril
of drowning you would first try to save Arnvid?"

"I should," said Gunnar, "and there would be no time lost
in making up my mind."

Arnvid stood upright in the narrow prow, steadying himself against the intricately carved prowstave. The crash and
hiss of the waves below, the salty smell of the spray, the cries
of swooping gulls might mean nothing to Gunnar, but filled
him with a wild delight. Already the events of his past life
were growing dim like the landscape he was leaving behind,
and he felt a joyous thrill of excitement as the oars creaked
in the rowlocks and the long ship cleft the white-tipped billows, bearing him toward adventure, perhaps to fame, wealth,
and the love of strange women. He was recalled from these
thoughts by a shout from Gunnar, who now stood on the
steersman's platform beside Sigfrith. Arnvid made his way
aft over the bales of wool and corded skins, past the barrels
of ale and water and up onto the platform. Immediately he
saw another ship coming behind them on the same course,
its dragon head rising and falling with the waves and foam
surging about the oar blades. It was still a long way astern,
but obviously gaining fast.

"There," said Gunnar, "may well be Grim Hareksson."

"A broader-built ship than this and short by a pair of oars,
I fancy," said Sigfrith, "but they are rowing their hardest

and mean to overhaul us if they can. Aye, it looks like Harek's ship, right enough."

"There will be weapon play if they come alongside," said Gunnar in a tone of pleasant anticipation.

"We want no manfelling on this voyage," said Sigfrith shortly. "If the weather gets worse we may want every man we have to keep the ship bailed. Fighting cocks like you and Grim had best settle your differences ashore." He shouted to the rowers to pull harder, but the other ship continued to gain, though more slowly. After a couple of hours it was within speaking distance. Another half hour and they could easily make out a big fair-haired man standing in the prow. He had a helmet on his head and wore a shirt of mail. Sigfrith swung the ship nearer inshore, where the Atlantic rollers spouted foam and columns of spray over the black rocks. They were drawing near to the tip of the headland and the empty ocean stretched before them, green and desolate.

"Is Arnvid Torolfsson aboard?" came a shout from the man in the prow of the other ship.

"Here am I!" shouted back Arnvid defiantly, but he felt his heart beginning to beat heavily.

"I am Grim. I have a message for you from Harek! You rode away so fast when he last saw you that he had no time to give it!"

Suddenly he drew a bow and took aim, but his ship heaved up on a big wave and the arrow went high over Arnvid's head. Sigfrith steered hard to port and out of the corner of his eye Arnvid was aware of a jagged pillar of rock overtopping the ship and not many yards away.

"Up with the sail!" shouted Sigfrith to the crew.

Grim shot again and this time the arrow stood fast in the stern.

Gunnar shouted: "You are no bowman to match yourself with your father Harek. His shaft did not go astray when he tumbled his servant from a galloping horse!" Snatching up a short spear he hurled it in a high arc at the oncoming ship. It passed over Grim's shoulder and wounded a man who stood close behind him. Quickly the great square sail rose on the yard and curved forward taut as a board. The ship rushed on like a dog obeying its master's whistle.

"Take in the oars," shouted Sigfrith. They watched a third arrow, caught by the wind, go into the sea a long way wide of its mark. A moment later the sail ran up on Grim's ship, but now it was clearly dropping further and further astern.

"You should have thrown that spear, foster brother," said Gunnar quietly. "Where we are going a man has to be quicker with his weapons than a peasant with a hayfork."

Arnvid flushed with shame and resentment. He thought to himself: Some day Gunnar may be surprised to see how I handle my weapons.

By nightfall Iceland lay behind them spread out along the horizon: a line of blue mountains with here and there a white glacier top. Next morning the land was gone, but there was still the dark hull and striped sail of Grim's ship a mile or so astern. The wind freshened with heavy showers of rain, then it died away and they ran into fog. For a day and a night they toiled at the oars. Then a breeze sprang up from the west and veered again northwest. The other ship was nowhere to be seen, but that evening land appeared on the starboard bow, the low, featureless outline of an island. Sigfrith said it was the first of the Orkneys. The sea was calm and that night

they rowed southward between a succession of islands large
and small. At many places on the cliffs or near the shore
Arnvid could see tall rounded towers, somewhat bulged below and tapering upward. Some were partly in ruins, some
were seemingly perfect. Sigfrith said they had been built by
island folk before the vikings took Orkney. In the afternoon
they cast anchor in the sheltered harbor of Kirkwall.

The land was bleak and treeless, but there were plenty of
farms with corn and cattle, and houses clustered thick about
the quay. Also there were more ships gathered together here
than Arnvid had ever seen before, not only trading ships
heaped with goods, but ships with brightly painted dragon
heads, gilded collars, and long lines of shields along the gunwales. Viking ships, said Sigfrith, who had taken care to give
them a wide berth.

"Even though traders here are protected by Earl Sigurd,
we want no dealings with those stiffnecks," he said.

Gunnar smiled at him contemptuously, but when they
went ashore in the ship's boat, which had been towing
astern, he said to Arnvid: "Here you must mind the saying:
'Wary should you be, though not too wary, wariest though
with ale and with another man's wife.' "

To begin with they were busy getting water casks refilled
and looking around booths where goods were for sale. Sigfrith
bought a coil of hemp rope and Gunnar a knife with a handle
set with garnets and a silver embossed sheath that took
his fancy. Arnvid stood by himself watching the folk that
thronged the quay and went in and out of the houses. He
felt ill at ease among all these strangers. Unlike in Iceland
he had no means of knowing what kind of men they were,
whether friendly or unfriendly, and when any of them spoke

to him he answered little. Toward evening he followed Gunnar and Sigfrith and some of the crewmen into a long low building with a thatched roof.

"Here we can have food and drink," said Sigfrith, "but each must pay in silver for what he has, and let us all sit together and come out together when we go back to sleep on the ship."

There were benches and tables down the whole length of the hall and several cooking pots hung over the fire. Casks of ale stood on tap and women went to and fro serving out food and drink. The benches were crowded and in the confusion of men squeezing in and elbowing their way out Arnvid became separated from his companions. Eventually he got a place and sat there, bewildered by the hubbub of voices about him and half-dazed by the heat, smoke and steam. Looking cautiously around, he saw a group of men in mail shirts sitting in a corner and regarding him with amused or scornful glances—doubtless some of the vikings. He flushed up and looked elsewhere. One might well be wary with those folk, he thought.

Suddenly a pleasant voice sounded in his ear. "Are you not thirsty, dark stranger? Here is ale in plenty if you have aught to pay with." A woman was leaning over him from behind. He turned his head and saw a pretty face, laughing eyes and moist red lips.

"As to that, I have silver in plenty," he said, and unloosing a pouch from his belt he showed her a handful of coins, part of a gift he had from Geirfin when he left Iceland. The woman took two and went away.

Arnvid had noticed a man opposite paying with a single coin, but he did not like to protest.

[13]

"A fool and his money are soon parted," said one of the mailed men.

"He might be parted from more than that before he leaves Orkney," said another.

Presently the woman was back with a horn of ale. Arnvid meant to ask her for something to eat—he was more hungry than thirsty—but she was gone again before he could say anything. He emptied the horn quickly as he saw other men doing, and thought it was good ale, much stronger than what they brewed at Geirfin's. Almost at once the woman brought him another horn and took away the empty one. He drank that and soon he had a third in his hand. A man opposite was regarding him with interest. He was a stout, good-natured-looking fellow with a sly twinkle in his eye. Now he raised his ale horn and said in a friendly tone, "Hail, stranger! What is your name and whence do you come, for I see you are not an Orkneyman."

"Arnvid Torolfsson I am called and I come from Iceland," said Arnvid readily.

"And I am Hallkel from Rousay."

They both emptied their horns. Arnvid remembered hearing Sigfrith mention Rousay. "The island will be yours, maybe?" he said.

"Nay, but I have a good farm there," said Hallkel.

"My foster father, Geirfin, has a good farm by the Breidi Fjord."

"You are doubtless a man of good birth, a champion on your way to win gold and goods in Scotland or England?"

"My father fell in battle beside King Olaf Trygvesson," said Arnvid proudly, hoping the vikings would overhear him.

porting him, half drawing him away toward the door. She took his hand and pressed it against herself so that he felt the hard breasts and nipples under the tunic.

"Come outside, Icelander," she said gently. "You are in no state to bandy words or blows with folk who are making sport of you. Come outside and you will feel better." He did not answer, but allowed her to lead him out at the door. It was nearly dark and there was a sharp air coming from the sea. A low bare hill and gabled buildings stood out blackly against a wash of silvery sky in the west. Arnvid leaned against the wall and was sick. He fumbled with his clothes and the woman helped him so that he could relieve himself. His head began to clear; he felt much better.

"Sleep is what you want now," said the woman. "Come, here you can have a bed." She drew him across the alley that wound up from the quay, and into the doorway of a house. They went inside. She kindled a splinter of wood from the red embers of a fire on the floor and lit a candle, revealing a small room with two beds, one on each side of the fire. He sat down heavily on a bench, now feeling very weary and depressed.

"What is your name?" he said.

She came and sat beside him. "Otta, I am called," she said. Her voice was gentle, with a lilt in it that reminded him of voices he had often heard by the Breidi Fjord; women singing while they spun, or churned butter, women who had come from the Isles or from Ireland. It seemed easy to relax with people like these; one need not always be on guard with curt, pithy phrases and bitter understatement, the sharp give and take practiced by the Northmen.

"Are you Irish?" he asked.

"My mother was Irish. It is that way with many folk here, even with Earl Sigurd of Orkney. His mother was a king's daughter from Ireland."

"Have you a man, Otta?"

"I had a husband, but two years ago he sailed away with some vikings and he has never come back. Maybe he is dead, or he has found another woman elsewhere. He was a little, ugly man, not noble-looking as you are."

He laid a hand on her thigh, but took it away again. Had not Gunnar said something about "another man's wife"? He could not remember clearly.

"Well, here is a good bed, as soft as can be had, stuffed with eider down." She pulled a rug away from the nearer bed and pressed her hand into the mattress. "Is it worth five pieces of silver to you?"

"That and maybe a little more," he said smiling as a tide of excitement and desire began to course through him. He handed her his pouch and she counted out six coins which she put carefully in a little bag hanging from her girdle.

"The bed looks good, but a bedfellow would be yet more to my liking," he said.

"Is that your mood?" she said laughing.

"What else?"

"Why then, take off your clothes."

"And you, too."

"Of course."

In a few moments they were stripped and stood facing each other by the dying glow of the fire. She ran her fingers over his skin and he thought that never before had a woman's touch given him so much delight.

With a sigh she said: "You are a fine figure of a man, strong and shapely; it is easy to see there is good blood in you, but I think you have much to learn about what you may expect from men and women."

"Aye, but I am learning fast."

She stooped and blew out the candle. Then their bodies touched and drew together eagerly; his sticky with sweat and sea water, hers soft and smooth, sharply scented with some herb from the wild moors. Once in the bed he was soon appeased, his breath came evenly again; a few enigmatic visions chased each other before his eyes. Faintly he heard Gunnar's voice shouting his name somewhere outside and made no answer. Then all at once he was drowned in sleep, but Otta drew off from him and stayed awake.

About half an hour later Grim Hareksson and a dozen of his men came up the alley from the harbor. They had brought their ship through the islands by a different route from Sigfrith's and not till nightfall had they cast anchor some way out in the bay.

"This is the place where we got meat and ale last time I was here," said one of the men. They went in one by one into the long hall where the fire had now burned low and many men were asleep on the benches, but some still sat up drinking. Among them was Hallkel, the peasant from Rousay.

"Welcome, strangers!" he said rather tipsily. Grim threw a searching look at him. "Is ale to be had here, friend?" he said in a curt tone.

Hallkel nudged a girl who was dozing on the bench beside him.

"Ale for these Icelanders!" he said.

"How do you know we are Icelanders?" said Grim, seating himself opposite.

"I guessed you might be by your speech. We have had a lot of them here tonight." The girl gathered up some horns from the table and the floor and began filling them and handing them out to Grim and his men.

"What names had they and whence did they come, these Icelanders?" asked Grim, when he had drunk out a horn at one draught.

"I forget now . . . aye, from Breidi Fjord I think it was, and one was called Arnvid. We had great sport with him when he was drunk. He told us of how a man called Harek had sought to kill him, but killed instead one of his own servants."

Grim's face set in a scowl. "Where are these folk now?" he asked.

"They went back to their ship, all except this Arnvid."

"And where is he? I have a message for him."

"He is safely bestowed with a harlot in the house across the alley," said Hallkel with a laugh.

"I will see him in the morning," said Grim indifferently.

Hallkel strove to draw Grim out in talk, but got only shorter and shorter answers. At last he staggered up and went outside. After a moment he crossed over and tried Otta's door. As he expected it was unbarred. Very quietly he set it open and stepped inside. There was still enough light from the fire for him to see Otta slipping naked out of the bed where a man lay asleep, breathing heavily. She came up to him.

"Have you Arnvid with you?" said Hallkel.

"Aye, there he lies. I have no mind to have you here tonight," she whispered.

"Why not, my pretty? I have no mind to go elsewhere and

I have to sail back to Rousay in the morning." He caught
hold of her with practiced hands.

"I will not have him wake up and find you with me. Do
you think I want an uproar in my house?"

They listened to the even breathing from the bed. "He
sleeps like a log," said Hallkel. "If he does wake there need
be no weapon play with a poor fool like that. Come into the
other bed, Otta; I mean to have you," he muttered angrily.
"Do you think I am going to let a naked woman out of my
arms?"

"Well, if you go early, before dawn."

He did not answer, feeling her body relax. It was not long
before they were both asleep, side by side, while Arnvid slept
on by himself.

It was when the night was at its darkest that Grim and his
men came out of the hall and went silently across the alley
to Otta's house. Grim tried the door and found it unbarred.
He was a little surprised, but reflected that a harlot's door
might well be so. The men stood behind him in a close group
and he went in alone. The fire had gone out and there was
only a faint grayness coming from the smoke hole. He listened
and heard a rhythmic snoring nearby. Drawing a dagger from
his belt he stepped forward cautiously, feeling before him
with his left hand. He touched a rug and felt there were two
sleepers under it. For a long minute he stood still; then he
moved his hand further and touched hair. Now his eyes had
grown more accustomed to the darkness: he could make out
the pallor of a face and that the hair must be a beard. He
lifted it up a little and made a sudden violent slash with the
dagger. There was a slight gurgle and then a splashing on the

floor. He wiped the dagger on the rug which had begun to heave convulsively.

A sleepy voice muttered: "Lie still, dear!" Grim pressed with all his weight on the struggling form; he knelt on the legs and caught a thrashing arm in a steely grip. Very soon all movement ceased, though the splashing went on steadily. He turned back the way he had come. Cold air streamed upon him from the doorway; he went out and stood among his men, listening for a moment. Then, without a word, he led the way down to the beach. He thrust his hands into the water that ran up the shingle and washed off the half-dried blood. Then they pushed out their boat, got in, rowed to the ship and climbed on board. The watchman asked them how they had fared ashore. "Well," said Grim, and added: "Arnvid got the message my father sent him."

Instinctively they all turned to look at the dark buildings across the water. There was no sound except for the chuckling of wavelets along the ship's side. A faint flush of dawn showed above the hill to the northeast.

"Wake up all who are asleep!" said Grim. "Clear the ship, set out the oars." He went up on the steersman's platform and in the growing light the men could see that his tunic was all splashed with blood.

"What course will you set, Grim?" asked someone.

"To Denmark," he said.

* * *

Arnvid awoke to see daylight streaming into the house through the smoke hole. He yawned and stretched himself luxuriously in the soft bed; he felt for Otta but she was no longer beside him. He closed his eyes again, but suddenly

sat up, remembering all that had happened during the night
and that Gunnar and Sigfrith might be searching for him.
With a stab of shame he thought of the agreement that they
should all sleep on the ship. He looked across the room and
could see Otta asleep in the other bed, but on the side nearest
to him a man hung over the side with his head dangling. The
face was Hallkel's, the fellow who had sat opposite him in
the hall, egged him on to drink, and then laughed at him.
The throat was cut from ear to ear and a great pool of blood
spread over the earthen floor and had soaked into the ashes
of the fire.

Arnvid sprang out of bed. He meant to shout, to wake up
Otta, when suddenly he stood still, panic-stricken. Anyone
would think that he had killed Hallkel after the quarrel in
the hall. Had he not said: "I'll be the death of you!" Silently
he put on his clothes, buckled on his sword, took a last look
at the dead man and then at Otta who was beginning to turn
over and rub her eyes. He slipped out at the door and ran
full tilt down to the quay. As he did so he fancied he heard a
scream from the house he had left. There was the ship. Men
were moving about on board. He could see Gunnar and Sigfrith talking together on the steersman's platform. He hailed
them in a desperate voice. Leisurely a man got down into
the ship's boat, cast off, and rowed to the quay. As Arnvid
climbed over the gunwale a few minutes later he saw that
all his shipmates were watching a commotion on shore. A
crowd of people were in the alley and beginning to stream
down to the quay.

"Up with the anchor and start to row," said Sigfrith, as
though nothing were amiss. Presently they were drawing

away from the landing place and following the coast round toward the open sea.

"What happened?" said Gunnar.

"I was with a woman at night. I woke up and saw her in bed with a man who had his throat cut. He was dead and she was still asleep. It was that man Hallkel I spoke with in the hall, but I did not kill him."

"You wanted to kill him when you were drunk, but someone else killed him, meaning to kill you. It would be Grim."

"Grim Hareksson! Has he been here?"

"That he has, and gone again an hour ago. If those folk on shore had laid hands on you they would have taken you before Earl Sigurd and you, not Grim, would have been paying blood money, and no small sum either. Well are you called Arnvid the Lucky, yet you may try your luck too far."

Gunnar threw him a glance of kindly contempt.

Chapter 2

YORK

As SIGFRITH'S MEN ROWED STEADILY up the long, placid reaches of the Humber, Arnvid could not take his eyes from the landscape on either shore. If he had been impressed by the fertility of Orkney he was amazed by what he saw here. Mile after mile of flat country, sometimes covered with forest or marsh, but more often lying under hay and corn, with here and there high-roofed halls and occasionally the tall stone tower of a church. He knew that some landowners had begun to build churches in Iceland in the last few years, but the only one he had seen was little different from an ordinary small house.

"What are these towers for?" he asked Sigfrith.

"There is often a bell in such a tower," said the trader. "Maybe the sound of it calls the people to hear the priest, but I have also heard it said that it keeps away the old gods who have no good will toward churches. Sometimes treasure is stored in towers to keep it safe from vikings."

"What think you of the Christians, Sigfrith? I have heard little of them in Iceland."

"Folk who have begun to believe in this God, Whitechrist, seem to me little different from what they were before except that they fast on one day and do no work on another and spend some time in churches listening to a priest who speaks in a tongue they do not understand."

"Are the priests good men?"

"It is said they are men with power, who can so deal with their God that dead men go either to a land of joy or to everlasting fire."

"Why should the dead go to everlasting fire and where is there such a fire?"

Sigfrith shook his head. "There are deeds that make this God angry, such as manslaying and consorting with harlots, but the worst thing is to believe not in Him but in the old gods. Such men, the priests say, will be punished in the flames, which are somewhere below the earth, just as the land of joy with the house of God, the father of Whitechrist, is somewhere above the sky, where Valhalla was commonly said to be. I sometimes think they must be one and the same place. Perhaps Odin has been driven out of Valhalla, as was foretold in the old poems."

"It would seem that most men must go into the flames," said Arnvid with a smile.

"There are degrees of punishment and with the priests' help some men may escape most of it. As to that, priests themselves are sometimes manslayers and live with harlots, for some of them are forbidden to marry."

"I see little sense in it," said Arnvid.

"Nor I, for I think no just god would burn a man for ever

or even for a week because he had avenged a kinsman or lain with a loose woman."

"Then you do not believe in the Christian priests?"

"I know that King Olaf Trygvesson believed in this Whitechrist and put men to death who denied Him, and Olaf was the greatest warrior and most honorable man in the northern lands, so he may have been right to think as he did. But as for me, I say nothing one way or the other. I am content to deal fairly in trade, to plunder no man who is not an enemy, and to fight if need be in defense of my goods."

Gunnar had been listening in silence. Now he said: "I think that what the priests say is mostly lies and that their God has no power, otherwise he would protect the Christians against vikings and men like Sweyn of Denmark, who burn churches and monasteries and take their treasure. But here in England the Christians are almost always worsted when it comes to a fight."

"Besides," said Arnvid, "King Olaf, as you say, did much violence to men who would not believe, and he built churches and brought priests into Norway who were said to be exceptionally holy men, but for all that he fell in battle against Danes, Swedes and Northmen, most of whom stood for the old gods."

"I doubt whether either Whitechrist or Odin could give a man victory with such odds against him," said Sigfrith.

They had now left the estuary and were rowing up a winding river, gradually drawing nearer to some higher ground on which appeared several church towers, taller than any they had seen yet, and a mass of houses set so thick that the smoke from all the fires drew a veil against the sunshine. More and more ships were to be seen moored by the riverbank, and it was hard to get near the quay—so many big vessels were laid side to side with planks from one to another and goods being carried to and fro. This, said Sigfrith, was York, the biggest and strongest city in England next to London, where Danes or Northmen had ruled for nearly a hundred years, though now there was an English earl in the city, King Ethelred's man. Clearly all was peaceful here: there were no warships about or sinister-looking figures in helmets and mail as there had been at Kirkwall, only harmless traders who seemed to be in no fear of their goods being stolen. Even an army might find it hard to win its way into York, for the place was girdled by vast walls of stone with many round towers, and though these works had decayed and parts had fallen into ruin they had been patched afresh and strengthened by timber palisades.

It was agreed that Gunnar and Arnvid should stay in charge of the ship while Sigfrith went up into the city to see his friend, the trader Audun the Stout. He was not gone long before he reappeared on the crowded quay walking beside an enormous man with a ruddy smiling face and a long yellow beard. He was wearing fine clothes under a scarlet cloak and carried a gold-tipped staff.

"Seldom does one see a man of that girth in Iceland," muttered Gunnar as Audun followed Sigfrith on board.

"I should guess there is no shortage of food and drink in York," said Arnvid. As Orkney had excelled Iceland in good things, so Orkney seemed of little account compared with what he saw now. Gunnar said: "England is stuffed with food and drink, with gold and goods. It is like a beehive where the bees have forgotten how to sting. That is what King Sweyn has found out."

Sigfrith was showing Audun the cargo. The trader walked along the ship; he poked some of the bales of fleeces with his staff, nodded, but said little. Despite his genial looks he seemed preoccupied, and not greatly interested in considering such matters as wool and skins. After drinking a horn of ale he shrugged his shoulders and said: "I have refused other men, Sigfrith, for trade is bad and grows worse year by year. We may be safe enough in York, for the moment, but it is risky to send goods elsewhere. King Olaf Trygvesson never laid his hands on ships sailing in trade, but King Sweyn is less particular. I will buy your goods because we are old friends, even though my warehouses are filling up with goods that I have little chance to market. I will send my men to carry this loading up into the city and there the wool will be weighed and the skins counted, and I will pay a fair price in corn and silver. You would do well to carry it back to Iceland as soon as may be."

Sigfrith thanked him and said that he desired nothing better, but he had on the ship two men, foster brothers, whose wish it was to seek their fortune in England. He beckoned to Arnvid and Gunnar to come forward. They gave their names and Audun received them well. He asked them what they knew of England.

"I know little," said Arnvid, "but my forebears had power in Westmorland." Audun stroked his beard and said nothing.

"I sailed last year with some Danish vikings," said Gunnar. "We came to land in Wight and harried far and wide in Sussex."

Audun looked from one to the other. He looked around to be sure that they were out of earshot of other men, where they stood together on the steersman's loft.

"Which are you for?" he said bluntly. "King Ethelred or King Sweyn?"

"What would you advise?" asked Gunnar.

"For Ethelred things go from bad to worse, yet Sweyn has few men's love," said Audun evasively.

"How does York choose?" asked Gunnar.

"Nearly all here are of Danish stock, yet we would stand for Ethelred if we could trust him as we could his father, Edgar. He was a king who will not soon be forgotten. We were better off under him than under our own kings who were always at war; but now all is different. When Sweyn raided along the coast a few years ago the leading men had no will to fight against him. If he comes again it may be that he will be accepted as king, as we took Olaf the Red and Olaf with the Brogues and Erik Bloodaxe."

"I am ready to serve King Sweyn," said Gunnar.

"And you?" Audun looked at Arnvid.

"I would sooner fight for my own hand."

"There are many that think that way, even though they do not say it."

"When a ship goes to wreck there are often pickings on the beach," remarked Sigfrith.

"Aye, the Kingdom of Westmorland, maybe." Audun looked at Arnvid, who flushed but did not answer.

For many weeks that summer the wind did not favor the voyage to Iceland and the harvest was cut and bound before Sigfrith rowed down the Humber and set sail northward. Arnvid and Gunnar had been asked as guests to Audun's house, which stood in a plot of land between two streets in the heart of the city. Like the hall of the earl, not far away, it was built in part of stone, with thick walls blackened by fires that had raged in York many times when the city had changed hands. Projecting into the street in front of the hall was a roofless portico with a pediment upheld by four columns of stone, their bases hidden in fallen rubble, refuse and mud. Here and there lumps of ruin stood up high above the thatched roofs of the houses, mantled with sprouting weeds and saplings, or sharp and ragged where stone had been torn out for church building. Audun shook his head when Arnvid questioned him about these mighty works. No one knew or cared, he said, how they came to be here, but such ruins were common enough in England and he had heard men say that much greater buildings were to be seen in southern lands, especially in Rome and Constantinople, some built with extraordinary skill and covered with carved figures of men and women. Perhaps folk from those parts had once ruled in England. Audun was not much interested in these speculations, but he did say that his house had once been the king's hall; and that not much more than fifty years ago Erik Bloodaxe and his witch wife, Gunhild, had sat in the hall and condemned many men to death or to loss of eyes or tongue; and that there were folk who could remember seeing Erik's seven sons standing in a group beside the pillars in the street, all handsome young men, arrogant as strutting cocks, but cruel and treacherous, steeped in their mother's wickedness. They had lost York and won Norway, but now they were all dead in battle or murdered by men that had good cause to hate them.

There was too much to see and hear in York for time to hang heavy on Arnvid's hands, but Gunnar grew impatient and kept asking Audun whether there was no warlike enterprise in which they might be employed. Audun said that so far as he knew the land was at peace, for contrary to expectation King Sweyn lay inactive in Denmark. One day, however, he had news that a formidable band of raiders had broken out of Westmorland and was pillaging in the Vale of York. It was to be expected, he said, after Ethelred's devastation in Cumberland and Westmorland two years ago. The folk there were short of corn and cattle and were not going to starve when there was plenty to be got on the other side of the moors. They did not meddle much with the Northmen settled in the upper dales, but fell on the big farms of the Danish landowners nearer York. Audun had several such farms; one had been burned and fifteen of his men killed and the raiders had cleared off all they could lay their hands on. Audun and others had made a complaint before the earl and a force was to be dispatched at once against the raiders. Would Arnvid and Gunnar care to go with it? Gunnar said that he had sat at food and drink long enough at Audun's expense and had nothing against striking a blow on his behalf, though Arnvid might think differently. Arnvid asked what manner of men these Westmorings were and Audun said they were mostly Northmen, but mixed with Welsh, and they had many folk drawn from Ireland and the Isles. They were reckoned to be men of the Welsh king, Owen the Bald, who was sometimes at Penrith in Cumberland, but more often in Strathclyde and hand in glove with the King of the Scots. When Arnvid's grandfather, Leif, ruled in Westmorland he and his folk had usually stood by the king at York, but so long as York was for Ethelred . . . he shrugged his shoulders.

Arnvid was silent. He knew he would lose face if he hung back; clearly he would have to go, and yet was he the man to succeed in Westmorland where his forebears had failed?

What quarrel had he with these Northmen and Welsh, folk with whom he had a bond in blood? And then Gunnar slapped him on the back and said gruffly, "This may be a step toward fame and fortune, foster brother!"

Next morning they bought themselves tunics of chain mail from a weaponsmith and late in the afternoon they set off with three hundred well-armed and well-mounted men furnished by the leading traders in York under the command of Dag Woodbeard, an elderly retired viking. Audun had made Arnvid and Gunnar each a farewell gift of a good horse and he had insisted that if they encountered the West-morings Arnvid should decide what was to be done, as he and not Gunnar or Woodbeard had a claim to be master of that country and the folk that dwelt there.

They rode out of the northwestern gate of York and followed a road that went straight as an arrow over hill and hollow and through field and forest. Gunnar was gay and talkative and Woodbeard threw out a few pithy understatements; they rode side by side, seemingly indifferent to the peaceful landscape, but Arnvid could not take his eyes from the fine farms with high gabled halls that were scattered thickly over the plain. Here was wealth, he thought, here was good earth bearing such crops of corn as he had not thought possible; earth, he heard it said, in which a man might plow all day without turning up a stone; here was house timber and firewood without end. Yet all this did not give him much pleasure, for somewhere ahead lay strife into which he would go untried as a maid going to her marriage bed, and decisions to take under the critical eyes of well-experienced men. He had chosen to leave Iceland in search of honor and he was going forward with fatalistic calm but with a heavy heart. And then the thought came to him that if only Gunnar were not here he would no longer feel this nagging self-distrust, he would feel a match for Woodbeard in word and deed; in fact he would be twice the man he was now.

After a ride of some twenty miles they reached a farm belonging to Audun. Here there was news of the Westmorings. They had done some mischief not far away, but were now withdrawing into Yoredale, the way they had come, driving a large herd of cattle with them and a train of pack horses laden with booty.

The steward of the farm was an Englishman; he did not seem overpleased to see the army assembling on the home field among the shocks of corn, many of which were pushed down and torn to pieces by the tired and hungry horses. Woodbeard had been here before; pointing to the river he said to the steward: "This is the Yoredale Water. If we follow it we should come into the dale ahead of the Westmorings who are moving on the road further north."

"Maybe," said the Englishman, "but forest grows thick along the river beyond Masham and there are few paths."

"Can you not find us a guide, friend?" said Gunnar.

"Not beyond Masham, but there will be folk there who could guide you further."

"Then the sooner we set off the better," said Woodbeard.

"Aye, for you will go slowly through the woods and the Westmorings will travel fast along the road. The sooner the better, surely."

The steward glanced at the riders letting their horses do what they would with the corn. Some had dismounted and were crowding round the hall door asking for ale.

"What say you, Arnvid?" Gunnar turned somewhat per-functorily to his foster brother, who sat silent in the saddle. He too was looking at the throng of horsemen dark against the ruddy glow of the sun that dipped to the western hills. He was conscious of mixed feelings which all tended to shorten his temper: a subconscious sympathy with the West-morings, an irritation with Gunnar and Woodbeard for the way in which they assumed he would fall in with their plans. He noticed how the grass-fed horses were lathered and drip-ping with sweat; a haze of steam rose round them in the chill evening air. One beast collapsed suddenly under its rider.

"I say that we shall stay here and rest for two hours," he said in a sharp voice.

"To what end?" said the viking, staring at him with an aggressive glint in his blue eyes.

"Anyone can see that we shall wreck the horses if we push on at once."

"Horses! What are they but like ships, a means of getting quickly from place to place?"

"Ships take no harm from hard rowing."

"I have seen rowing where the oar shafts snapped, but victory was snatched from defeat. What are a few foundered horses if we can get ahead of the Westmorings?"

"This is war, foster brother," said Gunnar tolerantly. "We are out to take men's lives, not to save hay at a threat of rain."

"If you delay here it will be dark when you come to the worst of the woods," said the steward.

"I am master of this expedition and I say we shall rest before we ask more of man or beast." Arnvid's voice rose to a shout.

[35]

"One hour then," said Gunnar.

"Two hours I said and so it shall be!"

Gunnar and Woodbeard looked at each other. They swung themselves out of their saddles. Woodbeard turned savagely on the steward.

"Get us food and drink or it will be the worse for you," he said.

Chapter 3

INTO WESTMORLAND

IT WAS TWILIGHT when they came to Masham and found the place deserted. The folk had taken fright at the approach of armed men, thinking that the Westmorings were upon them. It was a long time before a fresh guide could be found and in the darkness they went astray in the woods. The sun was well up when they came on the broad road up Yoredale and saw that the muddy places were churned up with fresh footprints of horses and cattle.

"We may yet catch up with them if we push on," said Woodbeard, but even he agreed that they would have to eat and rest for a while. The host was camped there about a burned-out farm, Gunnar and Woodbeard staring impatiently at the deepening trough of the dale that led westward through forest-covered hills, when there was a shout behind them. A flock of sheep had appeared on the road followed by a few riders and their dogs. Everyone sprang up and took his weapon. The sheep scattered this way and that before the rush of Woodbeard and his men, and the riders swung off the track. In a moment they were cantering away through a brush of saplings into the thick woods; their spears slanted down, their heads dipped as they vanished under the low-hanging boughs of oak.

"We have clipped off the tail of the Westmorings," said Gunnar, "but it is not much to boast about, that they will go short of a few score sheep."

"Let us ride on. Cattle are slow on the hoof—we may be able to deal a blow at these Westmorings before midday," said Woodbeard.

Arnvid had fallen asleep under a thornbush. Gunnar woke him up and told him briefly what had happened. "Seldom does wolf in lair a legbone get, or a sleeping man a victory," he said pointedly.

Arnvid made no answer but got on his horse. Already the men were closing into a long column and moving westward. The low sunshine flashed on helmets and spear points that began to dance up and down as the horses broke into a trot.

As they pushed further into the dale they came on plenty of clearings where the farms stood unmolested with men working at harvest and smoke going up peacefully from the house roofs against the dark walls of forest. They stopped several times to get food and bait the horses, but the folk were by no means friendly and would say little about the Westmorings. Woodbeard thought that many of the peasants had got some share of the looted cattle. Toward evening they came through stunted and wind-broken birchwoods and saw a few huts beside a round hill on which was a cross. One of the men said that these were the last houses in Yoredale, and when they passed over a deep ravine with limestone crags he said that now they were in Westmorland. They descended gradually into a much deeper and narrower dale. On either side blackish crags rose against the sky and autumn-tinted scrub ran up like surf among fallen rocks and shaly screes. Down on the flat floor of the dale a river looped its way among bogs and pools, edging past a steep-sided knoll and here again they saw work of man's hands in a low rampart founded on great upright stones like teeth sticking into the ground. There was an entry blocked with a few poles. Woodbeard turned his horse off the track and rode up to it. He gave a shout and drew his sword; the long column of men swung after him, kicking their tired horses to a trot, but at that moment Woodbeard dropped from the saddle and when Gunnar and Arnvid came up to him they saw he had an arrow in his throat. He scrambled to his knees, but fell back dead. Gunnar was off his horse in a flash; he threw down the poles and rushed through the gateway. Arnvid followed him and saw a circular space crowded with grazing cattle. On the opposite side was another gateway; a dozen men were cantering through it on horseback and disappearing down the bank to the river. In a few moments they were mounting the hillside beyond, following a twisting track into the woods.

As the men from York poured into the enclosure there was a shout of "Vengeance for Woodbeard!" but all quickly realized that on tired-out horses it was for the moment useless to pursue the Westmorings.

"It seems we have got back some of the cattle," said Arnvid, looking around. There might be about sixty, he thought. "Little to set against the loss of such a man as Woodbeard," said Gunnar.

Arnvid suddenly felt very weary. He sat down on a stone

and was aware of disillusion, of something approaching dismay. Here he was in Westmorland, the goal that he had set himself already before he left Iceland. He was at the head of an army, eager to fight. They would carry fire and sword across the land and make him king, if he gave the word, yet his heart sank at the thought. Was he a coward, then, dreading to put his life at stake, or doubting that he could cut the figure that Gunnar would think appropriate? If only Gunnar were not here . . . But it might not be that: it was as if some spell had fallen on him in this sinister-looking place, where a single flying arrow had brought death to Woodbeard. Doubtless many strange things had happened within the circle of these old walls, that now lay deep in the shadow of the hills while across the dale the glow of sunset still rested on crag and scree. He looked at Gunnar who stood there impassive, his hands thrust in his belt, watching while some of the men collected stone to make a cairn over Woodbeard's body and others picked out cattle for slaughter or went around trying them for milk. Others were already building fires. There would be a feast and a long rest tonight, and then, what of the morrow?

Suddenly a group of men came up to Arnvid dragging forward an old peasant with a halter round his neck.

"We caught this fellow hiding among the bushes by the riverbank," said one. "Maybe you would like to question him before we hang him."

Arnvid repressed an exclamation of anger. Could he build up power in Westmorland by hanging the first peasant they came upon? He glanced at Gunnar, who seemed likely to accept the idea without comment.

"What manner of man is he?" said Arnvid.

"He says he is a shepherd."

Arnvid rested his chin on his hand. He stared at the old man, a big broad-shouldered fellow with long grizzled hair and beard, and pale, finely cut features in contrast to the ruddy, brutal-looking faces around him. His clothes were dirty and patched, but there was an air of dignity about him, an aloofness, an almost contemptuous flash in his gray eyes.

"Are you a Welshman?" asked Arnvid.

"Aye, master. I am of the Cymry," he answered.

"But you speak in our tongue."

"Few have the speech of the Cymry nowadays, but it was not always so."

"Whose man are you?"

"I am a shepherd of Arni Arnisson in Ravenstonedale, yonder over the fell." He pointed to the skyline to westward, the direction taken by the twelve riders.

"He is a Northman?"

"Aye. All the great folks hereabouts are reckoned to be Northmen."

"What do you know about these cattle?" said Gunnar sharply.

"Only that they have been taken from the Danes, east beyond Yoredale. These that you see here should have gone on into Ravenstonedale tomorrow morning."

"There have been many more beside these?"

"Many a hundred, master."

"Where are they now?"

"They will be overnighted below Kirkby and then they will be divided up and go all over Westmorland."

"H'm, that is all we want to know." Gunnar yawned and turned away, but Arnvid still sat looking at the shepherd.

"Is there a king in Westmorland?" he asked.

"There has been no king since the days of King Jukil. He was a good man and friendly to the Cymry. He strove to keep the land at peace."

"Had he not a half brother called Leif?"

"That he had. I saw Leif once when I was a boy in Ravenstonedale. A hard man and a great warrior."

"He was my grandfather."

The shepherd looked at Arnvid in silence. The armored men also stared at him as though with unwilling respect. There were some muttered remarks that Arnvid did not catch. He felt a sense of power, but also a forewarning of doom.

"You will know of King Torfin, Leif's father?" said the shepherd at last.

Arnvid nodded.

"He built a hall here," continued the shepherd. "You can still see the place where it stood." He pointed to a patch of nettles in the center of the enclosure out of which rose some lumps of rotting timber. "He chose this place where he could best stand on guard against the enemies of the land. One day he rode up on the crag of Moel Fre, yonder, that black snout of rock against the sky. There three men sprang on him from ambush, but he killed them all. When he came down, hard-wounded, his foemen had come through the pass and set fire to the hall. He got away with his wife to Saint Helen's Well and there that day he lost his life fighting, in the same hour that his son Leif was born."

"So this place was a king's hall," said Arnvid. He looked at the circle of ruined wall and now within it he saw rings of rubble showing through the turf, here and there a leaning stone that might have been a doorpost.

"It was a king's dwelling long before the days of King Torfin," said the shepherd. "Here lived a great prince of the Cymry, Uther Pendragon, and here he was poisoned by a Saxon woman. He lies in a grave on the snout of Moel Fre and there the folk chose his son Arthur to lead them in the war. Twelve great battles he won against the foes of Britain, but in the end he was betrayed by his wife and his nephew, Modred."

Arnvid sat in silence. His gaze wandered away from the aloof figure of the shepherd and the jostling throng of helmeted men, from the crumbling walls of the old fortress to the sharp-edged ramparts of the fells, now almost black against the night sky in which stars were beginning to sparkle. A thin fog was rising from the pools and reed beds in the floor of the dale, rising higher and higher to form a white lake in the enclosing forest; its chilly breath flowed over him like a miasma of evil influences, the aftermath of what had happened here in past time. Perhaps only he and the old peasant were sensitive to this realization of man's futility. To what end did heroic figures appear one after another, in age after age, only to be betrayed and to have their work laid in ruins? Perhaps the Christians had an answer to this when they said that it was useless to strive for power and fame but only for the glory of God. And then he thought of his talk with Sigfrith and Gunnar as they rowed up the Humber toward York, when the beliefs of the Christians had seemed either repellent or absurd. He looked at the callous jeering faces of the men about him—all Christians, doubtless, and in what way were they the better for being so? Now they suddenly laid hands on the shepherd. A clamor of voices broke out.

"Come, let us make an end of him! Vengeance for Wood-beard! A life for a life!"

Arnvid stood up. He put his hand on the old man's shoulder and said: "This man had nothing to do with Wood-beard's death. Let him go in peace."

The men fell back a step with a growl of baffled blood lust, but one of them still kept a hold on the halter round the shepherd's neck.

"You are beguiled by this cunning old fox," said Gunnar, with a weary smile.

"Let him go, I say!" shouted Arnvid, and half drew his sword.

The man aimed a kick at the shepherd and turned sullenly away.

"May God reward you, master!" The old man bent and kissed the skirt of Arnvid's mail coat, then he strode calmly through the gateway, none hindering him. Before his figure vanished in the misty darkness they could see him beginning to run, northward on the road toward Kirkby.

"There he goes to warn the Westmorings!" said Gunnar. "By tomorrow morning all their booty will be hidden away where we shall never find it."

Arnvid thought that this was very likely true. He felt angry with himself, but angrier with Gunnar when he said, "You will never make a warrior, foster brother. It would have been better if you had stayed in Iceland."

"At least we have saved these cattle," he muttered.

"We have got back a tenth, perhaps, of what they have taken. So far we have not much to boast about."

"What plan would you make now?"

"Tomorrow we should push on into Westmorland and burn every house we come upon. We should seize men as hostages and then summon the big landowners to a council. There we can demand from them gold and goods; we can demand that they make you king, and in return we can offer them peace with York and protection against Owen the Bald and the King of the Scots. Is not this what you have had in mind ever since you came to England?"

"Maybe it is, but I see now that it is useless to seek power by such means as these. A land is not to be won except by the good will of those that live in it."

"The Danes won York with the edges of their swords, not by English good will."

"In the end it might be better for them if they had stayed in Denmark."

"To me it seems that many men would be poor who now are rich and many a song and saga would never have been heard by the fireside where men sit over their drink," said Gunnar, with tolerant good humor. To Arnvid it seemed as though this customary reasonableness cloaked a pitying contempt, the contempt that a warrior might feel for a peace-loving man even if he had the prestige of high birth. His temper flared up, and when Gunnar inquired what plan seemed best to him he answered very curtly, "Tomorrow we shall take the road back to York."

Chapter 4

AUDUN'S FEAST

ONE EVENING EARLY IN NOVEMBER, Audun held an ale feast at his house in York. Most of the richer traders and some Danish landowners were there and so were Arnvid and Gunnar, to whom Audun continued to show hospitality though he had little good to say of their expedition against the Westmorings. There was also an Englishman, Bermond by name, a trader from London, who had brought a case before the lawmen in York about an alleged theft of some of his goods put ashore on the quay. Audun had spoken on his behalf, but the case had gone against the Englishman as it seemed likely that the goods had been disposed of by some of his own men who were now missing from the ship. Bermond was a well-dressed and haughty-looking man. At first he made little response to Audun's friendly efforts to draw him into talk, but as more and more of the company pledged him in drink he began to speak more sharply and unguardedly, displaying an insolence which, to Arnvid's surprise, no one seemed disposed to resent.

As for Gunnar, he was concerned first and foremost with the food and drink and it was only when talk touched on King Sweyn that Arnvid saw his face harden and his eyes grow watchful.

It was common knowledge that rumors had spread in York, ever since traders from Denmark had been there in the autumn, that Sweyn was making ready for a fresh attack on England in the coming year. Several men asked Audun what he thought of this and he said that it might well be true. Bermond said, "We heard the same talk last winter and he did not come."

"But he came many times before that and did what he would, first in one place and then in another," put in someone.

"King Sweyn would have no such success in England were there not Danes everywhere who would sooner see him master rather than King Ethelred," said Bermond.

"All the same, friend," said Audun peaceably, "there are men of Danish race who have fought as well for Ethelred as any Englishman. You well know that in London."

"I doubt whether there are any such men in York," Bermond flashed back aggressively.

"It is no wonder that folk have little heart to fight for Ethelred when the best he can do is to pay Sweyn in gold and silver," said Kolben, Audun's nephew, who sat on the other side of Bermond.

"Aye, and as long as he gets paid for coming here he will come again," said another. "Was ever a king so generous in gifts as King Ethelred! Not only does he pour gold into the hands of Danes that fight against him but also of Danes hired

to fight in his service. Is it not true that Pallig the Viking is
to have twenty-four thousand pounds for this year's work?"

Voices broke out here and there among the guests:

"What work has Pallig done but plunder wherever his
men are quartered?"

"Is he not King Sweyn's brother-in-law?"

"Can Ethelred be such a fool as to trust him?"

Bermond glared about him. He now seemed very drunk
and banged his ale horn on the table.

"King Ethelred a fool!" he shouted. "Did he seem a fool
to you men of York when he sent his army into Cumberland
two years ago and burned it out from end to end?"

"It was like a man turning his back on the wolves and
striking at rats," said Audun with a laugh.

"The whole land is full of rats, but the King will make an
end of them, and that before long!"

Audun stroked his beard, his gaze wandered up and down
the table, his eyelids dropped and his brow, smooth a moment before, broke into furrows like a plowed field. There
was a short silence.

Then Kolben laughed and said: "That should be no small
task for Ethelred!"

Bermond got awkwardly to his feet. "The Danes are
vermin!" he shouted. "We shall treat them as such."

"Rats have sharp teeth. Ethelred found that out in Cumberland," said someone.

"No plan, no victory," said another.

"No plan, say you?" Bermond staggered and supported
himself against the table. "You shall see whether there is a
plan or not!" He backed down the hall. A servant opened
the door for him and he went out.

"It looks as though the next blow would be against us," said one of the landowners after an uneasy silence.

Audun shook his head. "Here we are too strong," he said, "but elsewhere something may be tried. For the last month I have heard a word here and a word there; it all points to one thing."

"Will you swear yourselves to King Sweyn?" asked Gunnar, speaking for the first time.

"King Sweyn is far away. The time may come when he will desire the land more than the gold he now draws from it. Then we might make good terms with him, but not till then." There was a murmur of approval. Arnvid sat deep in thought. How different this was from a night in Geirfin's hall! There the talk might have been of fishing and farm work and maybe of some unfriendly act by Harek's folk. Here men were watching and waiting while two kings strove against each other; a kingdom plunged down in ruin and inconceivable wealth went from hand to hand. Through this confusion must lie a path to fame and power for the man who had the wit to find it, and here was a moment of suspense when he sat eager and alert, careless with strong drink, in this old smoke-blackened hall, while outside, instead of the windy dusk and the waves breaking on the desolate beaches of Breidi Fjord, was the narrow street, the sharp smell of wood smoke and stale urine, a surly hum of voices and the clamor of bells from pale towers that thrust up into fog and darkness. . . .

The guests had gone. Audun was alone with Arnvid and Gunnar. He came and sat down opposite them at the long table, tracing patterns with a finger in some spilled ale. After a while he said, "You heard that Englishman, what he said when we taunted him about his king?"

"Empty threats perhaps? The man was drunk." Gunnar smiled nonchalantly.

"You think it would be folly for Ethelred to turn on his own men, even if they be Danes by birth?"

"Surely: there would be no better way of driving them into King Sweyn's camp."

"True enough; but if he destroyed them all he might then feel more secure."

"He could not do it! York with its great walls . . ." broke in Arnvid.

"Even so, it could be done. Maybe it will be done some day, but not by such a king as Ethelred. Yet even he could kill a great many of us, men suspecting nothing, scattered over all England. It is the mark of a weak king to give way again and again and at last to seek a desperate way out. I think Ethelred is such a man."

"What is your plan, then?" said Gunnar.

"I do not fear much for York and the great towns—Lincoln, Nottingham, Stamford, Leicester, and Derby—but elsewhere he may succeed. Pallig and his men—they too might be destroyed where they lie camped about London. But you are right. I have a plan. Will you two help me to carry it out?"

"We have eaten your bread for many a month and rendered you little service," said Gunnar.

"And you, Arnvid?"

"I would say the same. What you bid me do, that will I attempt," said Arnvid eagerly.

"I have a brother, Otkel by name. He got a grant of land from King Edgar, who was so strong a king that he was not afraid to show favor to Danes and Northmen. Otkel lives far away in Worcestershire. I would send him a warning to seek safety while he can. Will you set out with that message tomorrow morning?"

"Gladly!" said Arnvid, and Gunnar nodded.

"I shall give you two good horses. You should be well-armed and lose no time on the way. You ride south to Derby and thence along the road toward Worcester till you come over some hills. Thence it is westward through the forest, a place called Kinver."

"We shall find it," said Gunnar, "but where should Otkel seek safety?"

"There might be time to make back toward York, but if there be not time Wales is not far away across the Severn. It might be a little safer there than in England."

"I would not be sorry to see Wales," said Arnvid.

"You are half Welsh by birth, are you not?" Audun looked at him thoughtfully, drumming his fingers on the table.

"I am, and I say it without shame," said Arnvid, flushing.

Audun shrugged his shoulders.

When Gunnar and Arnvid went to their sleeping quarters in a loft Gunnar said: "The old man has found us a more risky task than going in search of his stolen cattle. I see little that we can gain from it, either in goods or fame, yet we could not honorably refuse."

"I had no mind to refuse."

"You have still much to learn, foster brother," said Gunnar, "much to learn as to what is to your advantage and what is not."

Chapter 5

INTO WORCESTERSHIRE

A FEW DAYS LATER Arnvid and Gunnar were in the heart of Mercia. All had gone well; there had been lavish hospitality both for man and beast, nothing but friendliness from Danish landowners and townsmen, but after they left the strong town of Derby behind them there were few more men that they could recognize as Danes, and after they had crossed the broad grassy track of Watling Street, the boundary of the old Danelaw, there were fewer still. Now they were come into Worcestershire and were approaching the hills of which Audun had spoken, the first real hills that they had seen since Charnwood showed up to southward as they rode out of Nottingham. Now every man they met seemed English and unfriendly and they had to lay out money even to feed the horses. Women eyed them with overt indifference, but in the absence of their menfolk with eager coquetry. The houses they went inside were slovenly kept; though there was food in abundance only buttermilk was offered them to drink.

There were no bath houses and everyone went about unwashed and uncombed.

The track led between two rocky heights smothered in birch and rowan and mounted a high ridge beyond. It was after midday when they drew rein on the crest and sat their horses for a while in silence, Arnvid on a big black stallion, Gunnar on a bay; two handsome and formidable-looking young men in an empty landscape: high gorse, withered bracken, dark cushions of heather, here and there a stunted thornbush. Both wore polished steel helmets; Gunnar had a skirted tunic of ring mail covered by a blue cloak, Arnvid a sleeved leather garment in one piece covered with overlapping iron rings and encasing each leg to the knee. It had no opening save for a laced strip down the chest; it was an admirable defense but not easy to put on and still harder to get off. Gunnar had laughed when Arnvid bought it from a weaponsmith in York. He was not going to cumber himself with that newfangled kind of armor, he said. He preferred the old skirted tunic that need not be taken off when you wanted to make water or do other business. "You would look a fool, foster brother, if a man assailed you at such a time, you with your mail coat pulled down to your knees and unable to get it up again in five minutes!" Though it was true enough, he added, that he had seen men killed by an upward thrust from below an open skirt of mail. Some day men would not dare to go into battle till they were sheathed in iron from head to foot, but it had not come to that yet.

Each of them had a round shield slung on his back and as for weapons each had a short throwing spear, Arnvid his father's sword and Gunnar the axe that were gifts from Earl Erik.

Ever since the start they had been off before daybreak and riding till after dark, and Arnvid was not sorry that Gunnar now seemed inclined to rest for a while and give him leisure to look at this vast landscape that had suddenly spread out to westward. The hill sloped down into a plain filled with oak forest, a dark sea of treetops that lapped against more hills rising like islands in the far distance, sharp and blue in the wintry sunshine, blunt peaks, humpy ridges, a solitary tilted crest. And far beyond these hills were the faint outlines of still higher hills that seemed whitened with snow.

"We are near our journey's end," said Gunnar. "Somewhere in that forest must be Otkel's land, and those far hills may well be Wales."

Arnvid did not answer; he sat motionless, letting his horse pull at the wiry turf. Wales—the word was as music in his ears. There, behind those hills, dwelt his mother's people, to whom in his fancy he was more closely knit than to these hard-headed and rough-tongued Danes and Northmen. What did all this mean to Gunnar? The high gorse sprinkled with yellow blossom—that was only cover whence a foeman might spring out; the dusky oak wood—a place where you could fell good timber for building hall or ship, or get a shot at a fat deer; the blue hills—landmarks that might save one from riding astray. Yet all this to Arnvid was inexpressible delight, such as one might draw from the sad song of an Irish servant or from a girl's laughing eyes. He threw a cold glance at his foster brother and felt a pitying contempt for him as a man who knew only the gross and not the impalpable pleasures that met one on the journey through life. But he was considerably taken aback when Gunnar suddenly declaimed some alliterative verse that neatly epitomized their doings and even gave a few subtle hints of lonely landscapes and food and drink in crowded halls.

"I had almost forgotten you are a poet," said Arnvid with a wry smile.

"I have to keep myself in practice," said Gunnar modestly, "but so far we have done little enough to make verses about."

They rode on down the hill. Soon the heath gave place to ever-thickening copses of oak and hazel and here was a goatherd's hut, sagging walls of wattle under heather thatch. A frowsy-headed girl stood in the doorway with a stained dress and filthy bare feet, but her face was pretty enough and her eyes full of admiration for the two warlike-looking young men on their powerful horses.

"Is there a man about here?" asked Gunnar.

"No, master. My father is up the hill with his goats," she answered in a singsong voice that reminded Arnvid of his mother's. Perhaps she had Welsh blood. He looked at her with grave good will, but Gunnar had a meaning smile when he swung from the saddle and said, "Why, that is a pity, perhaps, for we would ask the way to Kinver."

"I have heard of such a place, but it is a long way from here."

"Not to be reached before nightfall?"

She looked from him to his horse and said. "No, surely not, even with such a good horse as you have. You would do well to get as far as Chaddesley."

"Is that on the way to Kinver?"

"I think so. Once I stood with my father on the hill whence you have come and he pointed out what he called the Edge of Kinver and also some smoke that rose above the woods nearer at hand and he said that was Chaddesley."

[55]

"You are a girl with your wits about you," he said approvingly. "Can you give us some milk? We are thirsty men."

"Goat's milk will not be much to the taste of men like you."

"It will do," he said.

The girl went inside the hut and soon came out with milk in a dirty wooden bowl.

"Take it to him first," said Gunnar, indicating Arnvid who stood leaning against his horse. "He is the greater man of us two. He is a king's grandson."

The girl went demurely on one knee before Arnvid and handed him the bowl. He took a gulp and passed it back to her. Then she took it to Gunnar and he drank from the other side of the bowl.

"Now," he said, "do you take a drink and I shall notice where you put your lips." The girl fingered the bowl for a moment, looked up slyly, and put her lips where Gunnar's had been.

"That means you will give me a kiss," he said smiling.

"Would my kiss taste better to you than this milk?" she said.

"Well it might, for the milk is sour enough," he said with a laugh. He sat down on an oak log and drew her to him, making her straddle over his knees. He lifted her dress, wrinkling his nose a little. Now she began to laugh and soon they were settling themselves closer and more comfortably together. The girl's head was on his shoulder; she looked across at Arnvid and said: "He has a strange and shy look, your friend."

"Nay, he is as bold a man as I am, but he has too much mail about him for love-making."

[56]

She gave a little scream of laughter and Arnvid turned away, red and angry.

Presently Gunnar put the girl off him and got up. He took a piece of silver from a pouch and gave it to her, saying: "That will pay for the milk and what else there was." He got on horseback. Arnvid was already mounted.

Gunnar said in a gruff tone, "Now, which way to Chaddesley?"

"I will show you." The girl ran lightly in front of them as they put the horses to the trot. Soon she pointed to a slough of mud leading deep into the wood. "Along there," she said, "and keep on as straight as you can."

Gunnar struck the horse hard with his heels. Both animals broke into a gallop and mud and water flew up in the girl's face. They thundered away into the dimness of the forest without looking back.

Chapter 6

CHADDESLEY

THE SUN HAD SET in drifts of crimson and gold behind the heaved-up masses of oakwood and the mud was crisping with frost when Arnvid and Gunnar rode into the home field of Chaddesley. It seemed a prosperous place with long strips of stubble freshly turned by the plow, a double row of peasants' houses, a mill, a big hall and a small church, all built of massive oak timber. It looked old, as though the buildings had stood there in peace for several centuries. Cattle were coming up from watering at the stream, dogs barked, servants bustled about the haystacks and cow barns, smoke rose steadily from the hall roof, a vertical gray pillar in the bluish dusk.

Chaddesley was much the same as other manors they had passed on the long ride from York and yet Arnvid sensed something unusual about it, something vaguely disturbing. It might be the bearing of the people, who turned to stare at them but did not approach, muttered together and then went on with their work; or it might be something that he had felt in the old stronghold under Moel Fre, that here were echoes of things that had happened in the past; but as he looked at Chaddesley he could not imagine that anything of moment had ever happened here. And then a thought flashed into his mind. Was he sensing something that was yet to come, something of vast significance to him and perhaps also to Gunnar? As for Gunnar, Arnvid had never noticed him taking much interest in his surroundings; but now as they walked their horses slowly toward the hall, he too seemed suddenly alert and thoughtful, as though assessing all he saw. He began to wonder about Gunnar, the essentially insensitive man, ready to take all he could get of fame or of food and drink, or fine clothes and weapons, or pleasure with women, and yet when Gunnar had seemed most dull and indifferent he had suddenly spoken up, putting into verse much that Arnvid had thought about but could by no means have expressed so tersely in words. Again he had a shock of surprise when Gunnar said, drawing his horse to a standstill, "Now we must be within a day's ride of Otkel, but I very much doubt whether we shall ever reach him."

They dismounted and led the horses to the hall door. It opened and out came a big, red-bearded man with a beaked nose and a mustache that stood out aggressively on either side of his face. He had a heavily lined forehead and bulging blue eyes; he had a helmet on his head, a black cloak with silver brooch, shield on back and spur at heel; he was girt with a sword, the hilt and scabbard of which were inlaid with gold. Accustomed as he was to seeing proud and quarrelsome-looking Englishmen, Arnvid thought he had never seen one he liked the looks of less. He glanced at Gunnar and saw that his face had flushed and his eyes had a defiant glitter as the man came up to them in a few swift strides. For a moment he stared hard without speaking, then he said curtly, "What men are you?"

Gunnar and Arnvid gave their names and Gunnar added, "To whom do we speak?"

"I am Edwin of Chaddesley. You are Danes, I take it."

"No, we are not Danes. We are from Iceland," said Arnvid with sudden sharpness.

The Englishman scowled and shrugged his shoulders. "What is your business here?" he asked.

"We come with a message to Otkel at Kinver," said Gunnar.

There was a short silence. Edwin looked at them still more searchingly. He seemed to appraise their weapons and armor and he threw a covetous glance at the two horses. "You cannot reach Otkel tonight," he said. "It is a difficult way through the forest and a day's journey. You are welcome to stay the night here."

Gunnar and Arnvid thanked him, though there was little hospitality in his tone. Some men were now gathering on the opposite side of the yard and one came forward leading a horse saddled and bridled. Edwin went across and spoke to him in a low voice. Then he mounted the horse and rode away among the buildings followed by some twenty men on foot. It was getting too dark to see much of them, but Gunnar thought they were armed. The man to whom Edwin had been speaking came up to them.

"I am the steward here," he said. "My master bids you to food and drink in the hall and you will sleep in yonder loft. The horses shall be well cared for." He beckoned to a servant, who led the animals away. Then he preceded Arnvid and Gunnar into the hall which was empty. A big fire burned on the hearth in the middle of the floor; the steward threw on more wood which made it blaze up. He indicated where they should sit on a crossbench near the fire, and went out at another door behind a curtain. Before he shut it again there was a sound of women's voices.

"That will be the bower," said Gunnar. "He will be telling Edwin's lady about us." Carefully he laid his cloak, helmet and weapons on the bench beside him and Arnvid did the same. "We had best keep on our mail. I think there is peril here," he added.

"I think the same," began Arnvid, but was silent when servants came through the hall bringing bread and drinking horns and two pitchers, one of ale and one of mead. There followed platters of fish and meat. The servants withdrew.

"This is the best entertainment we have had since we left the Danelaw," said Gunnar cheerfully, but his eyes kept ranging round the hall from one door to the other. "A fine hall," he said thoughtfully, looking at the huge oak pillars and tie beams. "Geirfin would be proud of a building like this. I would not mind it myself. I could fancy living here, Arnvid. All seems just right: good land, a forest to hunt in, plenty of servants. It only wants the right woman to take to bed."

"I doubt whether Edwin would part with it all to you," said Arnvid laughing. They had finished eating and the mead was going to his head pleasantly.

"Edwin is not here."

"Nay, but his steward is," said Arnvid.

"I mistrust that fellow, and I can guess what Edwin said

to him before he went. Go easy with the mead, Arnvid. We must keep our wits about us . . ."

The far door opened and the curtain was drawn back. A woman entered the hall followed by two maidservants. She came to the table where Arnvid and Gunnar sat, each with his drinking horn.

"Hail, strangers!" she said.

"Hail, lady!" they answered and rose courteously to their feet.

She looked at them steadily, first at Gunnar, then at Arnvid. The firelight shone full on her face and Arnvid's first thought was that she was a very beautiful woman, young, plump and well-nourished, cleanly looking. Then he thought her full red lips and the droop of her eyelids reminded him of someone—yes, the woman at Kirkwall, and all at once he felt she was not a woman to be trusted. He had smiled at her instinctively, but now his face hardened. It was Gunnar who spoke.

"By your speech, lady, I should guess that you are Danish."

"You guess right." Her eyes widened a little. "I am Thyra of Chaddesley, married to Edwin, an Englishman. My father had a grant of this place from King Edgar and I was his only child. I hear that you are both from Iceland. What are your names?"

Now she looked inquiringly at Arnvid and he said shortly, "I am called Arnvid Torolfsson."

"And I am Gunnar Geirfinsson, his foster brother," said Gunnar.

"Then let us sit and drink awhile, Icelanders," she said, taking a seat opposite them. The two maidservants had meanwhile gone to the end of the hall where a lantern hung above the outer door. There they set to work on sewing and embroidery. Gunnar filled his horn with mead and passed it to Thyra. She drank it half out and passed it back to him.

"You have the look of a warrior in your coat of mail," she said.

"It is true I have been a viking, but I am also a poet."

"And your foster brother? He too has somewhat the look of a poet, I think."

"Nay, he is no poet, but he is the grandson of a king."

"What king?" She turned with more attention to Arnvid, who stroked his beard and looked away indifferently.

"King Leif of Westmorland, who fell in a great fight on Steinmor, up north."

"We know little of such men and places, here in Worcestershire," she said, and smiled to see Arnvid turn red with anger.

"We know something of Worcestershire where we come from," said Gunnar.

"And where is that?"

"We have ridden from York with a message for Otkel of Kinver."

"Ah, so that is it." She lowered her eyes and sat very still.

"You can guess what message we carry?"

"I can guess."

"We have two good horses. We should be able to reach Kinver tomorrow"

"Horses cannot take you through the forest of Pyperwood. You must ride a long way around and even so it is no easy way."

"Nevertheless we must go."

"I think you will be too late."

"Too late? How so?"

"Because Edwin, my husband, has gone ahead of you," she said deliberately in a low voice.

"What does that mean?" Gunnar reached across the table and took her hand.

Now her eyes met his intently. She said, "Do you know that tomorrow night all the Danes in England are to be killed? It is the King's order."

"We suspected something of the kind in York, but we did not know when—" He broke off and then said, "You are a Dane yourself."

"Thanks to Edwin I am safe. But there is little else I should wish to thank him for."

Spellbound, Arnvid watched the pair. Their hands were still clasped, they stared at each other with questioning eyes. Thyra drew her hand away.

With an effort Gunnar said, "We are pledged to warn Otkel. We must try to reach him tomorrow."

"Have you been told where you are to sleep tonight?"

"Aye, the steward said in a loft across the yard."

"There you will be killed before you awake. Edwin arranged it all before he rode away."

Gunnar began to laugh. "Well," he said, "if this be our last supper it has been a good one. And perhaps, thanks to you, we shall not be killed so easily as Edwin expects."

"I have a plan," she said, smiling a little.

"That is good hearing, Thyra!"

"I can keep you safe for tonight, but I cannot answer for tomorrow. Then you must do as you think fit. Give me some mead, Gunnar!" She drank a full horn, then stood up and called the maidservants. She said, "These guests are going across to sleep in the loft. Go to the bower and I shall come to you to make ready for bed." The girls went without a word. "Now come with me," she said. Gunnar and Arnvid followed her to the end of the hall where she unbarred a low door that was behind another curtain.

"Here is the cupboard bed where I sleep," she said. "There is ample room and the mattress is stuffed with goose down. Take your weapons and climb in. There you are safe, so safe that you can lay aside that cold and heavy mail." She laughed softly.

"And then?" said Gunnar.

"In a few minutes you shall let me in and we shall bar the door. Some of the folk will come afterward to sleep in the hall and some will go to the loft, but they will not find you. No one but me will know that you are here."

"That is something like a plan!" said Gunnar. He slipped an arm round her waist.

"Quick!" she said, beginning to laugh. "The servants will come soon."

"We should go outside for a minute," said Arnvid.

"You will be fools if you do, for there death awaits you! There is the fire," she said simply. "Get out of your mail and be quick!"

"The fire? That is a custom we do not have in Iceland."

"Here we are not so particular." In a moment she was gone through the other door into the bower.

In silence Arnvid and Gunnar made ready. They pushed all their belongings into the cupboard bed, got off their clothes and lay down under the sheet. Presently there was a slight tap on the door. Gunnar opened it and found the naked body of Thyra in his arms.

Chapter 7

SAINT BRICE'S DAY

EARLY NEXT MORNING Arnvid lay dozing in the cupboard bed, sometimes conscious that the pair beside him were talking in whispers. There was love talk to which he tried to close his ears. He felt a distaste for this affair between Gunnar and Thyra. Was it because he desired the woman himself? Surely not, and yet their shameless abandonment to lust and their complete indifference to his nearness seemed like a physical affront. Why was it that women gave him no more than a glance and then yielded everything to Gunnar? Did they sense an indecision in him, or some innate fastidiousness, while from Gunnar they accepted the practiced and confident attack, having no instinctive will to resist it? If Gunnar had not been there perhaps he would have taken that girl at the goatherd's hut, or perhaps he wouldn't . . . Anyhow it was surely a fortunate thing for them both that Thyra wanted Gunnar and was ready to betray her husband. He slept again and woke hearing a clatter of servants having breakfast in the hall. Soon they were gone about their business and there was silence except for the cheerful crackle of logs on the fire. He heard Thyra whispering again. Now she was giving Gunnar careful instructions on how to get to Kinver. They had to go around by the hills to the east . . . a place called Clent. It might be safe to ask the way there, for the people at Clent were friendly to Otkel. They were really Danes, but they had been there so long that they were now reckoned as English. No one would molest them. It was only Edwin who wanted to kill Otkel and his son Tord, and another man nearby, Steintor he was called. Most of the landowners hereabouts had no stomach for killing folk who had never done them any harm, but they did not dare to disobey the King's command . . . Then suddenly they started love-making again, then more whispering, and at last Thyra unbarred the door and slipped out. They heard her go into the bower.

"What now?" said Arnvid.

"We shall get on our clothes and mail. Thyra will have the horses brought around as soon as the steward is out of the way. She says he will be going to the mill in a little while."

They helped each other as best they could in the low cupboard and presently there was a knock on the door. They opened it and saw a girl with a broad smile on her face.

"Well, my pretty!" said Gunnar. "Would you like to come inside?"

His eyes went past her and saw that the hall was empty. She giggled and said they were to come through to the bower when they were ready. She seemed in no hurry to leave them so Gunnar pushed her out at the door behind the curtain. Then he made sure that the outer door was barred, and they did what was needful.

"I have a mighty hunger," said Gunnar as they went into

the bower and his face lit up when he saw a bowl of porridge, bread and ale set ready for them. Several women were at work with looms and spinning wheels and through another door they saw others cutting up meat and plucking birds in what seemed to be a kitchen.

"A king could not live better than they do here," muttered Gunnar. "England—is there another land like it?"

Quickly they finished their meal and went out into the open air. There was a man holding the black stallion, saddled and bridled, and Thyra was on the bay, trotting around the yard. A servant was busy feeding pigs in a sty, otherwise there was no one about. It was a fair morning, mild and windstill. Gunnar looked at the horses critically; they seemed to have been well fed and groomed. He nodded, well satisfied. Thyra came up to them at a canter. She reined in and dismounted. She and Gunnar stared at each other for a moment in silence and the servant stood there looking on with a wooden face.

"We have much to thank you for, lady," said Gunnar formally.

Thyra colored, but said only, "You should find your way if you mind what I told you."

"Shall I be welcome if I find my way back?" he said, smiling.

"Life is more worth having than love," she answered in a low voice.

"I am not so sure of that. Anyhow I am not an easy man to kill." He vaulted onto the bay. Arnvid had already mounted the black. They waved their spears aloft in a gesture of farewell and rode at a swift trot out of the yard, Gunnar leading. There were men plowing in the home field—they turned their heads, but did not stop work as the riders went by. Soon the furrows were dark with the shadows of broad-topped oaks, they went through a gateway in a stake fence and the forest closed around them, thick lichened trunks rising like monstrous trolls out of bare ground, silvery-stemmed saplings interlaced with twining honeysuckle and purple-leaved brambles, glittering hollies. A faint track wound on over hill and hollow past blackened places where charcoal had been burned, on and on until through the russet foliage they saw high ridges dark with gorse.

"Clent," said Gunnar. "So far so good."

They overtook a woodcutter bearing a load of faggots.

"Which way to Kinver, friend?" said Gunnar.

The man pointed in a direction at right angles to the way they were going and Gunnar nodded as though expecting this. They came out on a heath and made good speed across it, but soon the woods began again, thicker and wilder than ever. They had to get off and lead the horses under low branches; they all but stuck fast in a swampy ravine. After some hours they found they were heading back toward the hills of Clent. Again they changed direction and now they found a wheel-marked track that led to a small farm. Beside the buildings was a group of men, all armed.

"I doubt if we should find any welcome there," said Gunnar. They turned their horses and rode back into the forest, following a little-trodden path that was so narrow that they could not ride abreast.

"We are as well hidden in these woods as fish in the sea," said Arnvid. He found a pleasure in this tangled solitude, in the rustle of fallen leaves, the scent of autumnal decay, the companionship of a good horse.

"Fish are not hidden from other fish," remarked Gunnar shortly.

It was some time after sunset that they came to a rough

open place and got off to rest the horses and let them graze awhile.

"I wish Audun could see the task he has set us," said Gunnar discontentedly. "I grant that his horses have served us well, but even so it looks as though we must be too late at Otkel's, if we ever do find him." With the bridle over his arm he walked up onto an old grave mound, forcing his way through the withered bracken. On the top he gave a loud exclamation. The woods parted ahead and they could see that the land began to slope to a wide valley. On the further side was a sharp bare ridge. "I could swear that is the Edge of Kinver," he said. "We have come the right way after all."

"It looks a long way yet," said Arnvid.

"It is that and it will be dark directly. Let us ride, foster brother, and we may yet be on time. Then we have done all that man can do."

They went at a stumbling trot through bush and brake. Soon they were on a broader path. It was dark enough now and owls hooted in the thinning woods. The big hill loomed up blackly ahead and all at once they came to where two other tracks converged on a knoll above a stream. There stood a hall with a glow of light on the smoke that rose above the long low roof. They rode to the door, got off and passed their reins over crooks fixed in the wall. They knocked loudly and were aware of a murmur of voices within suddenly stilled. A man opened the door and they stepped into warmth and the bright glare of a fire and a pleasant smell of cooked meat. A great company sat along the benches on either side of the fire, both men and women. All had ale horns in their hands except for one or two who had fallen asleep with their heads on the board.

"Is this Otkel's hall?" said Gunnar in a loud voice.

An elderly man in fine clothes answered from the high seat.

"Nay, strangers, here lives Steintor, but you are welcome none the less, for this is the wedding feast of Tord Otkelsson and my daughter Astrid." He was clearly more than a little drunk.

"We come with a message for Otkel from his brother Audun in York. Is he not here?"

"He should be here, but as luck would have it he lies in his own hall, a mile away, with a broken leg he got out hunting. Sit you down, strangers! You must be weary if you have come all the way from York. Are you Danish men?"

"We are two Icelanders; I am Gunnar Geirfinsson and this is Arnvid Torolfsson, my foster brother."

"Then welcome, Icelanders! Come to the board and drink while there is yet something in cask and can!"

A place was made for them and friendly hands forced them down on the bench. A woman brought them ale. They found themselves sitting opposite a young man with flaxen locks and a surly, scowling face. He was enormously broad-shouldered and his hairy arms were like great oak branches. Arnvid thought he had seldom seen such a grim-looking champion. Beside him was a girl with fresh coloring and delicate features, with a childish beauty, but wistful-looking and with downcast eyes as though ill at ease. Now she raised her eyes and stared glancingly at Arnvid, but more fixedly at Gunnar. Some animation came into her face, a glow of interest and excitement.

This is the old story, thought Arnvid, but he nerved himself to raise his ale horn and say, "Do I drink to the happiness of Astrid, Steintor's daughter?"

She nodded gravely, but her gaze quickly returned to Gunnar, who had lost no time in emptying his horn at a draught.

"That message I have—" he began, but the young man interrupted him. "I am Tord Otkelsson," he said in a thick voice. "You can give your message to me."

"Then we would have you know that Audun warns his brother to be on his guard. More than that he counsels him to leave here as soon as may be and seek safety among the Danes in Northumbria, or at least to cross over into Wales."

For a moment there was silence; then voices broke out all over the hall. "Safety!" "Who is safer than we are here?" "These strangers are joking!" "Drink, man, and speak more sense!" Tord Otkelsson said gruffly, "What is it my father has to fear?" Gunnar answered in a loud voice: "You have all much to fear, for tonight, by King Ethelred's command, all the Danes in England are to be killed."

Again the company stared at Gunnar in silence. Then Steintor said, "It cannot be true! There is no sense in it! What harm have we done Ethelred, we who got these lands in gift from his father, Edgar?"

"You are Danes, and that is enough," said Gunnar.

"But who will be found to search us out here? We are friends with all our neighbors. Not a man has a grudge against us."

"Are you friends with Edwin of Chaddesley?"

"Edwin? Why surely. He was bidden to this feast, he and Thyra, but they have not come."

"We have had speech with Thyra, who wishes you well, but from her we learned that Edwin is coming tonight with a muster of armed men. He will kill you all or burn you in."

"Let him come then!" shouted Tord. "We are not afraid of Edwin of Chaddesley! If he comes as a friend we will give him drink. If he comes as a foeman we will meet him with the sharp edges of our weapons!"

"Aye, that is well said," added Steintor. "Danes we are, and afraid of no man. I tell you, friends, we have no quarrel with Edwin and we are true liegemen to King Ethelred, who, by what I hear, has many Danes in his service. Earl Pallig and his men, are they not in the King's pay and guard the land down by London?"

"Earl Pallig is King Sweyn's brother-in-law. He above all is doomed."

Gunnar shrugged his shoulders and drank. Arnvid leaned across the table and said to Astrid in a low voice: "Can you not persuade them to seek safety while there is yet time?"

"Who am I to give such counsel when all are sure there is no danger?" she answered with a faint smile.

"They are drunk," he muttered, and thought he had been a fool to imagine that Astrid either could or would attempt to make that company see reason. It was only that he felt a sort of agony at the idea of this girl being done to death.

Gunnar stood up and Arnvid rose with him.

"We have given our message," he said. He looked at Tord with an expressionless face. "No one can say that you have not all been warned. Thank you, Steintor, for the drink." Together they went out at the door into the sharp night air. The moon was rising over the forest. They picked up their spears and got on horseback. Gunnar pointed to moving gleams of light among the trees beyond the field fence. "Edwin coming," he said.

"Do you mean to stay for the fight?" asked Arnvid.

"Not I. No sense in throwing away my life among these fools. I have something better to do."

"What, then?"

"I shall ride back to Thyra. Will you come with me?"

"No," said Arnvid decisively.

"What is your plan, foster brother?"

"I shall ride to Otkel's hall and give warning there."

"And then?"

"I might try to reach Wales."

"I think my plan is the better."

"For you it may be."

"I doubt whether we shall meet again, Arnvid."

"Likely not. Farewell, Gunnar."

"Farewell!" Already Gunnar had turned his horse and was trotting away into the darkness. When he got to some rising ground he looked back. He saw a bright glare of fire leaping up in the direction of Steintor's hall and another one further away across the valley. He stopped and watched for a minute, aware of a faint clamor of voices. He wondered how many beacons of this kind were being lit throughout the length and breadth of England. He wondered where Arnvid was now and whether he was still alive. Then he jerked the reins roughly and rode on.

Next morning on a half-foundered horse he came into the yard at Chaddesley. All looked just the same as when he had left it twenty-four hours earlier. Men stared at him, but went on working. He got off stiffly and knocked on the door of the bower. A woman opened to him and he said with a smile, "I would see your mistress. Tell her I am both hungry and thirsty."

In a few moments Thyra was before him, her face flushed with joy.

"What has happened?" she asked. He told her in a few

words. "Come into the hall," she said. "There we can talk while you eat." They sat side by side near the fire. A girl brought food and drink and went out again.

Thyra said, "The steward sent a messenger after Edwin."

"To tell him how we had spent the night?"

"Most likely. From what I know of Edwin he will be here very soon, but I can have you well hidden."

"You need not do that. When he comes I shall be ready for him, but I would like to snatch a little sleep first. Will he meet me in fair fight, think you?"

"He will be too angry to think of anything else than to kill you with his own hands."

Gunnar yawned and lay down on a bench. "Wake me when he comes," he said. She gave him a kiss and left him.

It was an hour later, though to Gunnar it seemed only a few moments, that Thyra laid a hand on his shoulder. He started up rubbing his eyes and then instinctively felt for the weapons leaning against the bench.

"Edwin is here," she said. "He has just ridden into the yard on a horse covered with mud and foam."

"Well, now it is life or death," said Gunnar cheerfully. He picked up the heavy axe with its shaft bound with iron wire, the gift of Earl Erik. He looked doubtfully at the shield, but decided to leave it lying. Leisurely he walked across the floor and stood by the fire. The outer door opened and Edwin strode in, throwing off his black cloak that was plastered with mud. Immediately on seeing Gunnar he drew his sword and took his shield on his left arm. Thyra slipped behind him, closed the door and put up the bar.

"Hail Edwin!" said Gunnar in a casual tone. "You find me alive and not dead as you expected."

Edwin did not answer. He dealt a swift slanting blow at Gunnar's head, but Gunnar parried it easily with the axe shaft that he gripped with both hands. A second blow glanced off the shaft and fell on Gunnar's shoulder, but did not bite on the mail. Then Gunnar swung his axe backhanded so that Edwin could not cover himself with the shield. He guarded himself with the sword, but the heavy weapon beat it down and caught Edwin below the ear, cleaving the neck to the bone. Blood spurted high. The big man gave at the knees and fell sideways into the fire. The helmet came off his head and hair and beard shriveled up and burst into flame. Gunnar drove the point of the axe under his chin and pulled the body out of the fire onto the floor. He looked at Thyra who stood on the other side of the hall, pale and trembling a little.

"It was almost too easy," he said. He picked up Edwin's cloak and carefully wiped the axe head. A loud knocking began on the door. After a moment, Thyra took down the bolt. The steward and half a dozen servants came into the hall. The steward had a spear, but the others were unarmed. They looked in a sort of bewilderment at Thyra and Gunnar and at the dead man lying by the fire.

"Stand back and hear what I have to say!" said Thyra in a hard imperious voice. "Edwin is dead in fair fight. I am free of him and I am not sorry, for there was little love between us. This man, Gunnar Geirfinsson from Iceland, I choose as my husband. He is your new master. Obey him in all things."

There was a silence. The steward and the servants stood handfallen, with downcast eyes.

"Answer me!" she said sharply.

"It shall be as you say, lady," muttered the steward.

"Then take up the dead man, fetch the priest, and get him buried by the church."

When they had all gone out bearing the corpse with them, Gunnar and Thyra sat down side by side in the high seat.

"So begins a new life for us," she said.

Gunnar looked at the long splash of blood across the rushes on the floor.

"Has Edwin any kinsmen?" he asked.

"None in these parts. He came here two years ago from London on some business of the King's."

"Has he no children?"

"I doubt it. I have never borne him a child, but that does not say that I cannot bear one."

"How so, Thyra?" he said with a smile, though his eyes were shrewd.

"I had one once, but it died. A man took me when I was out hunting in the forest."

"And who was that man?"

"He was Tord Otkelsson."

"A man of more strength than wit. He will be dead now. Maybe it is as well. I am a jealous man, Thyra."

"There is no one of whom you need be jealous," she said, avoiding his gaze.

Gunnar stroked his beard in silence. I have found a lucky way out, he thought, though there may be more rocks ahead. And then his thoughts left the woman and he felt a strange void, a loneliness, because Arnvid was no longer with him. Obscurely he felt that he would have come if it had not been for Thyra.

Chapter 8

NIGHT BY THE SEVERN

ARNVID TURNED HIS HORSE onto the track that led toward the dark hill on the other side of the valley. The hall he had just left was not fifty yards away, across a little stream, but he was already in the skirts of the forest nearing some immense oaks which the woodcutters had left standing. He saw the hall door open and a man appear silhouetted against the glow of firelight within. Meanwhile a long column of men, riding and on foot, had entered the home field, plainly revealed in the light of torches they were carrying. The man in the doorway went back into the hall, from which came immediately a loud hum as from a disturbed hive of bees. Fascinated by the spectacle, Arnvid brought his horse to a standstill. He had little fear for himself: he had his weapons, he was well-mounted, and the forest was close. He drew his sword and sat passive in the saddle. A mass of men poured down to the hall door. The torchlight flashed on spear points and uplifted swords and axes, and there came a savage bloodcurdling roar of voices: "Death to the Danes!" Now Arnvid could see the huge figure of Tord Otkelsson in the doorway, gripping an axe, and there were screams and groans as he felled man after man and Steintor lunged past him with a long spear. The crowd of attackers recoiled and began to mill around the building. Some put their torches to the low eaves of thatch and suddenly the piercing screams of women sounded from the door at the other gable-end. A rush of figures was overwhelmed by men hacking and stabbing, but a few broke away closely pursued. Men flung themselves on some who fell in the stream. There were growling taunts and agonized cries, but one woman got across and ran on blindly straight toward Arnvid. A man came after her. He reached out and caught hold of her dress and she fell almost under the belly of the horse that began to rear in terror. Arnvid whirled his sword and dealt a sweeping cut at the man, who fell forward with a cloven skull. Frantically the woman scrambled to her knees. She stared upward at the rider. The hall was now well alight and in the flickering glare Arnvid recognized Astrid, the bride, whose husband still swung his axe amid gouts of flame and blinding smoke.

"Get up behind me," he said. "I may be able to save you." He sheathed his sword, calmed the horse somewhat with a hand on its neck, and took one foot out of a stirrup. He helped her as best he could and presently she was up astride the horse's quarters, clutching him round the waist. Now they were off at a laboring canter. Tree trunks closed together ahead, the light faded, the shouting died down and the crackle of flames and falling timbers grew faint in the distance. Soon he was only aware of the long drawn-out sobs of the young girl behind him, and presently she too was silent.

The track plunged downward in a hollow way full of mud and approached a river. A rider came splashing toward them through the water. The moon shone full on him as they met near the bank—a thickset peasant with a cudgel on a stout-looking horse.

"Will you sell me the horse, friend?" said Arnvid. "This one is overloaded with two to carry."

"That I won't," said the man, "for I know by your speech you are a Dane."

"What will you do then?" said Arnvid.

"I'd kill you, but unluckily I have no weapon."

"Then if you cannot kill me I may have a try at killing you." Arnvid drew his sword and drove it through the peasant's throat. He thought, this is the second time I have killed a man tonight—how easy it is, once one is in the mood. And he realized that what made it easy was having this girl to protect and the desire to win her admiration. Somehow, too, it was easier because Gunnar was not here to take command and to look slightingly at whatever he did.

They both got down and stood listening. There was no sound save for the bark of a fox far away in the woods. The peasant had fallen from the saddle and lay dead; the horse stood there passive. Arnvid perceived it was a gelding. It seemed a good sound animal, well-fed but ill-used. He was about to help the girl onto it when he had a thought.

"It would be best for you to change clothes with this peasant," he said. "You will be warmer and ride more easily, and you might pass for a man. That could be a help in what lies ahead of us."

"Yes," she said tonelessly, "if you think it best; but you have yourself to save and I cannot but hinder you."

"Our course lies together, no matter to what end," he said decisively, and thought it was a new man that spoke thus.

Astrid held the bridles of the horses while he took a thick leather coat off the peasant. Then he unlaced the leather leggings and drew off the linen breeches. He helped Astrid off with her long-skirted dress that was finely embroidered in colored wools and rolled it into a bundle while she struggled into the coarse dirty clothes from the dead man. There was a fur cap and he put it on her head after he had shorn off a good part of her hair with his sword. He surveyed her for a moment as she stood there looking at him with a fatalistic indifference which quickly cooled the excitement he had begun to feel when he saw her stripped of the wedding dress. He wondered how Gunnar would have dealt with this situation. Would he have snatched the opportunity to make love, without any tenderness, merely in a spirit of callous amusement, as he had done with the goatherd's girl? The sort of thing a viking might boast of doing. And would Astrid have tried to repel Gunnar as he was sure she would have repelled him, Arnvid? Perhaps not. He remembered how she had looked at Gunnar in Steintor's hall, and how she had avoided looking at her newly wed husband. Well, Gunnar had had Thyra and was now on his way back to her. What was the use of thinking about him and Astrid?

Meanwhile they had got on horseback and ridden on across the ford. The track climbed up onto a heath and away to the right was another fire blazing up with a trail of sparks swaying toward them. They could smell the burning and Arnvid guessed that there was more in that fire than wood.

"That is Otkel's hall," said the girl.

Arnvid had almost forgotten that he had been riding to

save Otkel. They might have got the lamed man away on a litter and hidden in some peasant cot. There might just have been time, if he could have found his way to the place, but then he could not have saved Astrid. They went on in silence and he began to think of the crazy wickedness of this act of Ethelred's, the destruction of hundreds and thousands of harmless people in time of peace. What would come of it? Surely nothing good for England. He longed more than ever to be out of a country where such black treachery was possible. Wales—it could not be worse there and it might be better. He began to urge on his horse and Astrid soon dropped behind. He dared not shout to her to hurry so he had to pull in and wait till she came up.

"Can you not ride faster?" he said almost angrily.

"Even if I had the will, I have neither whip nor spur," she answered. "To what end should we ride fast, for when daylight comes we shall meet our deaths. Anyone will know us for what we are."

"In Wales we might be safer."

"Wales is far away and there is the Severn to cross. Besides the Welshmen have no reason to like us Danes."

"They are not Ethelred's men."

"They are with him against the vikings. Anyhow, who will give us food while we are still in England? I am faint now and I can hardly keep in the saddle." She began to sob like a child.

He set his teeth. "Do you not *want* to live?" he said violently.

"What have I to live for? My father and all his friends gone."

He noticed that she said nothing about her husband. **Passion** began to burn in him.

"But *I* want you to live!" The words came without premeditation.

"You! Well, yes, I must do what you want, I suppose," she said resignedly.

On the far edge of the heath they saw in the moonlight a row of little huts standing in what looked like a new clearing.

"Now we shall try our luck," he said, and rode up to the first door. Dismounting he struck hard on it with his spear shaft, awaking a ferocious growling from a dog within. Presently a woman opened the door a little way.

"We would buy food and drink for ourselves, and oats and hay for the horses," he said.

The door slammed, but he kept it open with his foot. "Get us what we want and that quickly or we shall take it without your leave," he said and thrust the door down. He pointed his spear at the woman's breast.

"We have nothing," she said sulkily. Some small children behind her began to cry and the dog flew at him. He kicked it across the hut and it lay still, whimpering.

"Tell me no lies. Give me what you have!" he said.

Slowly the woman handed him two loaves of newly baked bread. He passed them to Astrid and said, "Open your coat and put them inside." The woman brought milk in a bowl. Astrid drank a little and Arnvid a great deal.

"We have no corn," the woman said, "but there is a haystack behind the house." He got out a bright silver coin and gave it to her. Then they led the horses to the stack and pulled out several armfuls while the animals helped themselves.

[83]

Arnvid took the rolled-up wedding dress, which he had tied to his saddle, stuffed it tight with hay and knotted up the ends. "Get on horseback!" he said to Astrid. "Now take this in front of you . . ." A moment later they were off, making down hill into the woods, battling their way through a brush of oak scrub and hazel, on and on till unexpectedly they came to water—a broad, swiftly flowing river, silvery in the light of the moon.

"The Severn," said Astrid.

"I wish we were across it," he said discontentedly.

"There is a ford somewhere hereabouts."

"We may be able to find it when daylight comes. We must stay the night here, Astrid, eat and sleep. Here we are well hidden." He looked around at the brushwood, thick with autumn leaves.

They took the horses to drink at the river, then led them up into a flat open space where from the look of the ground there had been charcoal burning. Here they took off the bridles, slacked the girths, and put out the hay in two heaps. It was coarse, thistly stuff, but the animals ate it greedily. Then at last they sat down side by side on a bank of dry moss and ate most of the bread. The moon had gone in and it was very dark and cold.

"Lucky there were no men about those peasant cots," he said. "I suppose they were all away killing Danes."

"They will be back by morning and then they will come and search for us."

"True enough. We must find the ford before daybreak. Are there Danes across the river?"

"I have not heard of any."

"The folk over there may not be so unfriendly. They may

not think of us as Danes if you speak to them in the way the English speak," he said hopefully.

"Yes," she said, and got up, looking about her.

"Do you hear anything?"

"No, it is only that . . ." She unbuckled the belt and began to struggle with the buttons of the leather coat.

"I too," he said. "I have to get out of this cursed mail."

"I will help you." Together they got it down and at last he stepped out of it. Then he helped her with the unfamiliar clothes. She seemed apathetic, without any preoccupation about modesty. It was as though they were man and wife. Presently he said, "Now you must sleep and I will watch," while his heart began to beat hard and he thought: There is nothing to prevent our lying together, only that she does not want me as I want her.

"I am not sleepy. Let us sit awhile," she said with a sigh. "Do you not want anything more?"

"Aye . . . of course . . ." he said hesitatingly. "But not now. Sometime you may be more in the mood."

"I am ready. I owe you my life."

"Some other time." He began to get back into his coat of mail.

"There may be no other time. Tomorrow we may well be dead."

She lay back on the bank with her hands behind her head.

Half to himself he said: "I do not know why it is, but I should like to keep you as you are until we are both in safety."

"You are a strange man," she said, without any emotion.

He sat down beside her and said, "Tell me, Astrid, are you very sad for what has happened at Steintor's hall?"

"Of course! I loved my father dearly and I was the apple

of his eye. I grew up with the servants, and some of them were my half brothers and half sisters."

"Your mother . . .?"

"She died when I was born. She was of high birth, from Denmark."

"Do you not grieve for Tord Otkelsson?"

"I could never fancy him, but in time it might have been different."

"He made a good end, fighting to the last."

"He was brave, of course," she said indifferently.

Why "of course," he thought. Did she realize how hard he found it to be brave, until now when he had her with him?

"I will sleep," he said. "But wake me in a little while."

He lay down. She spread the wedding dress over their knees as she lay down beside him. He took her hand. She held it without responding to his strong clasp. In a moment he was asleep.

Chapter 9

THROUGH WYRE FOREST

WHEN ASTRID AWOKE HIM it was perceptibly lighter and they were in a mist that blotted out the far bank of the river. He got up hurriedly and made sure that the horses were still close by.

"Now you sleep," he said, and she lay back obediently. He tucked the dress around her and tried to make her comfortable, but she took no notice. It was very cold and he walked briskly to and fro on the open space, thinking of the men who might soon come searching for them—two obvious fugitives from the massacre—and of the formidable barrier of the great river. So much depended on the horses. The gelding had a good thick coat and looked as though it had run out, but the stallion had been in stable every night since they left York. He spread his cloak over the creature's back and thought he might well have done this as soon as they dismounted. Much depended on Astrid. She sat on her horse and let it carry her, but she did not *ride*. Unless she put more heart into this business they would almost inevitably get caught, sooner or later. If only she felt for him as he did for her . . . but was it reasonable to expect that, when she was still half-stunned by the shock of a frightful experience? Again unwillingly he thought of how Gunnar would have dealt with her, probably to their mutual satisfaction. What was the old saying? "He who woos will win . . ." With a sudden shock of dismay he realized that day had broken; everything around him was distinct in the gray light and the mist had lifted so that he could see the woods mounting up across the water. Hurriedly he went to Astrid and stooped down. There she lay with open eyes, regarding him with calm detachment.

"We must start!" he said urgently. "It is late. Let us eat what is left of the bread and set off."

"Yes," she said, sitting up and beginning to roll the wedding dress into a bundle. For the first time he noticed that she had a slender gold bracelet on each wrist.

"Let me take care of the gold," he said. "Someone might snatch it from you."

Without a word she undid the bracelets and handed them over. He put them in his pouch. There was still some silver that Audun had given him; it had not been necessary to pay for anything while he and Gunnar were in the Danelaw, but now they were not likely to receive much free hospitality. The gold might be necessary to buy food—it might buy their lives. If only they could reach Wales . . . He could hardly swallow the bread, he had become so agitated, but Astrid ate without visible concern. When she had finished, she went down to the river, drank, and washed her face and hands. Arnvid got the horses bridled. He was glad to see they had finished all the hay and had filled themselves on the rough grazing. He was glad to see Astrid washing. Perhaps she was no longer so indifferent about her fate.

They led the horses out of the clearing and along the bank upstream. A glint of wintry sunshine lit up the tops of tall trees across the river, yellow twigged ash and dark crowns of oak. Very soon they came to a track going down to the water, not a track that was much used for it was almost grown up with brambles and gorse, still it must lead to a crossing of some kind.

"Is this the ford?" he asked dubiously.

"It may well be," she said.

By the water's edge, turned bottom-upward, they found a small coracle—plaited willow covered with skins.

"We could get across in this, but we should have to leave the horses," he said.

"If there is a ford the horses should carry us across."

"That is our best chance. If we get rid of this boat, though, it may hinder pursuit." He launched the coracle and pushed it out into the stream. Soon it was drifting away at surprising speed. He cut a hazel switch for Astrid and they got on horseback. The stallion held back at first, but the gelding walked into the water without much persuasion. It was as though it had been across before. Then all at once there was a rustling and snapping behind them, a loud shout, and a dozen peasants came running down the track—rough, dirty-looking men carrying spears. There was a shout: "Death to the Danes!" Arnvid looked at Astrid. She was going steadily forward into deeper and deeper water. Now it was up to her feet, now to her thighs. The horse stumbled and nearly went under, it was swept down a yard or two, now it seemed to be swimming; but Astrid was still firmly in the saddle. He looked back at the peasants; one man was well ahead of the others and coming on into the river, poising his spear. Arnvid wheeled his horse around and managed to get his shield on his left arm. The peasant launched the spear and Arnvid caught it on the shield. The point came through, grazing his hand, then it sagged down and dropped into the water. Wild with rage, Arnvid threw his own spear in return, but the horse swayed in the strong current and the spear went wide.

He turned the horse again and urged it after Astrid, but in a moment it went under and he realized that he was too heavy on its back. They were going helplessly downstream and the horse could barely keep its head above water. In a moment it would be drowning. He slid off backward and grasped it by the tail. At first he thought it would make for the bank they had just left, but now swimming hard it strove toward the gelding, which had emerged on the far side of the river. Soon it began to get a foothold again and splashed up onto the bank, dragging Arnvid after it. Well, the Severn was crossed and their pursuers were baffled, but Arnvid was angry at the loss of his spear, he was breathless and chilled to the marrow. For a moment he felt something like despair. He turned his eyes to Astrid who had ridden close and sat looking down at him. There was a hint of a smile on her face. The sun shone on them with a faint warmth, the sky was pale blue. He leaned against the saddle, considering her for the first time in full daylight, aware that she was indeed a very beautiful girl. He had thought a lot about her body. Now he began to wonder about her mind. What lay behind the mask of indifference, almost of apathy, with which she encountered hardship and peril? Gunnar had said that he had much to learn about life. Perhaps he had much to learn about women.

What was the old saying? "So is woman's love, like driving on slippery ice with an unshod filly, a wild two-year-old, badly broken in; or like sailing rudderless in gathering storm; or like a lame man's deer hunt on the rocky cliffs." A dangerous thing, to be committed to a woman so far as love was concerned; and yet that was what he desired, now more than ever, as he watched her face, calm, a little mocking, but not unfriendly. He thought of what he had seen in the firelight outside Steintor's hall. Well, he had saved her from that and now he wanted to keep her safe, like some precious possession, no matter at what risk to himself. The hope grew strong in him that he might succeed. Eagerly he vaulted onto the stallion and gathered up the reins. A track of sorts plunged upward into the woods and they rode side by side under the great mossy bows of oak that soon screened them from the group of peasants watching across the water. On and on they rode over high hills and deep darksome valleys, always among enormous trees and in a silence that seemed like some enchantment, a miasma more threatening than the ill will of human beings.

"Here we seem safe," he said at last, "yet maybe not so safe for we can die of cold and hunger if these woods go on without end."

"It must be the Forest of Wyre," she said. "The greatest forest in these parts, so I have heard, yet if we keep our course it must come to an end."

"The sun is right before us, but sinking fast. We must be riding toward Wales," he said, and broke off, thinking it was childish to suppose that they could expect safety anywhere except among people of their own race, and perhaps not even then.

It was growing dusk when the woods thinned away into brakes of gorse and broom. Dark against a fiery sky rose the bare, tilted crest that Arnvid and Gunnar had seen from the hilltop above the goatherd's hut, one of those faint blue heights that rose along the western horizon like groups of blunted sawteeth. Now, all at once there were wattled fences and stripes of plowing, a hall, church and cottages much as there had been at Chaddesley, but here they were compressed within a palisade. They drew rein and the horses reached eagerly for the green prickly shoots of gorse, their breath steaming upward in the still, cold air.

"A fine homestead, but our lives may be short if we seek its shelter," said Arnvid dubiously.

"All the same we must have food and dry our clothes."

"Look!" he said. "That blue smoke going up among the trees, far away yonder. That might be a woodman's cot where few folk are about."

Keeping out of sight of the farm they edged their way back into the woods and came after a while to a little low house with living room at one end and cow stalls at the other. An elderly man was milking when they looked in at the door.

"You can speak as the English do," whispered Arnvid.

Astrid said: "Can we do you some service, friend, in return for food and warmth? We are on a long journey and have fared through wood and water."

The man set down his bucket and came out into the open. He looked them over suspiciously, pursing his lips as he stared at Astrid, and frowning as he surveyed Arnvid's sword and coat of mail.

"Whence do you come?" he asked gruffly.

"From the west," said Astrid readily. "We have business with the Earl in Worcester."

"You would do best to ride to the hall; it is but a mile away."

"We have no wish to go before great folks in such a sorry state. For those perished with cold and hunger the first roof is the best."

"I doubt whether you are speaking the truth."

"And if we are not, at least we mean you no harm."

The man's wife had come out. She whispered to him, pointing at Astrid. He gave a sudden laugh and said, "Well, well! What service do you offer?"

"What would you have us do?"

The woman answered, "You can come in to the fire, but your man can first cleave some logs outside." She pointed to a heap of hewn oak.

"And the horses?"

"The horses shall be housed and fed," said the man.

Arnvid whispered to Astrid, "If they offer you any hurt, remember I am here with my sword." She nodded and said, "They seem to be simple and kindly folk. They think we are lovers."

"Do they not think we are Danes?"

"Maybe they know nothing about the killing of the Danes."

She followed the woman into the house; the man led away the horses, Arnvid picked up an axe beside the woodheap and began to split the logs. The work was easy enough with the clean-grained oak and he soon built up a neat stack as they did with the birchwood in Iceland. Then he went to the house door and looked in. There was a blaze of light from a fire in the middle of the floor and on a bench beside it sat

Astrid stripped of all her clothes. The woman was rubbing her all over with a dirty-looking cloth and the man sat nearby, silent and fascinated by the sight of a girl's breasts and thighs revealed in the ruddy glare of the fire. The clothes hung steaming from a sapling that spanned the room at head height. Arnvid thought he had never been in a dirtier or fouler-smelling house, yet instinctively he felt that there was no danger here. With the man alone it might have been different, but the woman was clearly in command and Astrid was as safe here as she would have been in her father's hall.

"Come you and strip too, if you be as wet as she is," said the woman in a friendly voice.

"He is far wetter," said Astrid. "He has been in up to his neck and nothing dries under a leather coat."

Arnvid hesitated, then he unbuckled his sword and worked himself out of the mail. He went outside for a moment, then came back, took off all his sodden garments and hung them on the rail. Stark naked he stood by the fire and never had he felt warmth so comforting. The women's eyes were fixed on him. Astrid's were calm and thoughtful, but the housewife's had a glint of lustful curiosity. He turned away from them.

"A modest and a silent man, your friend," said the woman.

"He does not speak in our tongue," said Astrid.

"He has the look of a Welshman, but it is easy to see he is of noble birth."

Astrid did not answer.

Presently the woman rubbed Arnvid down with the same cloth. The man began to make some unseemly remarks, but the woman quickly silenced him. She was not a young woman, but now Arnvid sensed a certain shyness about her and thought she handled him more gently than she had done Astrid. Then she brought out food in plenty and they all four ate till they were satisfied and emptied a bowl of buttermilk. The peasants plied Astrid with questions and she answered both wittily and evasively. Sometimes she flashed a glance at Arnvid as though seeking approval. He felt daunted that she could sit there naked beside him with seeming unconcern. Had she no desire for him as he had for her, or was her mind completely innocent, or was she still so dazed by what had happened at Steintor's hall that she was careless of everything, even of modesty? Now that he came to think about it there was not much modesty in England and the people were more easygoing, more unwary, more uncontrolled in word and deed than they were in Iceland. It might be because life was so easy here. There was so much to be got with little labor that folk did not naturally become hard in mind and body, proud of endurance, greedy of gain, careful of honor. The English were like the lush thickets rooted in rich earth as compared to the white-stemmed storm-beaten trees of Iceland. . . .

The woman made up a bed of straw by the fire and presently Astrid lay down on it covered with a deerskin. The couple went to their bed at the end of the room. Arnvid stood looking on. The fire had died down to a mass of glowing embers. He thought that now he could take Astrid if he wanted to. It was only what was expected and she would not resist him with her body, though her mind might be far away from his. Somehow the prospect did not please him. For one thing she was utterly tired out and already asleep, for another he had a fastidious or maybe a superstitious feeling that this was neither the time nor the place. It might seem safe here, but danger was not far off. He remembered what had happened when he gave himself up to pleasure with the Orkney woman at Kirkwall. And then, like the chill of frosty night stealing into the room, came the thought that it might be a paltry satisfaction to lie with an unwilling woman. He put on his clothes again, though they were still clammy with the Severn water, and lay down to sleep on a bench only a yard or so from Astrid, but with the fire between them.

Chapter 10

THE OUTLAWS

NEXT MORNING THE GRASS WAS WHITE with rime and a thin mist hung about the wooded hills above which the sun rose like a pale silvery disc. When Arnvid went outside the stuffy cottage he felt extraordinarily lighthearted. In the sharp air he had a sense of being keyed up for joyous adventure and his spirits rose still higher when Astrid came to meet him, flushing a little and dropping her eyes before his. She is more alive this morning, he thought, more content with our enterprise, more hopeful perhaps, more pleased to have me with her. Perhaps she has begun to want not only life but love. They went to see the horses in the stable. The gelding looked around in a disillusioned manner, but the stallion greeted them with a whinny of pleasure. There was fodder in plenty.

"We might take a bundle of hay in your dress as we did before," said Arnvid.

"It is easier to get food for the horses than for ourselves," she said. "I think the woman will give us bread and maybe meat as well."

"That should be worth a piece of silver," he said.

"Be sparing of silver. It may be more needful another time."

"You are a good housewife," he said smiling. "I think you will rule my house well."

"Where have you a house?"

"For the moment I have none. Where would you like it to be, Astrid?"

She looked away as though considering.

"I should like best where I was brought up."

"But there is no safety for us there."

"No," she admitted.

"I could have a farm in Iceland if I wished."

She did not answer and he thought the idea was little to her liking.

There was a good meal made ready for them in the cottage and when they had finished Astrid produced her dress. The woman filled it with loaves, cheese, and salted meat, enough to last them for several days.

"This is too good a dress to be used as a sack," she said. "A thane's daughter might be proud to wear it."

"It is my wedding dress," said Astrid.

"Then you are married?"

"Yes."

"Well then! Somehow I did not think he was your husband, but, to be sure, you are lucky to have such a noble-looking man. Perhaps he has killed someone and has to take to the woods? Aye, a proper man and no mistake. I could see that when he had his clothes off." The woman smiled broadly and made a coarse gesture.

Astrid did not answer, but she showed neither shame nor

resentment. Arnvid, however, cut short the talk by presenting the woman with a substantial silver coin minted with the head of King Erik Bloodaxe, one that he had got from Audun in York. The woman exclaimed with delight and her man snatched it from her, tried it with his teeth, spat on it, rubbed it on his sleeve, but soon had to give it back. They continued to stare at it together and hardly looked up when Astrid said farewell. In a few minutes she and Arnvid were on horseback. They were careful to start riding in what they supposed to be the direction of Worcester, then circled back through the woods and pushed on westward.

They went high over a bare hill, then down into flat country with many halls and villages. Peasants were working in the fields, but no one paid them any special attention. They rode over another crest into a deep valley full of forest. The hills on the far side were steeper than any they had yet come to, but there was a notch in them and the track climbed through it into a landscape that grew ever wilder and more desolate. The wintry splendor of the morning had faded and toward dusk snow began to fall in big wet flakes. Near the top of the pass they saw the charred wreck of a shepherd's cot. It looked as though it had been burned fairly recently. Now they were descending over a scrubby track into the next valley where everything was whitened over. For an hour they had scarcely spoken and Arnvid was oppressed by an instinctive feeling that this was dangerous country, where it was a good thing to be armed and on the back of a swift horse. It was the same feeling that he had had when riding down to Harek's farm, but there at least he knew where the danger was and how to escape from it.

Suddenly he said to Astrid, "I see nothing here to harm us and yet I feel that something is going to happen."

"I too," she said in a level voice.

"Why so?"

"We must be getting near Wales and from what I have heard there is often peril for folk when they reach the frontier of an unfriendly land."

"Are the Welsh so unfriendly?"

"Men say that all England was once theirs and they hate those who have taken it from them."

He was silent, thinking it might have been better not to have come this way but to have made back toward Derby and York. But there they would come on people who would be ready to recognize them as Danes and kill them at sight. Danger was everywhere, but hitherto he had not minded much, for his thoughts were centered on Astrid. Now a sort of panic was stealing over him and he had a violent inclination to urge the stallion to its utmost speed. He gathered up the reins and struck in his heels, but Astrid was immediately left far behind. He pulled up and waited for her, and then, just as she came up, he heard a drumming of hoofs on the track behind them. Through the veil of snowflakes two riders emerged at a canter. Had he been alone, Arnvid might have tried to outdistance them, but it was useless to think of that with Astrid on her sorry animal. With one accord they reined around and awaited the oncoming pair, Astrid with fatalistic calm, Arnvid in a sudden access of rage. The riders came to a halt fronting them. They were two men mounted on fine-looking horses. They wore no armor, but each carried weapons and had a shield at his back. One was a fair-haired and handsome man wrapped in a scarlet cloak, much torn and travel-stained, the other was a villainous-looking fellow in a leather coat, with black bushy eyebrows meeting above a crooked nose. Both had an air of recklessness and sneering defiance about them.

"These are robbers," said Arnvid in a low voice.

Astrid nodded and said, "It was to be expected."

"Hail strangers!" said the handsome man. "Whither do you ride?"

"That is our affair," said Arnvid, laying a hand on his sword hilt.

"In a place such as this it is well to ride in company."

"That depends on what manner of men you are."

"As for that, we are outlaws, and from your speech I take it you are Danes and therefore outlaws too; for the King has decreed death to all Danes in England."

"That we know, but our lives are not to be taken cheaply."

"All the same, friend, we are two to one."

"How so?"

The handsome man gave a laugh and pointed at Astrid. "A woman may be a match for a man in bed, but not in battle. Come, there need be no quarrel between outlaws. Join with us and share alike; we shall share our food with you and you shall share your woman with us."

Arnvid turned crimson. He looked at the two men and reckoned that with his coat of mail he had a fair chance against them both, which was doubtless what they were thinking also. To gain time he said, "I do not see that you have any food to offer."

"That is true, friend. We travel light, but we shall soon have food in plenty. Come our way and you shall see."

"And if we do not?"

"Then, as I said, we are two to one."

Now the other man spoke. "It is cold work bandying words in the snow. Let us set about our business." In a flash he unsheathed his sword and leveled the point at Arnvid's throat.

"Make up your mind quickly, friend, or there will be a Dane the less in England," said the other.

Astrid laid her hand on Arnvid's as it gripped his sword hilt. "Let us ride with them. Why die to no purpose?" she said in a low voice.

"We agree," said Arnvid and took his hand away.

The dark man looked inquiringly at the other, who shook his head slightly. In a moment they were all riding on, Arnvid between the two outlaws, Astrid close behind. It was almost dark and the snow fell thicker than ever. Now they were off the track and plunging through thorny brakes, down and down till suddenly there was a level stretch of snow-covered ground and on the far side of it a long, low, new-looking house. The dark man jumped off his horse and struck on the door with his sword hilt. A man opened it and the dark man whirled the sword in instant attack. There was a loud clash as the sword fell on the broad-bladed head of an axe. The man inside stepped out into the snow and struck in return. A woman screamed in the house. The dark man seemed to parry the stroke, but he reeled backward and nearly fell. In a trice his companion was off his horse and rushing forward with uplifted sword. Three figures swayed, struck, closed together and fell apart amid shouts of rage and pain.

"Now!" said Astrid urgently.

Arnvid had caught hold of the bridle of one of the horses.

"Get off your horse and get onto this one!" he said. Astrid looked at him in surprise, but obeyed. Then he drew his sword, struck the two loose horses with the flat of the blade, pricked them hard with the point, sending them careering off at a gallop. "Now ride!" he said. Coming alongside Astrid he goaded her new mount and together they plunged away at a reckless pace into the darkness, letting the horses take them where they would. Black mud spurted up out of the snow, trees went past like misshapen trolls with outstretched arms. Lowering their heads to the horses' manes they went full tilt down a hazel tunnel into swirling water, out again and up a bank so steep that they could hardly keep in their saddles. At the top they floundered through a fence and found themselves close to what looked like the gable-end of a house, but it turned out to be a haystack, half of which had been cut away. They pressed up against it, sheltered from a bitter wind that swept up the snow like gusts of sea spray and combed the forest with a muffled roar. They seemed to be in a little field with no sign of human activity save the haystack.

"Have we not fled fast and far enough?" said Astrid.

"Aye. Here we may as well overnight," he said. "Here is fodder, here we can eat some food and pull out hay from the stack to make a sleeping place inside." They got down from the panting beasts and set to work to make a deep cavern in the tough vertical wall of hay. Then they took off saddles and bridles, and listened to the horses chewing contentedly. Soon they were unpacking their food and crawling under cover to eat it in comfort, side by side on a soft fragrant couch. He put out a hand and caressed the girl's cheek, but she seemed to take no notice. Nettled by this he was about to handle her more forcefully when he remembered the dry, almost sarcastic tone of her remark about their flight. He also remembered the dread he had felt when they were in the power of the two robbers and the enormous relief it had been to give them the slip. Yes, he had been fairly panic-stricken, but Astrid had shown no alarm. He had been expecting death, and she must have been expecting rape. What did a woman think about rape? He did not know. He had never seen it, unless what Gunnar did to the goatherd's girl had been rape, and that girl seemed to have had nothing against it.

"Did you think we should have stayed with the robbers?" he asked coldly, and a suspicion crossed his mind that Astrid might have taken a fancy to the handsome outlaw.

"I did not think you would ride away when the fight began. I thought you would have helped the peasant to kill those two villains."

With something of a shock he realized that this had never entered his head. His one thought had been escape. Stiffly he said: "I did not think my business was to defend Englishman against Englishman. What I have set out to do is to preserve your life and honor."

"I know," she said. "You want my life and my body for your own pleasure, but just now I thought you were perhaps overcareful about your own life. It would have been a good deed to rid the land of those men."

"This is not my land."

"But I still feel it is mine, the land in which I was born and bred. It is a good land even if it has a bad king."

"From what I know of England I would sooner be among my own kin in Wales."

"Always Wales! Wait till you have seen it. I have heard little good either of the land or its folk."

"That is why you are against me!" he said bitterly.

"It is not for me to complain of the manner of man you

are, when I owe you my life. As I said before, you can do with me what you will."

"But it would be no pleasure to you to lie with a man whom you think a coward?"

"A woman can seldom have what she would like. A man can command her in everything except love."

"Have you ever seen a man you could love?"

She was silent a moment, then she said, "I think so, but what is the use of talking about it?"

Anger flooded through him, quickly coupled with lust. Why should he not take her at her word and have done with it? Everything was in its favor, except for this accursed coat of mail that had never yet done him any service. He remembered Gunnar laughing at it. Gunnar—he remembered how Astrid had looked across the board at Gunnar when they sat at the wedding feast in Steintor's hall. Yes, perhaps she could have loved Gunnar. Well, he could punish her for preferring Gunnar to him, but would that be a manly thing to do? Was he such a poor stick of a man that he could not rouse passion in a girl? Sullenly he turned away from her as far as he could. Wait till he had another chance! He would show her something that might surprise her . . . He heard her breathing deeply and peacefully, and in another moment he himself was asleep.

Chapter 11

INTO WALES

NEXT MORNING WHEN THEY SET OFF Arnvid had an impulse
to say: "Now we shall ride in search of the robbers and make
an end of them if you think that so important," and then he
thought shamefacedly of what a foolish gesture this would
be, particularly if the peasant had managed to kill them singlehanded.

It was a day of blustery snow and sleet showers. They
worked their way slowly westward over wilder hills and into
thicker forests. The tracks they found often petered out in
impenetrable thickets such as Arnvid and Gunnar had skirted
in Pyperwood. Again and again they had to turn back and
try afresh, and there were neither peasants nor robbers of
whom they could ask the way. They ate sparingly of their
food, uncertain of how long it would have to last. Astrid
was more silent than usual and Arnvid alternately sulky and
irritable. The new horse, a stallion, was both restive and slug-
gish, and when Arnvid in a temper punished it with his

switch it reared up and threw Astrid into a gorse bush. However she came out smiling, remounted and dealt with the horse in such a way that it gave little more trouble. Arnvid reflected that he had intended to surprise Astrid by some desperate deed, but now it was she who was surprising him with a show of spirit and ungirlish ruthlessness. Now, too, it was she who took the lead and either by luck or judgment hit on a path that brought them out of the woods at nightfall onto snow-covered slopes that rose against a black sky flashing with stars. The wind had dropped and it was freezing hard. To Arnvid it seemed a wilderness as absolute as any in Iceland. They could see for miles to right and left, but nowhere was there a trace of man's handiwork—no light from a peasant's cot, no fence rising from the snow-laden heather in which the path lost itself without a sign of a footprint. The horses were utterly spent; there was no getting any further without rest, but to overnight here might mean frostbite before morning came.

"We are facing westward," said Arnvid, after a long look at the stars. "Shall we leave the horses and walk to keep ourselves warm? Perhaps Wales is the other side of that hill."

Astrid sat drowsily in the saddle. Now she got off and lay down in the snow. "I have not the strength," she said.

"Nor have I the strength to carry you more than a little way."

"Without the horses half our chance of safety is gone."

"We might drive them before us." He got off and tried to thrash the horses forward, but they only moved a few yards and then stood obstinately with lowered heads.

"We must go back into the wood," he said. "There it will not be so cold. If we could make a fire . . ."

"A fire? I have flint and tinder in my pouch." Her head fell back and he saw she was asleep.

He gathered her in his arms and began to carry her into the wood, thinking that this was the first time he had held her close to him and now that it had happened he felt no desire, only pity and tenderness. True enough he held in his arms a precious possession, a creature who could give him pleasure, work for him, bear him children. Yet now he saw Astrid as something more than that, a girl with as much right to live as he had, but defenseless, strained to the utmost limit of her endurance, someone whom it would be a good deed to help even if there were no return; even, perhaps, at the cost of his own life.

There was little snow on the ground inside the wood and it was very dark. Vaguely he could make out enormous stunted and distorted trunks with low-branching crowns and he set Astrid down beside one of them. With numbed fingers he unfastened her leather coat and felt for the pouch at her girdle. The little bag contained scissors, comb, flint and steel, and tinder. For a long time he fumbled with the flint and steel, but in the end he got it to strike sparks freely. Then he took dry moss from the tree trunk and found to his surprise that there was a yawning rent in the stem and a hollow space within big enough to hold three or four people. Moss and dead twigs from the low branches, scraps of dry fern, withered grass and leaves—he collected a fair-sized heap in front of the opening. Then he struck sparks into the tinder, got it to glow, and finally started the fire. Flames shot up, a flickering radiance caught the monstrous trunks of oak, the drifts of brown leaves, pale fungi and glistening acorns. Now he hurried to and fro, collecting fallen branches, snapping them underfoot, and piling them on the fire. He fought hunger and weariness, intent on feeding the fire as though their lives depended on it, as perhaps they did. Then he went and led back the horses. They came willingly enough under the shelter of the still leafy trees. He took off the bridles and put out two small heaps of hay, the last that was left stuffed into Astrid's wedding dress. He also took out half the food they had left. He filled his helmet with snow and set it near the fire to melt. Bread, meat and cheese and a drink of snow water—they might be faring worse. He woke up Astrid and soon they were eating and drinking, man and woman crouched beside the fire as their ancestors must have done thousands of years earlier. A great content came over Arnvid. It was pure pleasure to look at Astrid's face, the flame-tinted flesh set in silky corn-colored hair, the full, red lips, the eyes that sometimes met his, the windows of her mind that revealed neither joy nor sadness but perhaps a grave appraisal of the man to whom she might choose or be forced to bear a child. Yes, this was the same face that he had seen first in Steintor's hall, aglow in the firelight, the eyes that had glanced at him and then rested fixedly on Gunnar. . . . With a sigh he got up, stretched himself and said: "There is room for us to sleep within the tree, a little room warmed by the fire under the forest roof."

Her lips parted in a smile, amused if not cheerful. She said, "Warmer than the grass beside Severn, sweeter than the peasant hut, not so soft as the haystack."

"But the best so far?"

"Perhaps," she said.

They lay down inside and put their arms around each other for warmth and comfort, though not for love.

Next morning there was still a glow among the ashes of the

fire. Arnvid made it up with fresh wood and they sat by a cheerful blaze while they ate all that was left of the food. Then they collected the horses that had found their way to a stream and grazed a bit on rushes and sedges. Arnvid shook his head at the sight of them, for they still looked hollow and exhausted. They mounted and emerging from the wood they rode slowly up the hill. The sun was rising behind them and threw long shadows from the pair over the sparkling snow. They were utterly alone in a white and silent world under a blue sky and instinctively they rode close together so that their stirrups sometimes clashed, each thinking that this was perhaps a crisis in their journey. For the moment they were rested and well fed, and very soon things would be better for them or else worse. All depended on what they found on the other side of the hill.

They reached the crest and there running along it as far as the eye could reach was a great rampart drifted deep with snow but almost bare on the top.

"That," said Astrid, "should be Offa's Dyke. Across it lies Wales."

The horses plunged and scrambled and got them to the top. There they halted and the man and the woman gazed out westward. The hill dropped steeply into woods through which ran a river. Though they did not know it, it was again the Severn, now flowing north instead of south. Across the valley were more hills, some wooded, some bare, range beyond range like a stormy sea breaking into crests of white foam. Arnvid looked at it all with shining eyes and his heart beat heavily with a strange emotion. So this was Wales, his mother's country, so often assailed by Englishman and viking, but never completely conquered. How often had those hills and forests withstood the shock of invading armies and seen them engulfed and destroyed or flung back whence they came?

"It pleases you?" said Astrid.

"To me it looks both sad and beautiful, a land that calls to something in my blood, like a song or music on the harp."

"I had thought you reckoned yourself a Northman rather than one of the Cymry," she said drily.

"So I did till I had speech with an old shepherd, a Welshman, on the verge of Westmorland. Are you sorry that I am what I am?"

She smiled and said, "That is a strange question for a man to ask a woman. Should not a man be sure of himself?"

"And I am unsure?"

"Yes, because you are not altogether either Northman or Welshman."

He flushed, thinking this sort of talk unseemly, as indeed she implied. If Gunnar talked about himself it would be to boast of what he had done or could do. He would not let a girl say that he had a flaw in him. And yet, because he loved this girl he very much wanted to know what it was that might hinder her from loving him in return. Was a woman worth so much consideration? Gunnar would laugh at the idea; but to Arnvid it seemed reasonable to share all thoughts with one who might be his dear companion and lifelong mate. He persisted. "Am I so different from the men you have known, Danes and Englishmen?"

Her face seemed to cloud with annoyance. "Yes, you are different," she said. "You are warm where they are cold: you are too gentle, too kind to man and beast, unless you fall into a rage. You are too much afraid for others, too much afraid for yourself. You are soft when you should be hard, and in such a world as this things will not be easy for you."

"And this is little to your liking?"

Now she smiled a little. "Sometimes I like you for it, sometimes not," she said.

They rode over the snow-filled moat on the far side of the rampart and down toward the tangled woods. It struck Arnvid sharply that this was the time to make a plan, not to talk about himself.

"There must be a king in Wales," he said after a time. "I think I should try to find him and enter his service. I heard Gunnar say that Northmen were sometimes hired to fight here out west."

"I have heard my father talk about Wales. He said there were once three kings, but that now there was only one and he ruled the whole land. Llewelyn ap Seisylt he is called, a good king who keeps the land at peace, but who has little support among the folk except in his own realm of Gwynedd."

"And is this Gwynedd where we are now?"

"No, I think it lies farther to the north. This would be Powys."

"It looks a good land and full of folk." As the woods opened out they could see houses clustering everywhere on the hillsides, some of them long houses as in England, but mostly little round huts like toadstools with their pointed roofs of thatch. There was no snow in the valley. The land looked green with rushy pastures and many little fenced fields. Now they were near enough to a group of huts to see people standing about and hear a chatter of voices and the sound of a song.

"Will you seek for food here?" she asked.

"These folk on the border will be the most suspicious of us. It might be best to ride further into the land, but I doubt whether the horses can do much without food," he said, frowning in uncertainty.

They passed on, crossed the river at a lonely ford, and turned up a side valley. Here there was a well-trodden path through high forest. Down it came three men riding bareback on little ponies. Their looks were friendly, they reined in and spoke in lilting musical voices which conveyed no meaning to Arnvid, but to his surpise Astrid answered them readily. They all talked at once; the men looked at her curiously and began to laugh. She asked a question and they looked grave, but soon smiled again and pointed up the valley. All the time their eyes had been returning constantly to Arnvid. They muttered together, nodded, looked wary, and then laughed. They shook their bridles and went off at a fast trot, the long manes and tails of the ponies streaming in the wind.

"How is it you can speak with these folk?" exclaimed Arnvid.

"I can hardly help knowing some Welsh," she answered. "Many of our servants were Welsh and I was brought up amongst them."

"These men seemed to bear us no ill will."

"All the same I would not trust them far."

"What did you ask them?"

"The way to Gwynedd."

They rode up into marshy moorland and soon came to some little knolls where there was very good grazing.

"Here is something for the horses," said Arnvid, brightening up. "Here we shall stay awhile." They dismounted and took off the bridles. Arnvid went to the top of a knoll and looked around. He came back and said, "I can see no one here to harm us, but on the other side of a bog there are some huts. I will go there and try to get food."

"Had we not better both go?"

"It would be best for you to stay with the horses. Tell me some words of Welsh and I shall say to the folk that I ride with a message to the King in Gwynedd and will pay for what they give me."

Astrid chose a few words that seemed suitable and he learned them carefully. Then with a last look at the horses he set off half-running among the gorse bushes.

Astrid wrapped herself in her cloak and lay down. She was tired and hungry; the horses were all right, filling themselves greedily. She would like to have slept for a little, but she felt uneasy at being left alone, realizing now more than ever how much she depended on Arnvid. She felt a little ashamed of being so critical of him. What would happen to her if he got killed? Well, what did usually happen to a lonely woman who was young and good-looking? Some man took her and kept her, and anyhow a woman who could choose her man was lucky indeed. She had not chosen Tord, but she would have had to have him, and now it was the same with Arnvid, only he put off taking her, waiting till all seemed to him exactly right. Perhaps that was one reason why she sometimes felt exasperated with him, and with herself as well, because she could not be with him day after day and night after night without wanting what was natural for a woman.

Now she began to think he had been gone a long time, and her anxiety grew. She also noticed that the horses had moved out of sight. Abruptly she sat up and then as quickly ducked down again, for above the gorse bushes she saw a man riding on a white horse accompanied by another man on foot. They were not fifty yards away; perhaps they had not seen her; but they had, for here they came straight to where she was lying. She got to her feet and looked around, but there was no sign of Arnvid. Then she looked at the man on horseback. At first he reminded her of the handsome outlaw; he was a fair-haired, formidable-looking man, but unlike the outlaw he was dressed in very fine new clothes and high leather boots and his sword hilt, scabbard and stirrups were inlaid with gold. Obviously a man of high rank—in England she would have thought him a thane or even an earl. He looked both haughty and cunning, but there was certainly a charm about him. He had a mustache and a small pointed beard, his eyelids drooped a little as though in arrogance or disillusion, his eyebrows slanted down toward the bridge of the nose giving him a sinister aspect, but his expression was more mocking then fierce. The man with him was in contrast stunted and dirty-looking with pitch-black hair, and carried a hooded hawk on his wrist. A master and his servant out for sport, and it was clear that they regarded her as their quarry. The fair man dismounted gracefully and stared at her in such a way that her cheeks flushed scarlet.

"What do you seek here?" he asked in Welsh.

"I am on my way to King Llewelyn in Gwynedd," she answered.

"And whence do you come?"

"It is not to be denied that I come from England."

"I know very well what has been happening in England and I can guess what brings you here."

"You can guess, but that is not to say that you guess rightly."

The Welshman laughed a little and his eyes had an appreciative twinkle.

"Why then are you wearing man's clothes?" he said.

"What else should I wear?"

"There are more ways than one of perceiving that you are a woman."

She reddened again with a mixture of shame and pleasure such as she had never felt when with Arnvid, but she said boldly, "Whether I am a woman or not, you have no right to molest me."

"A Danish woman can claim no protection, and as for my rights, you are on my land. All that you see is mine."

"Nevertheless there are folk who can protect me."

The Welshman glanced around composedly. "I do not see them," he said. "But I would like to see proof of whether you are a man, as you would have me think." He made a sign to the servant, who set the hooded hawk adroitly on a thorn branch and laid his hands roughly on Astrid. Rage flamed up in her, but she knew it was useless to resist. Besides she was in a way hypnotized by the glittering eyes and subtle smile of the chieftain. Better he than some rough dirty peasant who would take her to his hut and work the life out of her. Now her cloak and leather coat were off and the servant took her tunic at the neck and tore it downward bringing her breasts into the light of day. He was proceeding further when his master told him to stop.

"I can protect you from harm," he said, not unkindly. "You shall come with me to my house, you can have food and proper clothes, you can be washed clean; but first we shall try how things go between us here." He drew her down onto the turf, slid an arm around her and caressed her with a practiced hand. The servant turned away with assumed indifference and went to hold his master's horse. Astrid lay there, letting herself begin to kindle at the assured touch of a man who had a certain delicacy but no scruples. This is only what had to be expected, she thought with fatalistic calm. Her mind surrendered and the weak physical defenses of her clothes were being quickly overcome, when her ears, close to earth, caught the sound of rushing footsteps . . .

Arnvid had not found it easy to make himself understood at the huts. Men, women and children swarmed around him, curious rather than hostile, and keeping up an incessant chatter. He showed them silver and they brought out food readily enough, but when he put out a coin their voices became indignant. Two coins, and the clamor became louder. The people began to shout at one another, eyes flashed, some young men slipped away and came back with weapons. Then in desperation Arnvid unsheathed his sword. In sudden fury he shouted: "Give me the food or I make an end of you all!"

Oddly enough he seemed to be understood. The uproar died down somewhat and a woman put the food in a basket and pushed it toward him. He put down a third coin, pointed with his sword to a pony tethered to a stake and made a motion of eating. A man went away and returned with oats in a sack. Arnvid indicated that he wanted more, and more was brought. He took the sack and basket and backed away. A man sprang at him with a knife, but Arnvid dropped his burden and shot out a fist that caught the fellow on the jaw and he went headlong into a dunghill. There were shouts of rage, but also of laughter, and the laughter seemed to predominate. Arnvid put his sword between his teeth and picked up the sack and basket. He glared at the peasants, but saw that they were now disputing about the three pieces of silver. There were shrill voices, savage gestures, knives flashed out and cudgels rose in the air. Arnvid walked off with ostentatious leisureliness, but once out of sight of the huts his retreat verged on panic. He splashed through the bog and came up toward the knolls. Now he saw the two horses grazing a long way from where he had left Astrid and he was gripped by a fresh anxiety. How was it she had let them stray off? Had something happened to her? And then, just about where he judged that Astrid should be, he saw a man holding a white horse. He set down sack and basket, took his sword in his hand and ran with great leaps over the gorse bushes. Yes, here was Astrid, unresistant in the arms of a stranger, her clothes pulled open in preparation for the act of lust. The man raised his head. Arnvid saw his teeth clench, his eyes glint with surprise and rage, and then Arnvid's sword fell on his neck just below the ear. Blood spurted out in a torrent over Astrid's bare breasts; the man heaved himself to his feet, then he sagged at the knees and went down on the turf in a crumpled heap. Arnvid turned toward the man with the horse, but he was already in full flight, his black head bobbing up and down until it became a mere speck on the duncolored moor.

Astrid sat up. She pulled handfuls of moss and tried to wipe away the blood, then suddenly she was sick and lay crouched on hands and knees, shaking all over. Arnvid pushed her with his foot. "Get up!" he said violently. "Help me to catch the horses! Why did you let them go? I have got food, but I dropped it over there. I had something like a fight with the peasants, and then I find you letting a strange man play with you!"

"How could I help it?" she said coldly. "It was your plan to go away and leave me."

"Perhaps you would have been pleased to be his mistress."

"He was maybe as good a man as you," she flung back.

"Who was he?" Arnvid turned the dead man over. He looked covetously at the beautiful sword, and also at the white stallion, but let them both alone.

"He was the lord of all the land hereabouts. He was hawking. There is the hawk on that bush."

"Then it was a notable deed to fell him," said Arnvid, thinking that Gunnar would have taken that view of the matter. "Do you not think so?" he added.

Astrid was struggling into her thick coat. "It is what a man would think," she said in a bitter tone. "I think it is the worst of ill luck that you killed him. Such a deed calls for vengeance and we shall be safe nowhere,"

"That is true. We must anyhow get away from here as fast as can be." He picked up the bridles, took her roughly by the arm and hurried her across the moor. Presently he found the bag of oats and took it over his shoulders and Astrid carried the basket. The horses were in a little green hollow. Arnvid gave them a few handfuls of oats and slipped on the bridles while Astrid crammed the food into the wedding dress. When all was fastened on they mounted, but the horses had turned lazy and moved at a snail's pace until Arnvid in a temper jumped off and got two branches of gorse. After that they went fast enough, but Astrid was so exhausted that she could hardly keep in the saddle. When they had got well into the shelter of woods they stopped, drank from a stream and had some of the food. A new valley opened before them, again with a river running north, and across the water they could see several big halls and a multitude of small buildings all enclosed in ramparts and stockades.

"Could that be the palace of Llewelyn?" asked Arnvid.

Astrid shook her head. "Gwynedd is far away from here, across high mountains, so those horsemen told me," she said.

It was growing dark, clouds had dropped on the hills and a steady drizzle had begun. Arnvid thought it would be a very good thing if they could spend the night under a roof, but he was daunted by his reception at the huts and he realized that in any case they could not safely show themselves to folk after killing a chieftain close by. So it must be another night in the open, knowing that men would be searching for them, perhaps with bloodhounds. He had begun to hate these hills and woods, and the valleys full of folk who might be akin to him, but whom he found incomprehensibly alien in all their ways. Wales! Now he would be glad to be out of it as soon as possible, even as Astrid had hinted before they got in.

Everything was sodden with wet. They could not make a fire even if it had been wise to make one. It was hardly wise to sleep, but sleep they did in a fashion in the poor shelter of a holly tree. It rained in torrents, but toward morning it cleared somewhat and there was a soft, almost summery air. They ate in silence, each out of temper with the other. Astrid had begun to feel that their position grew more and more hopeless and that she at least would have been better off if that Welshman had got her away before Arnvid came upon them. Nor did she forget that Arnvid had given her something like a kick when she was doubled up with sickness and horror. He might be good at making plans, but he lost his head when they went wrong. Then he was unmanly, almost childish . . . As for Arnvid, he could not get over the thought that Astrid had been much too ready to let the Welshman have her. Perhaps the fellow had beguiled her in some crafty way, but it looked more as though Astrid had been hoping to secure a better protector for herself, doubtless a wealthy landowner with a good hall and scores of servants, instead of a homeless man who had to hide with her in woods and haystacks.

Bitterly he thought that women might seem helpless enough, but that did not prevent them trading their bodies and making a good bargain when they saw the chance. What a lot he had learned since he left Iceland, imagining himself a match for any situation, imagining himself the equal of Gunnar!

Chapter 12

IN AND OUT OF GWYNEDD

THEY RODE THROUGH THE VALLEY on their dispirited horses, keeping well away from folk and houses until they could no longer avoid a stream of people flocking down to a flat beside the river. There on a knoll stood a young man, bareheaded, but girt with a sword and wearing a coat of mail, and beside him stood a standard planted in the ground. The device on it seemed to be a wildcat. He was haranguing a growing crowd of men, all of whom carried weapons. They seemed to be peasants for the most part, but there were also some men of better quality mounted on good horses.

"Let us ride in among them," said Arnvid. "In numbers there may be safety."

The young man spoke passionately in a loud, musical voice, he spread out his hands and gestured to right and left, he unsheathed his sword and waved it aloft, evoking roars of approval from the gathering below. Weapons were brandished, there were persistent shouts in which Arnvid detected the words "Llewelyn" or "Gwynedd."

"What is he talking about?" said Arnvid, impressed somewhat against his will by the man's martial looks and fiery eloquence. Astrid had been listening intently to an undercurrent of talk around them. She said in a low voice: "I think he claims to be a son of the King of Powys and he urges the people to make war on Gwynedd. It is what is always happening in Wales. The great men turn upon each other instead of uniting to fight Englishmen and vikings."

"They are too manstrong for these narrow dales," observed Arnvid. "Folk everywhere, living like beasts, but rearing swarms of children. Different is this from Iceland—a farm here and a farm there, winning life from the land with hard labor."

"If we join this army we shall be provided for and it will take us to Gwynedd, if you are still set on that plan," said Astrid.

"It is maybe the best we can do," agreed Arnvid.

The young man had come down from the knoll and was now mounting a horse. The army began to stream forward, a long serpent of men with the standard at the head. From the disordered ranks there burst forth song, deep-throated, melancholy, yet with a glow of fury about it. Arnvid thought he had never heard anything more moving. His eyes grew bright, his cheeks flushed, but Astrid's looks were dulled by a weary contempt.

"Do you not like the singing?" he said as they edged in among the mounted men.

"A good singer may be a poor fighter," she said. "I do not fancy this war band will get far, but it may get us safely out of Powys."

Arnvid could imagine Gunnar saying much the same, and

again he felt sharply the difference between himself on the one hand and Northmen and Danes on the other; a difference to which Astrid might not show the same kindly tolerance as did Gunnar and Geirfin. He looked at the men about him and thought Astrid was probably right when she called them unreliable. But were they any more unreliable than he was himself? The army moved slowly, collecting both men and food as it went down one valley and up another, cooking and camping by big fires when darkness fell. Though not a few men joined the host during the day it did not gain much in strength, for many seemed to disappear during the night. There was singing around the fires, but there were also violent arguments. There was thieving and murder.

On the third day they came to the head of the valley and went up a pass through the mountains. Rain fell steadily and the clouds hung low. Sometimes they lifted a little to show patterns of snowdrift and gray rocky slopes. At the top they came into a raging blizzard. Arnvid had the feeling that they were half defeated already. There seemed to be fewer men now than when they had first set out. However, now they were going downhill and Astrid said that this might be Gwynedd. The first huts they came to were deserted and were soon set on fire amid exultant shouts. Men looked about for booty, but only a few goats could be found. The weather cleared as they went down and down through scrubby forest and at last came to green meadowland and patches of plowing, but still no folk were to be seen. It grew dusk and the army came uncertainly to a halt on a flat beside a foaming river. Then suddenly a horn sounded and a sleet of arrows came from the thickets across the water. At the same moment a mass of spearmen charged out of the woods on the other side of the valley. There were shouts and countershouts, the men of Powys ran together like sheep, they swayed this way and that, the standard vanished, and in a few minutes the battle was over. The invaders started running back the way they had come, the mounted men spurring their horses and treading down those on foot.

Arnvid and Astrid had been in the van. They were the only ones who did not turn back. They got their horses into a gallop and went on down the valley. A few arrows sang past them, but no one appeared in front. Evidently the men of Gwynedd, with the confidence of practiced warriors, had resolved to cut off the retreat of their foes rather than to bar their advance.

"Now we have to find King Llewelyn," said Arnvid when at last they paused to breathe the horses. The valley had opened out, the dark mass of cloud-capped mountains was far behind them and to the left appeared a lake with low wooded shores. Night was upon them and firelight twinkled here and there on the edges of the woods. He gave a sigh of relief. "Half our difficulties are over," he said. "We have come safely into Gwynedd."

Astrid did not answer. She sat inert in the saddle, desperately stiff and weary, exasperated by what seemed to her facile optimism. A broad river flowed from the lake; they followed it down and soon came to a big farm. After a short consultation they knocked on the door of the hall. A servant opened it and Astrid spoke with him explaining that here was a man from England with a message for the King. An elderly woman came to the door and asked for news. There had been a fight, Astrid said, and the men from Powys had been routed. The woman seemed pleased and said her husband and her sons had gone up the pass to give battle. There were only servants and women in the hall. They looked at Arnvid with respect and exerted themselves to make the guests welcome. When the meal was over the woman asked Astrid whether she wished to sleep with her companion. Surely they were lovers, she said. Astrid did not deny it, but said that she was very tired and would like to wash herself. Then she would rather sleep alone. The woman nodded understandingly and said she could sleep in the same bed with her. She took Astrid into a small room off the hall that served as a kitchen and brought a wooden bucket with warm water and a cloth. Astrid began to take off her clothes and then suddenly remembered that her breasts were still caked with blood. It had run down all over her belly. She had wanted to wipe it off, but Arnvid had not given her time. It would never do to let the woman see that—what would she think? Instead of undressing she merely stripped off her hose and put her feet in the bucket of water. The woman showed no surprise.

"It is as well to wash hands and feet sometimes, but little else," she said.

Astrid thought that they had been a good deal more particular in her father's hall, though latterly Steintor had begun to fall in with English customs and use the bath house less and less. She would have liked to wash away that blood and with it the recollection of the dreadful moment on the moor when lust and death were intermingled. Was it possible that the blood would remain unavenged? Deep down in her she felt that there ought to be some retribution. Natural it might be for Arnvid to kill the man who was going to lie with her, but he might have challenged him to fight instead of striking him down when he was defenseless. She realized now that in a way she had shrunk from Arnvid ever since, just as she had shrunk from Tord when they were out in the woods together not long ago and he had forced her to lie with him in the most brutal manner possible. They happened to be alone, the hunters had gone on, and in a day or two they would be married . . . Arnvid did not know about that and she would never tell him. A woman's chastity—how did men regard it? A bargaining counter for land and power; something that it was their pleasure to destroy. What a woman felt about it was seldom considered.

That day they rode over a hill into the valley of the Clwyd and followed it northward toward the sea. Here was the most fertile and thickly populated land they had seen since crossing the Severn, and riding unchallenged past hut and hall Arnvid began to have a feeling of complete security. No one seemed to doubt that they were on a mission from England to the King of Gwynedd, hospitality was offered them without question and they were told that Llewelyn might be found in the palace of Deganwy, westward along the coast.

There came a morning when they were riding beside the tidal reaches of the Clwyd in a thin mist that silvered the grass and strung jewels along the spiders' webs spread like nets upon the gorse bushes. The track narrowed and twisted among the stone walls enclosing little fields and folds, and suddenly out of the mist ahead came the trample and splashing of horses' hoofs. A company of mounted men trotted swiftly toward them and Arnvid and Astrid drew their horses in to the side to make way. The leading rider was a big man in a yellow cloak. He swept by on a white stallion, glancing disdainfully at the pair and giving them no greeting. He was

followed by half a dozen armed servants and in a moment
they were all out of sight in the mist. Arnvid was riding on
without comment, but Astrid put out her hand and clutched
him by the arm.

"Did you see that man in the yellow cloak?" she exclaimed
breathlessly.

He looked at her in surprise and saw that she was deathly
pale. He said, "Of course I saw him. A proud-looking man,
doubtless a rich landowner."

"But he was the *same man*—the same pointed beard, the
slanting eyebrows, the corn-colored hair—the man you killed
on the moor in Powys! Can it be that he was a ghost? The
white horse, that looked the same too."

"I did not take much note of that man's looks, but I know
this, that I left him dead. This must be some other man," he
said drily.

"I feel the sight of him was a warning."

"A warning of what?"

She did not answer. As so often happened, a vision floated
before her eyes of that scene on the moor: the man bending
over her with a smile that showed his white wolfish teeth,
the smell of wet heather, the chilly air on her naked flesh,
the first tremors of delight and surrender, and then the swish
of the sword stroke and the spurting blood. To Arnvid it
seemed that he had struck in time, before lust could have its
way; but to her it seemed that he had struck too late, for her
mind had already accepted what the man intended, even if her
body had not. And now, sooner or later, Arnvid would have
her, but she would never forget that he had killed the man
whom she herself would have chosen. There would always
be blood between them, the blood that was still caked on her

bosom. And then she wondered whether she had not persuaded herself that she loved the Welshman as a means of
thrusting back the love that Arnvid offered her. . . .

They came down toward the river mouth where there was
a homestead and several boats drawn up in a sandy creek.
Beyond was a glimpse of the open sea.

"There is something you will not have set eyes on before,"
said Arnvid cheerfully.

"The sea?" The blood was still on her mind. "Could we
go there and wash?"

He laughed and said, "The sea is not so good for washing
or drinking, but it has other uses. There is the path to Ireland and the Isles. To Iceland for that matter. With the
right wind it is easier traveling than sitting stiff on horseback
and toiling through brake and briar." He turned his horse
away from the friendly-looking house and followed a track
that went westward toward blue hills, beyond which, so they
were told, lay Deganwy.

They had ridden a mile when Astrid said, "Surely the sea
would be a safer path than the one we are now treading."

"Why safer?" he said.

"Because if you go to the King there must come a time
when a complaint will be laid against you for the killing of
that man on the moor. A man such as that is not killed without there being a case for the law court."

"But that was in Powys and this is Gwynedd."

"Llewelyn is king of all Wales."

He drew rein. "There is something in what you say," he
conceded reluctantly. "Come, let us ride into that copse,
eat some food, and think it over."

They had not been long within the screen of withered oak

leaves before they saw a company of riders going past at a canter not twenty yards away. They leaned forward on hands and knees, peering out.

"The man in the yellow cloak and his six servants," said Arnvid.

"Now there are seven servants. Do you not see the little dark man? He is the falconer who ran away over the moor when his master was killed. Now he is here. What does it mean?" said Astrid.

"I think it means they are searching for us," he said, watching cautiously while the riders disappeared along the track to westward. He stood up and climbed into the saddle. "You are right," he said. "Our only chance is the sea. Let us ride to the farm where we saw those boats."

They rode out of the copse and urged the horses to a gallop. In a few minutes they were at a gateway among the buildings. There was the hall and out of it was coming a middle-aged man with a shrewd, smiling face. Somehow he did not look much like a Welshman.

Arnvid did not wait for Astrid to speak. In his excitement he called out in Norse: "Will you sell us a boat, friend?"

"That depends on who wants to buy and what he has to bid," answered the man in the same language.

"You are a Northman?"

"I am an Orkneyman, Saemund by name."

"I am Arnvid Torolfsson from Iceland. My grandfather, Leif, fell fighting for King Erik Bloodaxe on Steinmor."

"So did mine. I can guess that it is urgent for you to have a boat." He opened the gate and they rode through.

"Why do you guess that?" said Arnvid, jumping off his horse.

"Because a man came here not an hour ago asking if I had seen a warrior in a mail coat and a girl dressed in man's clothes." Saemund smiled significantly.

"What man was it who came?" burst out Astrid.

"He was a servant of Caradoc ap Einion, a mighty man in these parts, high in favor with King Llewelyn."

"And what did you say?" asked Arnvid.

"I said that I had seen two folk of that sort ride by on the road to the west. Do you not wish to meet with Caradoc ap Einion?"

"I know nothing of him, but if he means me ill, one man has little chance against eight."

Saemund stroked his beard reflectively. He said, "Perhaps you know his twin brother, Cadogan ap Einion, the King's right-hand man in Powys?"

Arnvid and Astrid exchanged glances. Arnvid said slowly, "It may well be him that I met on a moor in Powys, soon after we had got clear from England. I killed him."

Saemund nodded. "A pity," he said. "Your days will not be many if you stay in Wales."

"How is it that you, a Northman, have a good homestead here in Gwynedd?"

"I have been hired by Llewelyn and I did him good service fighting against Danish vikings in Anglesey."

"I too had thought of hiring with the King."

"As things have happened you will have little chance. Come and see the boats." A servant took the horses into a stable. Arnvid and Astrid went down with Saemund to the beach. There on the sand lay a three-seater with a mast and sail, and a four-seater without a mast, besides some coracles.

"Will you take the two horses and such silver as I have

here for the three-seater?" said Arnvid. "It is all I have to offer."

There was a twinkle in Saemund's eye. He said nothing, but looked appraisingly at Astrid. Suddenly she said without reflecting, "Leave me with the horses, Arnvid. I have brought you little luck."

Arnvid flushed and said, "The boat is worth much to me, but I will not have it as the price of my woman."

"That was to be expected, friend," said Saemund. "Keep your silver as well. The horses are two good beasts. Can you manage the three-seater?"

"I have sailed worse boats on the Breidi Fjord." Arnvid began to push the boat out over the wet sand and Astrid came to help him.

"Food and drink you must have," said Saemund, and went back to the hall. Presently he came with two servants, all three running. They put a cask and baskets of food in the boat. It was now half in the water, with Astrid sitting in the prow.

"The wind blows from the southeast," said Saemund. "It will soon freshen and blow from the south and then southwest. There may be a rough sea, but it is a stout boat with a high gunwale. Farewell, friend. North lies Cumberland and northwest Man. You have little time to lose." He pointed over his shoulder and Arnvid saw riders coming down from the hall. The servants heaved and Arnvid thrust with an oar. "One more thing you may find of use," said Saemund. He threw a bow and a bundle of arrows into the boat. Arnvid gave him a look of gratitude, but there was not much time for words. Now the boat was drifting slowly with the tide ebbing down the river. Arnvid hauled up the square sail and made it fast, he stood in the stern, gripping the rudder pole, keeping the boat in midstream. The sail filled, they glided between the sand hills into the open sea. The bow rose and fell with a crunch among the choppy waves. He looked back and saw a number of men launching the other boat and getting out oars. Saemund stood apart, his hands thrust into his belt. Pursuit—Arnvid counted three pairs of oars, a man to each oar. They were not very good rowers, but the boat was coming on fast. With a throb of dismay he saw that it was gaining on them, even though their speed increased as the wind blew harder away from land. He shipped the rudder. "Come here!" he shouted to Astrid. She came, walking unsteadily over the thwarts. "Sit down and hand me those arrows," he said and strung the bow. The other boat was within fifty yards and closing fast. In the prow was the big man in the yellow cloak. As Arnvid watched he cast off the cloak and took a throwing spear. Arnvid stood up, balancing himself as best he could and shot an arrow, but it went wide. Another, and it went high over the boat's crew. The sea was getting rougher. He loosed three more arrows. Only one went anywhere near the boat. It was almost impossible to aim, the pitching and tossing in the stern was so violent. He went forward and stood beside the mast. Here it seemed a little better. He shot again and hit something; at least one of the oarsmen caught a crab and the others began looking over their shoulders. The boat dropped back a bit, but the man in the prow shouted in fury and now the rowers were pulling harder than ever.

"Six more arrows," said Astrid. She knelt beside him with her thoughts on the Welsh nobleman. He was near enough now for her to see again how exactly he resembled his twin brother. She remembered hearing it said that when twins of the same sex were very much alike their minds also were alike in every way. Then this man, Caradoc, would want her if he got the chance, just as Cadogan had done. She felt a curious excitement at the idea. One brother would complete what the other had begun. Was that what she had hoped for when she urged Arnvid to leave her behind? Perhaps, but so long as she stayed with him she could not break the bond which had grown between them, the bond of shared hardship and shared peril. She could not wish to see that bond broken by his death. Gratitude, but not love. Even now she could watch him without love in her heart as he stood beside her, a fine, manly figure in the rocking boat, handling his bow in growing desperation. And then she thought: It was the worst of ill luck for him to find me and desire me. But for that he might be safe with King Llewelyn instead of standing here at bay like a stag caught by the hunters. She handed him another arrow, a second, a third, and he shot them away in quick succession. One went so near Caradoc that he thought it wise to cover himself with a shield. The boat drew nearer and he poised his spear to make a cast at Arnvid. Then Arnvid thought of the shield hanging at his back, but he could not hold it and shoot at the same time. The little dark man had crept up beside Caradoc. He held a boat hook ready to grapple the sailing boat. Here came the spear. Arnvid ducked and it went through the sail. Caradoc was handed another spear. His face was alight with the lust to kill. Arnvid thought that he had never been so near death. On dry land he knew that he would have turned and fled, but here there was no escape. He took another arrow and shot wildly. The boat heaved up and even as his fingers slipped the string he knew the arrow would go high, but the other boat also mounted on a wave. There was a loud thud. Caradoc clutched at his face, he fell backward with the arrow sticking fast in one eye. At once all was confusion on the boat. The rowers stopped rowing and gathered over the fallen chieftain. There was a shrill chatter of dismayed voices, growing fainter as the sailing boat plunged forward on its course, leaving the other far astern.

Arnvid sat down on a thwart, breathing hard. He could hardly realize that it was all over, that the other boat was now turning and making back toward land. Already the sand hills by Saemund's hall had almost sunk below the horizon, but out west towered up the blue wall of the mountains of Gwynedd, seemingly sheer from the sea.

The sun was going down behind them, throwing a red flush here and there on a crag face or on the long snowy tilt of an upthrust peak. Arnvid's exultation was tinged with sadness. This might be his last sight of Wales, the land on which he had looked with romantic pleasure when he and Astrid rode over the snowdrifts on Offa's Dyke. What had he accomplished in that country, of which he had begun to dream already when his mother spoke of it at their last meeting? Merely the killing of two of King Llewelyn's liegemen. Two notable men, and the more notable they were, the greater the honor. That was how Gunnar would have looked at it, but to Arnvid it seemed more a confession of failure than a deed in which he could take pride. True, he had said to Geirfin that he was going overseas to seek honor and here it was, in a guise that did not please him; nor, he fancied, did it greatly please Astrid. He sighed and looked at her where she sat pale and silent, clutching the gunwale and watching the blue mountains and the green rolling waves. Well, after all these hazards he still had her. His mood changed to a joyous excitement. First he lowered the sail a little, for the boat was now meeting the waves with such force as to fling heavy showers of spray aboard. Then he got out of his coat of mail and flung it under the stern seat. There were no perils from which it could shield him, nor was there any point in Astrid going on wearing those dirty peasant clothes. He undid the corded wedding dress that Saemund's servants had put in the boat, emptied out some leavings of hay and held it up to her with a laugh. It was a bit torn and muddied, but it still looked a dress of which a woman might be proud. Gently he helped her out of coat and breeches and put the dress over her head. When it was on he had a curious feeling that she had returned to womanhood and that now their bodies were free for something different from the rough sexless companionship while they struggled through forest and fell. He took out food from the baskets and opened the cask of ale. She drank from his helmet, but would eat nothing, while he feasted in great content. The sea darkened and rose higher, the mast creaked, the boat rushed on. A few stars appeared and he dipped the rudder, aiming their course due northward. His kisses fell on cold lips and salty cheeks, but their warm bodies closed together and all seemed as it should be. When it was over she was very sick and moaned miserably, but that was only to be expected with someone in a tossing boat for the first time. He laid her down flat and covered her with the cloak and the leather coat. He sat in the stern, one hand on the rudder pole and the other clasped in one of Astrid's. That firm handclasp seemed to him to signify complete trust and confidence between them.

Chapter 13

HOUGUN

BY DAWN THE WIND had freshened a good deal with heavy
showers of rain and Arnvid judged that it had shifted more
to the southwest, as Saemund said it would. Far astern he
could still make out the blue mountains of Gwynedd under
a dark bank of cloud, a row of blunted teeth strung out along
the horizon, but now land appeared to eastward, a long low
coast backed by flat-topped hills. He wondered whether the
folk there were English or Danes, and if Danes, whether they
had been strong enough to escape the massacre. As he
watched, he realized that he was being driven nearer and
nearer to this unknown country and he swung the boat as
far as he could on a more northerly course toward another
group of mountains showing dimly across the sea. That, he
thought, might be Cumberland, with a promise of greater
safety. Astrid was awake, but little interested in what he had
to tell her. As soon as she sat up she was sick, and he saw she
was flushed and feverish. He made her as comfortable as he
could, disappointed that she could not share his mood of

hope and growing excitement, the pleasure of sailing fast in a good boat, the lure of adventure in new lands. Well, she had been tried hard enough lately; it was not surprising that she was ill now when the worst was perhaps over. He felt some pity and tenderness for her, but the painful, absorbing emotion was gone. He had had her at last and a sick woman was not a very attractive companion. For the moment the thing to do was to concentrate on getting them both safely to Cumberland. The sea was decidedly rough and sometimes a wave slopped over the gunwale. He set to work to bale the boat, then he ate and drank and sat down in the stern, indifferent to gusts of cold rain. The rain increased and all land was lost to view. Toward evening the wind was beginning to back, the sky cleared to west and north and a low watery sunlight flooded across the green waves to a line of shore, yellow sand and brown woods overhung with mist and shreds of blackish cloud. He lowered the sail and took to the oars. With short spells of rest he rowed all through the night, but with little idea of direction. Morning broke clear, sunny, and cold. There was the land away to port, seemingly not much nearer than it had been at sundown. He started to row toward it. Astrid was very weak and apathetic and could not keep down any food. She will die, he thought, if I cannot get her ashore very soon and put to bed under a roof. He rowed harder. It did not look an inhospitable land; there seemed to be green clearings among the woods, though further back were bare, craggy hills whitened with snow. Soon he saw sandbanks lifting above the tide and the water grew shallow and muddy with strong currents. It was a hard row, but at last he sighted a small jetty and some huts from which went up trails of smoke. He drew in cautiously beside the weed-grown posts of the jetty, put on his mail coat, went forward and hailed the men who were gathered in a knot at the water's edge.

"What land is this?" he shouted.

The men looked like Welshmen, but one of them answered him in Norse.

"This is Asmund's land."

Arnvid thought that there was no reason to expect ill will from a man of that name. It sounded a good deal better in his ears than Caradoc ap Einion, though at one time he might have thought differently.

"Is Asmund your master?" he asked.

"He is the master of all folk hereabouts."

"If we come ashore can you take us to him?"

"That we can easily; he is not far away."

Arnvid made fast to the jetty. He took Astrid in his arms and passed her up to the man, then he scrambled up after her.

Silent and shivering, Astrid allowed herself to be sat on a short plank and carried between two men. Arnvid and the others walked behind. Soon they left the shore and followed a track inland with a bank of forest on one side and a great stretch of salt marsh on the other. Arnvid fixed his eyes on a conical height rising abruptly from the waste of reeds and brush. It was encircled by a palisade and at the top appeared some timber buildings.

"What is that place?" he asked the men.

"That is Hauksborg," they said. "That is where we shall find Asmund."

Arnvid began to wonder about this man Asmund and whether it was wise to expect a friendly reception in that little fortress. It looked a sinister sort of place, a viking nest, an abode of evildoers. Still, what choice had he? With Astrid more dead than alive he could not range about the country trying to keep out of harm's way as he had done in England. And then he thought that perhaps this was still England and that Asmund might well be a liegeman of King Ethelred, like Edwin at Chaddesley . . .

Now they were crossing the marsh, where tree trunks had been laid down in mud and ooze. A steep path wound up to a gate in the palisade. Arnvid, looking northward, saw that the marsh narrowed into a long forest valley. Pale and un-substantial as a cloud in the far distance rose a solitary tent-shaped mountain.

"Whither goes that dale?" he asked.

"That," said one of the men, "is the way into Westmor-land."

Arnvid thought to himself: I turned away from that land when I had an army at my back. Shall I fare better now when I have only a sick woman with me?

On the top of the knoll was another opening through an earthen rampart within which stood the cluster of buildings. An armed man let them into a hall where about a score of people sat at meat. One of the fishermen went up to a man in the high seat and said: "Here, lord, are two strangers, a man and a woman, who have landed from a boat at the quay."

Astrid was stood on her feet and pushed forward beside Arnvid.

The man in the high seat looked them over in silence for a while, continuing to eat and drink. Arnvid did not much like his looks. He was neither dark nor fair, tall nor short; his nose was too thin and his eyes too close together, eyes that never seemed to meet Arnvid's for more than a passing glance. His clothes were very fine, but dirty and patched. The whole household looked slovenly, though there seemed to be plenty of good food.

"Whence do you come?" said the man at last.

Arnvid said that they had sailed in a small boat from Gwynedd, but before that they had been in England.

"You are Danes, I take it."

"The woman is Danish, but I am from Iceland. True I have been among the Danes in York and when I rode through English Mercia I was lucky to get out with life and limb. Arnvid Torolfsson I am called and my forefathers ruled in Westmorland; Torolf, Torfin, and Leif."

The man's gaze flickered over Arnvid as a peasant might look at a horse he had a fancy to buy.

"My name is Asmund," he said. "It is a name well-known both here in Hougun and in Westmorland. My grandfather stood side by side with yours in the fight at Grasmere Pass. They stood for King Dunmail, the Welshman, against Edmund of England. What errand have you in this land?—that is what I should be glad to know."

"It so chanced that the wind brought me here from Gwynedd, but I should be glad to know whether it has brought me to safety."

"It has at least brought you far from the power of King Ethelred. You shall both sit down with me to eat and drink," said Asmund with a smile.

"I am not unwilling, but the woman is only in a poor way. Sleep and warmth may do her good."

Asmund told his servants to make up a bed near the fire

and Astrid lay down on it. A girl brought her milk. She drank a little and closed her eyes.

Arnvid sat long at table with Asmund, who now seemed exceedingly friendly. After he had drunk a good deal of ale Arnvid began to think that he was indeed lucky to have come on a man so hospitable and so full of good will toward him. He agreed gladly when Asmund said that they should ride together to a farm he had up country and keep Christmas there in greater comfort than was possible in such a place as this Hauksborg. Then he looked at Astrid, thinking she could not travel any further at present. Asmund said reassuringly that she would be safe and well cared for. "She can be brought to you later on when she is well again. For the moment—there is not much pleasure to be had from a sick mistress," he said, with a shrug of the shoulders and a crooked smile. Arnvid could not but agree with him. A few days ago he could not have borne the thought that they should be parted, but that was when she was strong and healthy, a good comrade and counselor. That was before they had lain together; and now she was ill, only a shadow of her former self. Could that make so much difference if he really loved her? Or was his new mood of detachment, almost of indifference, the result of being a little drunk and excited by the prospect of adventure in company with this man Asmund? Already there was the bustle of departure. Horses were being collected outside and he found himself left alone in the hall with Astrid. He stood looking down at her, wondering what to say, wondering whether she would mind his leaving her here defenseless among strangers, wondering that he did not mind more.

"I have much to thank you for," she said, "but I have paid

as much as I could. You have had your desire. Now it is best that you go, for I do not think I shall bring you much luck."

"But for you I should not have got alive out of Gwynedd."

"But for me you would not have run into danger." Her flushed face turned toward him and he read in it a sense of gratitude, perhaps some affection, but hardly love. All the same, something seemed to turn over in his heart. Perhaps he had built up a bond between himself and this woman that he could never unloose, even if she preferred to go her own way without him. Abruptly he stooped and took her in his arms, but she turned away from his kiss, saying, "Asmund was right: love and sickness do not go well together."

"But you will be well soon," he said hopefully.

"Perhaps, but by then you may have other things to think of. You are trusting yourself to this man Asmund?"

"I have little choice, but he seems to me a good man and a useful friend."

"Was that what you felt when you first set eyes on him?"

"No," he admitted. "I thought there was some flaw in him, but now I think I was wrong."

"The first thought often goes nearest to the truth."

"You are shrewder than I am. Perhaps I shall be lost without you," he said smiling.

Asmund came into the hall. He was cloaked for the journey and had a fur cap on his head. "Come, Arnvid!" he called. "Now we must ride."

Arnvid rose from his knees. "Farewell for the present," he said with a sigh.

"Farewell, Arnvid. Keep your wits about you," she answered.

He went out, reeling a little when he came into the cold

air and wishing he had not drunk so much. Astrid was right; he had to keep his wits about him and he said little in answer to some broad jokes that Asmund made about women as traveling companions.

They were mounted on small but sturdy horses and rode northward up the dale, two by two, well-armed men both in front and behind. Arnvid looked at these men. They rode in silence and seemed sullen in contrast to Asmund's friendly loquacity. One or two had bandages as though they had been in a fight not long ago. They looked very different men from those bright-eyed, excitable servants who had ridden by in the mist with Caradoc ap Einion. He felt a qualm of apprehension and loneliness and he realized what a lot it had meant to him having Astrid by his side, a delight to the senses, a spur to action, no matter what peril lay around them or ahead. Now there was this man Asmund . . .

Suddenly he said: "If you are not for Ethelred what king do you serve?"

Asmund smiled appreciatively. "You go straight to the root of the matter, friend!" he said. "That is what every man in these parts asks himself. Long ago this was the land of the Northumbrian king in York. Then the Danes took York and the Welsh from the north won back Cumberland. Then King Athelstan fought against Danes and vikings and Welshmen at Vinheithi and beat them, and his brother Edmund beat the vikings and Welshmen again at Grasmere Pass, but he did not take back Cumberland or even Westmorland; he gave them to the King of Scotland, who let the Welsh kings go on ruling much as they had done before—Dunmail in Strathclyde, Malcolm in Cumberland, and Jukil in Westmorland, but here in Hougun the folk were reckoned to be under York and so after Erik Bloodaxe had fallen they could by rights be claimed by the King of England. But the King of Scots and his Welsh friend, Owen the Bald, were nearer at hand. Their power spread southward while Ethelred battled against Sweyn. Then Sweyn stayed away, the year that he won Norway from Olaf Trygvesson, and Ethelred sent an army to harry the men of Cumberland and those who had lately gone under Owen the Bald. Nearly all my farms were burned, though Hauksborg they failed to take. Now we are wondering whether it is better to be burned out by Scots or by Englishmen."

"And which do you choose?"

"We hate Ethelred, but we fear him little. It is Sweyn we shall have to reckon with in the end, for he will surely make himself master of England in a few years' time."

"What you want, to my mind, is a king of your own, strong enough to withstand the Scots and strong enough to make good terms with King Sweyn when the time is ripe. Is Owen not man enough for the task?"

"He is bound by marriage to the King of Scots."

"Then can you find no other man who would serve?"

"That is the question, friend," said Asmund with his crooked smile.

They fell silent, each busy with his own thoughts, and it soon grew dusk. The little horses only moved slowly, the forest thickened, and then opened out into rocky wastes dark with gorse and juniper. It seemed strange to Arnvid that there was nothing to fear, no sleeping place to look for, no plan to make for the morrow; Asmund led and he followed, confident that all was well. If Astrid had been with him perhaps she would not have been quite so confident. Astrid —he turned his head almost expecting to see her riding beside him, the familiar figure in man's clothes, grave, seemingly indifferent, whether they went through the gloom of English oakwoods or down the winding valleys of Wales, but all the same the treasured woman, snatched from murderous hands, guarded from rape, his dear companion. He wished she were here and yet he was angry with her because she had shown him no passion, and angry with himself that he should be so obsessed with a woman who only yielded to him because she had no choice. And now he had no choice but to let Asmund use him as he thought fit, a pawn perhaps in a game played for high stakes. He remembered hearing that a Northman had once come to Harek seeking winter bed and board and Harek had taken him with him to kill a neighbor, but it was the Northman who got killed.

They came to a clearing where a new house stood beside the half-burned ruins of an old one. "Ethelred's work," said Asmund, "but it has been made good. We shall overnight here and push on tomorrow to my farm at Ambleside. There is a good household with many servants and all is prepared for Christmas feasting."

"Have you a wife and children?" asked Arnvid.

"Some children I have here and there, but my wife is dead and she left me with an only daughter. Maria she is called and it is said that her forebears were kings in Ireland." Asmund swung himself from his horse, a door opened, there was a glow of firelight and a smell of baking bread, a smell of cattle, a smell of wood smoke. Arnvid forgot about Astrid: he was not so tired or hungry that he did not look with interest at the women within the hall, especially at a girl with bright eyes and fair silky hair, but she seemed to be heavy with child. He wondered what Maria would be like.

Chapter 14

AMBLESIDE

Next morning they rode on northward, mile after mile within sight of a long narrow lake, forest on both sides to the water's edge. Ice lay on the sheltered bays, the sky was leaden and now and then a few snowflakes eddied down through the bare branches. Except for ducks and swans out on the water, the occasional flight of a heron, and some red deer feeding on the opposite shore, there was little sign of life. It looked a land in which it would be hard to get a living. It was not much different from what Arnvid had seen of Wales from Offa's Dyke, but that had turned out to be a land swarming with folk and this seemed strangely empty and forbidding. He found no joy in it as he had found at first in Wales, but then he thought of the danger and disappointment that had followed. Things might go better for him here; they could hardly go worse.

Now they were drawing near the lake head and above the dark forests stood out craggy hills splashed with snowdrifts;

but now there were some boats to be seen on the water and many columns of blue smoke rose languidly in the still air. The horses pricked up their ears and moved faster. A few gruff remarks spiced with bitter understatement came from the riders.

"How like you the look of this country?" asked Asmund.

"I have nothing against mountains and forests, but I would like it more if it had more folk," said Arnvid guardedly. His impulse was to say exactly what he felt, but Astrid had implied in one way or another that this was seldom advisable. "Are we now in Westmorland?" he said.

"Most men reckon this end of the lake to be in Westmorland," was the answer.

Arnvid thought of several remarks he might make, but each seemed in some way likely to offend Asmund. Then he thought it might be as well to show his host that he was not a man to be content with all that came his way, thankful only to have a full belly and a whole skin.

He said, "I would guess that this is the worst part of Westmorland and that the folk here must be hard put to it if they do not live at other lands' expense."

Asmund smiled and nodded. "There is some truth in that," he said, "but the land is maybe better than you think. Anyhow the poorer the land the harder the folk and the more they make themselves feared elsewhere."

Arnvid thought, These men are little more than robbers, and then he asked himself whether he was right to condemn them on that score. No one thought ill of Gunnar because he had been out as a viking. That meant killing strangers and taking their goods. Why should not Asmund be such a man? He at least had the excuse that his land had been wasted, and if he struck back at Englishmen, who should blame him? Then Arnvid thought of his foster father, Geirfin. He was reckoned an honorable man though he lived off what he could get from his farm and sought no disputes with neighbors. And what of Audun, with his great wealth all won in trade and farming, no warrior but all the same one of the most powerful men in York? Even Gunnar had obviously been impressed by him, though as a rule he was scornful about traders. And all at once Arnvid perceived the contradiction in his own nature, which had doubtless been noted long ago by Astrid, that he was at heart a man of peace yet fretted by desire to appear a warrior and to be admired as such. The warrior's path to honor was both the easiest and the most dangerous; he only had to be both brave and lucky. It was harder to cut a fine figure as a man of peace, though it could be done, as he had seen for himself. He shot a glance at Asmund. He clearly was not a man of peace. But was he both brave and lucky? Arnvid would like to have thought he was, but he had an inkling that Astrid would straightway have said that he was neither.

They rode between a scattering of huts, all new and makeshift. Folk stood on both sides of the track watching the riders, but there were no shouts of welcome. Their looks were dark and lowering like the wintry woods and leaden sky. The horses broke into a trot and swept up a hillside above the reedy shallows of the lake. Here stood the hall, a fair-sized building of split oak trunks, but not as big as the burned-out ruin of the old hall nearby. Asmund rode forward and spoke to a group of men by the door, tall, grim-looking men with their hands thrust into their belts. Arnvid saw the beetling brows, the hard, unwinking stare of eyes like hawks' all fixed on Asmund; he heard the short, almost contemptuous answers, and there came back to him a vision of those Westmorings in the old fort under Moel Fre, the men who had killed Dag Woodbeard and then ridden leisurely away.

The company got off the horses and went into the hall that was full of smoke and a smell of boiled mutton. A woman who seemed to be the housekeeper came forward, a dark woman with a shifty glance and an agreeable voice. Beside her was a young girl, small and elfish-looking, very dark with an upturned nose and bright inquisitive eyes, not comely or very clean, but full of irrepressible vitality. Arnvid had seen not a few faces of that stamp in Wales, but this one had a more mocking and lighthearted air. He thought that all these folk had long ago taken Asmund's measure and knew what manner of man he was; it was only he who did not yet know for certain.

"Welcome to Ambleside! This is my daughter Maria." said Asmund. He turned to the girl with his crooked smile and she smiled back, not at him but at Arnvid. "Here I have brought a guest," he said, "a man who has traveled far by sea and by land. Arnvid he is called, son of Torolf, son of King Leif of Westmorland. Treat him with honor as befits his birth."

The smile faded on the girl's face; she gazed at Arnvid, and it seemed to him that something glowed in her as it had done in Astrid when she looked at Gunnar across the board in Steintor's hall.

"Food is ready, master," said the housekeeper.

"Let us sit down and eat, Arnvid," said Asmund courteously.

"First I could do with a bath and a change of clothes."

"The fire is lit in the bath house," said the housekeeper.

"That is well," said Asmund. "Maria, take out clothes from the chest. Let Arnvid have the best you can find. Now, friend, off with that mail coat; no weapons will bite on you here. A horn of ale before you go to the bath!"

Arnvid struggled out of his mail, he emptied the horn, hesitatingly he unbuckled his sword and hung it on the wall. It might be unwise to part with it in the house of a stranger, yet not to do so must seem an affront to Asmund. This was not Chaddesley. The folk here might not be as friendly as they seemed, but they could hardly be planning to take his life.

An old woman led him out of the hall to the bath house and Maria, who had been delving in a chest below the cupboard beds, followed with an armful of clothes.

They went into a little building where a pot of water stood beside a glowing fire of logs. There he began to get off his clothes, stiff and clammy with grime and sweat. The old woman took red-hot stones out of the fire with a pair of tongs and put them in the pot of water. Steam belched forth and filled the hut, somewhat veiling his nakedness from the curious eyes of the girl, but now the old woman pushed her out abruptly and shut the door. Soon the heat was almost unbearable and sweat broke out all over him. The old woman set to work to rub him down with a bundle of birch twigs, she put more stones in the water and switched harder and harder till his body was scarlet and stinging all over. Then at last she opened the door and said with a malignant grin, "There is the lake if you are man enough for it."

Naked he ran across rush tufts and sedge. Thin ice snapping under his bare feet, he waded painfully out through the shallows and finally ducked and swam with violent strokes, aware that the two women were watching him from the shore. He turned back and saw Maria walking slowly toward the hall, the bundle of clothes left behind on a rock. The old woman came with a coarse cloth and dried him. He put on the clothes and felt an extraordinary stimulation and a delight in his tingling body—the body that had not been properly cleaned since he left York and had been preserved as it seemed now miraculously from the weapons of foemen and from the hungry waves of the sea, the body that had clasped and enjoyed Astrid and was now keyed up for fresh adventure. He pulled on his shoes and buckled his belt, then he started to overtake Maria.

"Now I am a new man!" he said joyfully.

"Now you will eat and get drunk," she said with a smile, and he thought her smile, like Asmund's, was a little crooked.

"I am ready for more than that," he said recklessly.

"For what then?" She looked at him out of the corners of her eyes and he felt a distrust for her giving place to desire, but he answered vaguely and with more caution.

"To seek power and honor where it may be found."

"That may not be an easy task for you in Westmorland," she said shrewdly.

"Few tasks that I have set myself have been easy!"

"That I can believe, for it seems you come of a line of great champions, though by all accounts they were not lucky men."

"Arnvid the Lucky, I was called in Iceland."

"Doubtless you have done some notable deeds since you came thence." She handed him the pouch which had hung at his belt. "Two gold arm rings I saw in this. Did you take them from some foeman in battle?"

He flushed with vexation, for he had forgotten all about the presence of Astrid's two rings. Had she thought of them when he left her at Hauksborg? Perhaps she had reckoned them as part payment to him for saving her life—a very distasteful idea. He would give them back to her, of course, but how? Asmund had said she could be sent for when she was well enough for the journey, but as he glanced uneasily at Maria he fancied that Asmund might not be so eager to restore his mistress to him.

Slowly he fastened the pouch to his belt. Should he tell Maria about Astrid and how he had got her out of England? She was staring at him, her lips parted, her color rising, curiosity giving way to admiration. He thought that but for Astrid he might have been ready enough to make love to this girl, even to marry her if that offered some good prospect, as doubtless it would. Asmund might well have such a plan in mind. As it was, the hot excitement in her inflamed him, though her somewhat unpleasing features chilled the lure of her lively spirit and healthy body. He said nothing about Astrid, but he allowed himself to boast that he had felled two great men in Wales.

"Tell me about it!" she said eagerly.

"One I killed with an arrow when he sought my life, following me in a boat from Gwynedd," he said shortly.

"And the other?"

There flashed upon him a vision of Cadogan ap Einion, defenseless for a moment, arrested in his rape of Astrid, the swift sword stroke and the blood pouring down over the girl, her look of horror and disgust, almost of anger. It had been a black deed and now he shrank from the thought of it. He said nothing and they went into the hall together. Asmund and his men had finished eating, but there was plenty left for Arnvid. He sat down and filled himself greedily, while Asmund, already a little drunk, clapped him on the shoulder and shouted for more ale.

Maria and some servant girls went into the bower and Arnvid did not see her again that day.

Chapter 15

TEMPTATION ON THE MOUNTAIN

For the next few days Arnvid did little but eat, drink, and sleep. Strong as he was he had been tried hard, perhaps nearer to the breaking point than he had realized when borne forward by peril and anxiety. Now there seemed to be a breathing space and it might be wise to relax and make the most of it. No wonder Astrid had collapsed: it was a marvel that she had endured so long. Invigorated, however, by another bath, he soon grew restless. Lying alone in his cupboard bed he thought of the nights he had passed wtih Astrid, sometimes holding her hand, but separated from her by the coat of mail he dared not discard. Impatiently he thought that she might now be well again and falling into other hands than his, perhaps not unwillingly. He spoke to Asmund about her and Hougun and that he would be instructed to call at Hauksborg. heard that a man would shortly be riding with a message into With this Arnvid had to be content. That night, however, a naked servant girl was slipped into his cupboard bed. At first he had thoughts of pushing her out, annoyed by Asmund's idea that any woman could be a substitute for someone like Astrid, but when he laid hold of the girl he could not but help that his hand grew gentle feeling her body young and ardent and in the end he took the pleasure and appeasement offered him. After that she was with him every night as a matter of course, and when a message came from Hauksborg that Astrid was somewhat better but hardly fit to travel he was not greatly concerned. Of Maria he saw little though sometimes she sat by him in the hall, under her father's eye, asking questions about Iceland and what he had seen and done elsewhere. Arnvid was a good deal more outspoken to her than he might have been to Asmund, but even so he spoke with caution, building up a picture of himself that would better have suited Gunnar. He almost believed that he was such a man—harsh, resolute, wary and fearless. On fine days he rode out with Asmund carrying bow and spear in search of deer and boar in the woods. Sometimes they went far up into the mountains on foot. There came one evening when they stood side by side on a peak watching the sun dip behind a tangle of blue mountains split by deep dales and snowy gorges.

"A wolf-haunted land, useless except for hunting and hiding in," said Asmund, "but look the other way, Arnvid. There lies Westmorland, wide valley and green hills, yet sheltered from England by that long mountain range, snow-crested like a breaking wave at sea, dipping there for Steinmor where the road goes through to York, where Leif fell fighting beside King Erik Bloodaxe. There, below that snout of rock, they say your ancestor Torfin housed in an old fortress, guarding the frontier against his foemen."

"A better land it looks than this," said Arnvid, "yet I see little but dark heath, scrub, and forest."

"There is more than that; there, out of sight, are big farms and rich land under the plow. On those hills go herds of cattle and vast flocks of sheep. There dwell many sturdy landowners of Northman stock with tenants and servants, both Welsh and Irish, and men brought from the Isles. There is a land that awaits a new master, even as you said when we rode up from Hauksborg."

Arnvid stood leaning on his spear, well aware whither this talk was leading, aware too of the lust for power that had again begun to kindle in him, the desire that had brought him from Iceland, the plan he had taken up halfheartedly when with Audun at York and then abandoned when he stood in talk with the shepherd, away over there under the snout of Moel Fre. Perhaps he was a different man from what he was then, hardened by desperate undertakings, ready to put his fortune to the touch, ready to lose if he could yet cut a fine figure as his forefathers had done. All the same he answered coldly.

"It looks to me too small a land to stand alone."

"If we light a torch here the fire will spread, far beyond those barren peaks to the sea in the west and north to the Solway shore; further still, perhaps, where there are folk of our race and customs, men who hate the English and despise Scot and Welshman."

"And who is to light the torch?"

"Why should not you do it? You whose forebears won the land for themselves, ruled justly and will not soon be forgotten."

"They would be bold men who took me as their king, an unknown Icelander."

"*I* know you, Arnvid," said Asmund smoothly. "I have many friends to whom you can show what manner of man you are, for they are bidden to the Christmas feast at Ambleside. If they are in agreement with me we can go forward and hold a council at Hep according to old custom."

This, thought Arnvid, is only half the story. He cloaked his excitement and stared hard at Asmund whose eyes were everywhere except on his.

"What will it profit you to do this for me?" he said bluntly. "What do you ask for yourself?"

"Why, as to that, I had hoped you would make me an earl," said Asmund slowly. "And then, if we are in agreement we might further strengthen our bond. I would have you wed my daughter Maria."

So that was Asmund's price, surely not an unreasonable price to ask of one who had as yet done little to prove his worth either as warrior or leader of men. Earl Asmund—there might be other Westmorings better-fitted for such a climb to power, but for good or ill he was committed to Asmund. Nothing could be done otherwise. Maria . . . that was where he felt most reluctance. He liked the girl; he thought she had a good head on her shoulders even if her face did not please him, but at the back of his mind was always the prospect of making Astrid his wife. True he was annoyed and daunted by her coldness toward him, but he had reckoned that the status of a wife would be more to her liking than that of a mistress.

Asmund seemed to read his thoughts. He said, "The chance

of becoming a king is not to be thrown away lightly and in most ways one young woman is as good as another."

"Could you not make yourself king?" said Arnvid brusquely.

"Too many men would think they had as good a claim as I have, but with you it is different. You come of a line of kings both loved by their friends and feared by their enemies."

"You have only my word for that."

"I see no reason to doubt your word."

"Aye, men who can make use of me may not doubt who I am, but to my mind it is useless to go forward with this enterprise unless—"

"Unless what?"

"Unless I am freely accepted by the folk."

"Of that we can soon judge. Now that Ethelred has harried the land and Owen has failed in its defense I think your chances are good."

"Maybe." Slowly Arnvid overturned a stone with his spear shaft and pushed it down the slope. It rolled a few yards and went over an edge. In a moment it was bounding high in air among the crags, then it hit a rock and was shivered to fragments. My downfall, he thought, might be as swift as that if Asmund fails me. He thought of that army which had been raised in Powys and of how it had gone to pieces at the first clash with the men of Gwynedd.

"Then you will try this venture?" said Asmund eagerly.

"If your friends stand by me I will go with you before a council of the Westmorings. If they take me as king you shall be an earl."

"And the matter of Maria?"

Arnvid hesitated. Was a man fit to be a king who would let a woman stand in his way to power? After all he had not given overmuch thought either to Astrid or to Maria since he had that servant girl to bed with him. He had thought himself in love with Astrid, and love was a serious matter for any man, but was love disposed of in such a simple way as this?

With an effort he said, "If the maid be willing, it shall be as you say."

Chapter 16

MARIA

A GOOD MANY LANDOWNERS came to Asmund's Christmas feast at Ambleside, some from Hougun and some from Westmorland, but scarcely so many as Arnvid had expected. However, one and all were prepared to accept him as king and they promised to go to Hep, armed and manstrong, ready to support him and Asmund when the time came. There was much talk of who might be for and against them and Arnvid heard questions asked about Orm Torkelsson. Asmund was evasive in his answers, but Arnvid gathered that this man Orm carried much weight in Westmorland and that there was some headshaking about his not being present.

After the guests had gone home there was a long delay while further soundings were taken among landowners both west and north. The replies that came in time to Asmund were not all to his liking, yet on the whole he professed to be well satisfied.

"We shall make a good showing at the council," he said,

"but much depends on how you speak to the folk. Ready you must be in word and deed, quick of wit, generous with promises, yet you must not pledge yourself to more than seems possible; for we are shrewd men hereabouts, and not to be carried away by mere words as the Welshmen are, and we hold that what a man swears to, that he should perform." This I would say, and that, he went on, and Arnvid could not but admit that Asmund's advice was both sound and subtle. He saw, too, that the task might be harder than he had thought, especially as he had some suspicion that Asmund did not reveal the whole truth or all the risks that might have to be run. Nevertheless things had now gone so far that to draw back would be to make himself a laughingstock. That would be ten times worse than the humiliation he had felt when he turned back to York with a paltry herd of cattle, leaving Woodbeard unavenged.

It was the first day of spring, a morning of hazy sunshine with a breeze from the south. Arnvid had sat in the hall listening impatiently to Asmund's plans for how they should conduct themselves at Hep in a few days' time. To Arnvid the whole matter was now familiar: he thought he knew all the ins and outs of it so far as Asmund would let him. He was tired of words and he had begun to want an end to this long interlude of security and easy living. At last he got up and went out. The freshness of the morning cleared away the nervous irritation from his mind; he looked about him with renewed confidence. This is the land that I shall make my own, he thought. Never has it looked so fair. His gaze wandered to the lake. The water lay like dark burnished steel in the sheltered bays, but in the path of the wind it was a jeweled carpet, glittering with a million flashes of light. It seemed to him that the water acclaimed him as its future master, the brooding reflections of forest breaking up into a tumult of joyful welcome. It was to this end that he had been borne on the great ocean rollers from Iceland, through the swirling waters of Severn, and battered by wintry breakers on the Irish Sea. Here was peace and friendliness, here all his desires might be satisfied. Power would be his, honor in the eyes of men and love from women. He would have sons who would ride through the forest bow in hand and sail down the long reaches of the lake—Maria's children, but who was to say that he should have no children by Astrid? This was something he had never felt before. Not even when with Astrid beside him in sunlight and sparkling snow he looked out over Wales, had he felt this lightheartedness, this harmony of spirit and body, this fusion of his being with sky and water, with rock and wood, with all living things on the earth around him. And then he remembered a time in York when he heard a tonsured monk say that such joy as he felt now was all a delusion of the Devil; that men's desires for earthly power, for pleasure, gold and goods, were strong chains that drew them inevitably down to hell; that the body flowered and faded, and that only the spirit was eternal, coming to peace after it had been purified by the mercy of almighty God. How sure he felt now that the monk had lost his way in life and was himself deluded, a traveler following a will-o'-the-wisp across darkening swamps.

Strolling aimlessly along the track that led westward, Arnvid found himself beside an old fortress. The outer wall, some three yards thick and built of squared stone, was topped with thorny scrub. What buildings there had been inside had vanished and the place was used as a cattle pen. He was reminded of the fort under Moel Fre, but these works were far more carefully constructed. Idly he wondered what had been the purpose of this stronghold that looked as though it would last for ever and yet its builders were gone and forgotten. No one knew or cared what manner of men they had been and the thought brought him a momentary sense of disillusion. These old walls were a memorial of people who must have been far more patient and skillful than any that dwelt here today, yet it was plain that some disaster had overwhelmed them. Perhaps there could be no permanence in anything on which man set to work with hand and brain. All he could do was to hand on life and then vanish from the scene, leaving to others the quest for achievement. He might be lucky enough to see his children grow to manhood; luckier still if he saw his children's children . . . He heard his name called and looked up. Beyond the fortress was a low crag and on the top of it sat a woman. Maria. He climbed the rocks and sat down beside her, half-unwillingly, yet with a sense of relief, for here was a living being whose fate was linked with his and who might build for him the only kind of immortality of which he could feel hopeful.

Maria glanced at him archly. "Thoughtful you seem today, Arnvid," she said. "Is there anything amiss?"

"Nay," he protested. "I am filled with joy at the thought of being king."

"Yet no king can live without care."

"True enough; yet even so, few men would not choose kingship if it were offered them."

"A wise man might refuse it."

"Maybe the world is ruled with little wisdom, yet to me

your father seems a wise man and what he plans for us both is not likely to fail."

"I have nothing against what he plans for us two," she said, and the color deepened on her cheeks, "though I do not think it is much to your liking."

"Nay," he said awkwardly, "I have nothing against it either. To me it seems a good plan in every way."

"Except that the thought of me gives you no pleasure."

"A man does not live for pleasure alone, least of all a king. Do you think it will be no pleasure to me if you bear me a son?"

"I had thought there should be more to it than that," she said, sucking her lips and looking bleakly at the glittering lake and white blossom breaking like foam on the dark tangle of thorn. "Perhaps I am not as pretty as the girl you have down at Hauksborg."

He frowned and was at a loss what to say.

"You need not fear that I shall be a jealous wife," she went on, "and I think that you will be a gentle husband, too gentle, maybe."

He flushed. Astrid had said that. "Is it a bad fault in a man?" he said shortly.

"Not when he is a great champion, as you are, yet a king can be too gentle, and too trusting."

"It would be hard for me if there were no folk I could trust," he said.

"Then do not trust too much in my father."

He was taken aback and exclaimed: "Surely *he* means me welll!"

"Oh, surely. But remember you are a strong weapon in his hand and he will use you for his own advantage. As you say, he is a wise man, but I doubt whether he is wise in his plan to make you king and himself an earl."

"Are we not men fitted to take power and hold it?" It was the question that he had often asked himself, but of late his self-assurance and his confidence in Asmund had so dominated him that to hear Maria raising this question caused him sharp annoyance.

"Whether you are or not, it is doubtless too late to turn back now. Nor would I urge you to, for on this plan hangs my hope that I shall be your wife." She laid a hand on his arm and said: "Can you not think kindly of me, or is it that your heart is given to the woman at Hauksborg and your body to the servant girl that shares your bed and I am only a step on your path to power?"

He was silent, angry yet ashamed that she could put her finger so exactly on the truth.

"This is foolish talk," he said at last. "Nor do I think it seemly that you speak against your father."

"I should not do so to any man but you."

"And why to me?" he said, willfully obtuse.

She flashed a look of scorn at him, but he thought there were tears in her eyes. "You know the answer to that, just as I know the answer to what I asked you. You are right: this is foolish talk. I was wrong to think that a man such as you are would not be too proud to take advice from a woman. I forgot that my birth is not equal to yours, and that I have a turned-up nose and a crooked mouth; that what would be my delight can never be yours, or that I can expect nothing other than to be my father's tool and breed when it is required of me, while you have your pleasure with other women."

He looked at her unhappily. It had never been a pleasure to him to give hurt to man or beast if it could be helped and least of all to a woman.

"I am what I am, and not altogether the man you think me," he said. "I know that give and give back make the best friends. But it is not always possible to give back love for love. My trust I would as soon give to you as to anyone in this land and I am not too proud to listen to your advice. Much I have heard from Asmund, seeming to show that the way lies clear ahead, yet there are times when I feel that I am on a dark path full of pitfalls."

"Pitfalls there are in plenty."

"You think this enterprise hopeless?"

"Not hopeless, but very dangerous."

"You mean that I shall have to reckon with Owen the Bald, the King of Scotland, King Ethelred, and maybe King Sweyn?"

"Those men are like great mountains far away and it may be possible to slip past them, but there is a hard crag to climb before you get so far. Have you heard of Orm Torkelsson?"

"I heard him mentioned at the time of the Christmas feast and I saw men shake their heads. I gather he is a Westmoring whom it would be well to have on our side."

"He will never be on your side so long as you are hand in glove with Asmund."

"He is your father's enemy, then?"

Maria plucked three rush stalks and began to plait them together with deft fingers.

"Once he was his best friend and I was promised to Orm's eldest son, Rolf, but now we can only consider him an enemy, and a dangerous one, for he is knit close with many friends and kinsmen, besides being in favor with Owen and his Welshmen. It fell out in this way. Year after year Asmund and Orm used to sail as vikings together, sometimes to Ireland, but more often against England. Once they went as far as Normandy. Usually they had good luck and they did much mischief to the lieges of King Ethelred, so much so that men say that was the reason an English army was sent to harry here in Cumberland. After that we were short of corn and short of cattle. Last year some of Orm's friends made a raid overland toward York, but Orm and Asmund sailed again as vikings and each had three ships. They went south and plundered in Devon and Somerset, but they did not get as much booty as they expected. On the way home Asmund proposed an attack on Anglesey, but Orm spoke against it. However, in the end they went ashore, agreeing not to go far from the ships. They were busy taking corn and casks of mead from the farms when King Llewelyn came upon them with a host of picked men. Asmund and his folk left all they had taken and got back on board with little loss, but Orm put up a hard fight. In the end he lost many men and the Welsh boarded and cleared two of his ships. After that they sailed back to Hougun and Orm was very bitter about Asmund not having stood by him in the fight. Then they quarreled about the division of the booty and Orm having few men had to give way and take less than he thought his due. Asmund was not ill pleased at first at the way things had gone, for he is greedy for goods and he reckoned that he had come off better than might have been expected. But after you came to him at Hauksborg and he made this plan to have you as king he would gladly have come to terms with Orm. He bade him to the feast and offered to share goods with him as Orm should decide, but Orm returned no answer. So there the matter stands and at Hep it will be a trial of strength between Orm and Asmund."

"This is bad news that you give me, Maria," he said thoughtfully.

"It is best that you know it. Then you may be ready with some plan of your own."

"What kind of man is this Orm?"

"He is a great warrior, stubborn and revengeful. One thing is both his strength and his weakness—his leaning toward King Owen, who is little liked by the Westmorings since he did nothing to defend them against Ethelred. If you, he, and Asmund were knit firmly together you would be chosen king at Hep without a doubt." She took the plaited strand of rushes and showed that it was too strong for her to break between her hands.

"Is there no way of winning Orm to my side?"

"You could offer him what you have already promised my father, but Westmorland is too small a horse to carry two earls and a king."

"Could we get help in Cumberland?"

"King Owen has too strong a grip on Cumberland for it to be loosed without war."

"If Orm were to be killed?"

"That might be the easiest way, but it would win you many enemies, let alone his three sons who are already famous champions."

"What does Asmund think of all this?"

"I do not know what he thinks."

"He seems confident that all will be well."

"Some plan he has, no doubt."

They fell silent and sat looking at each other. Her large gray eyes met his unwaveringly, and gazing into those eyes he found that he forgot the other features that were unpleasing to him, while he became conscious of her rounded bosom, her small hands and feet, and a wholesome smell about her like new milk.

"It does not look as though we should become man and wife," he said, and did not know whether he was glad or sorry at the thought.

Her eyes dropped and she stirred a little toward him. "It is spring," she said in a low, passionate voice, as though she could not control herself any longer. "For those that are mateless life becomes a torment."

He could not doubt what she expected of him and he found that his reluctance had begun to shrink away like snow before a south wind. They were pledged to each other; her instinct was right and natural. If he thwarted it her love might turn to hate and he would lose the only sure friend and counselor he had. She might even seek his destruction. He took her in his arms and at once she seemed beautiful and desirable in every way; yet even now his will resisted hers and he looked round half-hoping to see someone coming so that they would have to separate. But all the folk were working in the fields on the other side of the hall and he and Maria were utterly alone: he saw only big hills and glittering water. The warm wind and the soft thymy turf drew his senses toward pleasure, yet because pleasure was forced upon him he felt a kind of exasperation and he was rougher with her than he need have been. When it was over he could see that she would have liked some tenderness from him, she would have liked to sit and talk of all manner of things, but she recognized the sullenness of his mood and went sadly away. He stayed on the crag thinking if only Maria had been Astrid. Then it would not have seemed so intolerable to be tied to a man like Asmund and moved to and fro like a piece on a chessboard in a game that was probably already lost.

Chapter 17

NIGHT AT HEP

A FORTNIGHT LATER came the day which had been fixed for the journey to Hep. Arnvid, since his talk with Maria, was less than ever inclined to share Asmund's seeming confidence about the outcome. The prospect of being made a king was alluring enough; nor did the other part of the bargain now appear so distasteful, to have Maria as his wife. At least he would have a woman who was desperately in love with him, and his nature craved love from women and admiration from men. Nevertheless his spirit quailed at the thought of what lay ahead. Once he emerged from his present obscurity he must inevitably find himself confronting an ever widening ring of enemies, and the only support on which he could reckon was Asmund and his band of friends—a handful of landowners, the liegemen of Owen or Ethelred. Well, that sort of thing had been done often enough: Harald Fairhair, master of one small province, had won all Norway, never losing a fight. His descendant, Olaf Trygvesson, had started as a viking leader, harrying here and there in England, Wales, and Ireland. He sailed to Norway with half a dozen ships and not only got himself made king but forced Christianity on an unwilling people. Many other men had won kingdoms and lost them again, but their names were not unhonored in song and saga. Was he, Arnvid, such a man? Sometimes he thought he was, sometimes not. But one thing was certain: all these kings had been fired by ambition; they had made their own plans, they had led men to conquer or die, whereas again and again it seemed to him that he was little more than a pawn on the chessboard handled by a crafty player.

Arnvid had lain awake most of the night, but toward morning he slept heavily and woke with a start when Asmund knocked on the door of the cupboard bed.

"Time to get up, Arnvid!" he shouted in a cheery voice.

Arnvid undid the door and slid himself out, bringing his clothes with him.

"Early shall arise he who will take another's life or goods," quoted Asmund. "Here are fresh clothes, more fitting for a man such as you are to wear at the council." He handed Arnvid a silken tunic dyed scarlet, black linen breeches, a belt with a gilt buckle, and a well-polished helmet. Arnvid laughed. "Whether I am chosen king or not, at least I shall look kingly."

"Never fear," said Asmund, "you will be taken as King of the Westmorings and you will ride back to a loving bride."

It was chilly and dark in the hall, but the fire was beginning to burn up. Arnvid went near it to put on the clothes. He looked hard at the tunic which seemed a very fine garment, but he noticed it had been slit on the left side and carefully mended. He guessed that it was viking loot and that its last wearer had got his death wound through that slit.

Asmund hurried him through breakfast, saying it was urgent to reach Hep before nightfall. All was confusion in the buildings, men and women coming and going, sorting over goods and weapons, and outside was a great trampling and whinnying of horses. When Arnvid went out he saw that some horses were saddled and some loaded with packs and some were merely haltered. It looked as though the whole household was to be on the move, everyone seemed to know his or her part; it was only he who stood there somewhat at a loss in his splendid clothes, observed by all but getting orders from none. Maria came up to him, dressed for riding and carrying a little whip in her hand. For a moment his thoughts went back to Astrid with a pang of regret. Then there had been only the two of them in the chill of early morning, the ground soaked with dew, the sky reddening in the east, the girlish figure beside the horses, a sense of peril and of high adventure. Peril and adventure were before him again but in a different guise and now he did not embrace them so wholeheartedly. Astrid—no, he must put her out of his mind.

"Do you ride with us to Hep?" he said.

"No. I ride to Hougun. Are you sorry?"

He was not sure whether he was sorry or not and did not answer.

"Most of the servants go with me to a farm we have down by the sea."

"Why so?" he said in surprise.

"My father says that here we are running short of food."

From the tone of her voice he divined that this was not the real reason, and said so. She shrugged her shoulders.

"There we are near our ships," she said.

"In case this plan miscarries?"

"All is thought out, you see."

"Then your father is not so sure of success as he would have me think?"

"Success may depend more on you than on him. Now they are getting on horseback. You must go, and good luck go with you." She looked at him fixedly and it seemed to him that her face was transfigured, that its uncomeliness had vanished like the gray tints of night before the rising sun.

"I wish we could have had this night together," she said with a sudden blush. "But as it is I may be carrying your child."

"Would that give you joy, Maria?" he said mechanically, while the intuition flashed on him: She thinks she may never see me again.

"It is you I want, rather than the child," she said sadly. "Farewell."

A servant brought her horse; she mounted and rode away without looking back. He wished he could have said something to please and comfort her, but somehow he could find no words that had the ring of truth. Stroking his beard he looked moodily at the throng of riders moving southward toward the lake shore. She had a good seat on horseback; he liked the way she had swung herself into the saddle; all she did was spirited, graceful and decisive; but his heart gave a leap when a vision came to him of Astrid in dirty man's clothes on a big black horse, her lovely face turned toward him in silent, unfathomable appraisal. . . .

Now he was mounted and riding beside Asmund. They turned eastward, and there followed fifty picked men, all well-armed and on good horses, each man with a spare horse on a halter. To begin with there was a straight hard road, but once they were through the strips of plowing and the fenced grassland it shrank to a narrow pathway hardly perceptible in a sea of dark gorse and withered bracken. Asmund said that this was the place where a stand had been made against Ethelred's men and where Kenneth MacMalcolm's Scottish raiders had been thrown back thirty years earlier.

It was a long toilsome ride, over rocky mountains and down into deep forest valleys, but here and there they came on a bit of the old road, firm under its covering of thyme and turf, with curb stones showing up in the encroaching ling. By late afternoon they had reached a dale where the fells rose in steep folds under scrub and scree to bare, rounded crests like mighty haunches and upthrust knees, and here on a green patch above the river was another stone fortress encircled by earthworks, almost perfect and exactly like the one at Ambleside. Asmund said that they were now in the gorge of Lune. They rode below the walls and over a rushing stream by a bridge with stone piers, following a broader road that went northward out of the mountains. Asmund pointed to a great stone and said that at one time it marked the boundary of England, but where the boundary was now it was not easy to say. A strong king and it moved one way, a weak one and it moved the other.

The scrubby woods died away in scatterings of white-stemmed birch and they rode into a great heath. To eastward were low hills topped by old grave mounds and to westward, sharp and black against the sunset, rose fells like billows on a stormy sea.

"This is Hep," said Asmund, "and here are the Westmorings coming to meet us." He pointed to groups of men on foot and on horseback threading their way through the wilderness toward a cluster of booths and tents where fires were lit and a crowd was gathering like bees flowing into a swarm. Everywhere amid brake and briar stood up reddish stones, some of them set out by human hands in circles and avenues. It looked to Arnvid a place where much had happened in past days and where perhaps much was still to happen.

Asmund turned his horse toward a booth at the foot of a solitary knoll. Here were some of his servants who had come in advance to make the roof weather-tight and gather firewood. Here was food in plenty for man and beast and here in a growing throng were his friends, mostly from Hougun, men whom Arnvid had already seen at the Christmas feast. They greeted him respectfully and as more and more men streamed toward Asmund's booth, all well-armed, and the murmur of talk grew into a loud and friendly clamor, Arnvid began to feel himself borne forward on an unexpected wave of confidence. All seemed to be going as Asmund said it would. He sat down to meat in the booth that was overflowing with folk, and when ale was passed around man after man rose and pledged himself to stand by Arnvid and Asmund at the council tomorrow. After a while Arnvid went out, a little drunk with ale and also with an unaccustomed sense of power. It was nearly dark, but he could see groups of men sitting everywhere around fires that shone out like beacons far over the heath. He walked aimlessly, glad of the cool air and the pleasant smell of wood smoke and the stars showing dimly overhead. Instinctively he made toward one of the fires which threw a flickering radiance over the trampled ground and long shadows from the great stones, and suddenly he was aware of a group of men walking close behind him. He turned and saw there were four of them, ruddy, monstrous figures in the glare of the fire. First came an elderly man with a high forehead, beetling brows and a long red beard. His hands were thrust in a belt from which hung a sword, and from both there was a glint of gold and silver. Behind him were three young men, sturdy and sinister-looking. They, too, had long red hair and they carried long-shafted axes. Their looks were surly and arrogant, but the older man seemed to have a frank, goodhumored air about him, and Arnvid felt drawn toward him, little as he liked the aspect of the other three. "Hail, friends!" he said, suiting his tone to the dignity and the shade of aloofness he imagined proper to a king.

It was the older man who answered gruffly, "By your looks I should guess you to be a stranger here in Westmorland."

"That is true, yet I am already known to many, and more will know me tomorrow."

"Are you Arnvid Torolfsson, whom Asmund will put forward as king?"

"I am he, and I claim the kingship that was won by my forebears, Leif, Torfin, and Torolf."

"Boldly answered!" said the older man with a smile. The other three closed round him muttering words that Arnvid could not hear.

"To whom do I speak?" he said, stiffening with a sudden realization of danger.

"To Orm Torkelsson. Have you heard that name before, young man?"

"I have," said Arnvid. He glanced around. Men stood in groups not far off, silent and watchful, but he had come a long way from Asmund's booth and he fancied that the folk here were not his friends. Suddenly fear gripped him and then rage that he had got himself into peril without the least necessity. Here he was, alone with Orm and his three sons, the very men against whom Maria had warned him. At the same time he could not help feeling that this Orm was a more honest and trustworthy man than Asmund.

"The men you speak of are not without honor in this land," said Orm, "but you must know that we Westmorings are now the men of Owen the Bald, whatever folk in Hougun may want to think."

"I know that you are ill content that Owen did not defend you against Ethelred."

"That is as may be, but for good or ill an oath is an oath."

An honest man, thought Arnvid, yet he now had a suspicion that he might not be as honest as he seemed.

"Is there no way on which we could come to terms?" he said.

One of the young men spoke up. "The easiest way for us to come to terms with King Owen would be to bring him your head," he said, shifting his grip on his axe shaft.

"In Iceland it is not the custom for men to bear weapons against each other at a council meeting." Arnvid spoke nonchalantly, but a cold sweat broke out all over him.

"This is not Iceland," said Orm, putting a restraining hand on his son's arm. "But," he continued, "we shall offer you no violence now. All the same I warn you that if you persist in claiming kingship tomorrow there will be bloodshed." He turned away abruptly. With enormous relief Arnvid watched the four tall figures striding off across the heath from fire to fire till they came to some horses. There they mounted and rode away into the darkness.

He lost no time in returning to Asmund's booth. He went inside and saw it was almost empty. By the light of a candle Asmund was sitting at one end with six of the men who had been his guests at Ambleside. They were talking in low tones, but fell silent when Arnvid took a place amongst them.

"I have met with Orm Torkelsson and his three sons," said Arnvid, with assumed indifference, and was pleased to see all eyes turn upon him with keen interest.

"Did they know who you were?" asked Asmund.

"They soon guessed."

"Then you are lucky to have got back here alive."

"Orm seemed to me an honorable man."

"That is what he would have folk think, but his sons are not so careful of their honor. All three of them are killers and used to every kind of violence and lawlessness."

"I can believe that, but I would like to have made a friend of Orm."

"Will you offer him friendship at the council tomorrow?" said Asmund, a note of exasperation in his voice.

"I had thought of it," admitted Arnvid. He stared from one to another of the company, but saw only furtive and gloomy faces.

"It would be a waste of words," said Asmund. "Orm has taken his stand against you and he is not to be shifted by any offer you can make him."

"He is your enemy, not mine!"

There was a silence, then Asmund said smoothly, "You may think, Arnvid, that you would get better support from Orm than you would from me, but if he comes to the council tomorrow you will see one man in his party for three in mine."

"Has he not King Owen behind him?"

"I would say that he is the only man in Westmorland on whom Owen can rely, and the only man who can hinder you from being made king. My spies have been busy and I know all his plans. He has sent to Owen for help, but so far none has come."

"Where is King Owen?"

"He is thought to be with the King of Scots at Stirling; there is some talk of an attack on Northumbria. Now is the moment to seize land and power, when Ethelred has to meet a fresh Danish invasion. There is news that King Sweyn will sail against England this year with more men and ships than ever before, eager to avenge his sister killed on Saint Brice's Day. A bold step now, Arnvid, and who knows what may fall into your hands!"

"And only Orm Torkelsson stands in our way? King Owen's watchdog guarding the sheepfold."

"Rather than see you made king he will force matters to a fight."

"Rather than see you made earl."

"Put it that way if you like."

"Then what is our plan for tomorrow?"

"I have a plan for tonight. Orm and his sons sleep with Sigurd Longchin at his house in Rossgill. In less than an hour we can be there, make a ring around the house and burn them in."

"No!" said Arnvid violently. "I will not have Westmorland at that price."

"It will cost you dearer if it comes to a battle at the council place. With Orm out of the way the land is yours."

"Has he no kinsmen to avenge him?"

"There is no leader among them. A deed such as this will cow his party as much as it will cheer ours."

Arnvid looked from face to face. "Are you all agreed on this plan?" he said.

"We are," said several men at once. "It is the best we can do."

"Then I will not have it done!" His voice rose to a shout. "I shall not begin to rule in Westmorland with a deed such as this!"

"You are little likely to rule otherwise," said Asmund sourly.

"Orm could have ended this business by taking my life out there on the heath; his sons urged him to, but he forbore. I shall not repay that by having him burned in."

"And how will you hinder us if we are resolved to make an end of him?" Asmund's shifty eyes sparkled with malice.

"I can ride forthwith to warn him of your intent."

"That you cannot, Arnvid, if, for your own good, we hold you here under guard," said Asmund carefully. He threw a significant glance at the others, who rose to their feet.

"At least I can refuse to speak at the council tomorrow, and then there will be no one to make you an earl, unless you persuade King Owen that you are his man; but that, I fancy, will now be no easy task for you." Arnvid folded his arms and leaned back with a look of inflexibility. He saw well enough that Asmund's plan offered a good chance of success. It was the sort of swift, decisive act that might be expected of a king. It might make him some enemies, but it would vastly increase his prestige. All the same, he had said instinctively that he would be no party to it and surely it was impossible now to retract his word without loss of face. If he had not seen Orm and taken a liking to him he might have agreed. After all, his talk with Maria had prepared him for something of the kind. . . .

"You would wreck the whole enterprise to save the lives of this man and his three villainous sons?"

Arnvid looked straight before him and did not answer. He wondered whether he were more actuated by regard for Orm, his enemy, or dislike of Asmund, his friend, and a foreboding came over him. How could a man who yielded to every whim and scruple ever make good as a king? What would Gunnar do if he were in his shoes? First do away with Orm and then, when he was sure of his ground, put an end to Asmund. And he would go to bed quite cheerfully with Maria after he had killed her father, and most likely Maria would make no fuss about it. Right or wrong, her husband would come first. He said to himself: The thing is to be hard, but I am only hard to my own disadvantage. I should be crafty, but I wear my heart on my sleeve. When I should be subtle I am only obstinate, but I am what I am and will be no other.

There was a long silence. The candle guttered and burned low. The clamor of voices outside had died away; there was only the sighing of the wind, a patter of spring rain on the roof and the sizzling of drops falling through the smoke hole on glowing embers.

At last Asmund said, "So be it, then. We shall meet Orm at the council tomorrow and if we are manstrong enough we may win through."

Chapter 18

THE COUNCIL

ARNVID STOOD BESIDE ASMUND at the foot of the council mound. Their supporters were ranged in a solid mass to southward of the mound, about Asmund's booth. To eastward in a looser array were Orm and his friends, sturdy, war-like-looking folk though scanty in numbers compared to Asmund's. Between the two parties and more in the background was another fairly large body of men. These, said Asmund, had not yet committed themselves to either side. The sun shone, a mild breeze blew eastward over the heath and larks sang high overhead. Nature seemed to smile on this gathering of armed men, confident, angry, or perplexed, but glancing around him Arnvid noticed gray veils of rain passing across the western mountains and a group of gnarled ash trees caught in a yellow glow against a black sky in the north, whence came a faint growl of thunder. Asmund chewed his lips, staring hard at Orm and his company, but his gaze often shifted to the north where the heath stretched empty and desolate toward a thickening of forest below a pale limestone scar.

At last a youth went up on the mound and blew a horn four times, to east, north, west, and south. He was followed by a very old man, grimly handsome with long white hair and beard. Asmund said he was Kol the Old, the senior lawman of Westmorland. The raucous murmur of voices died down. The old man raised his arm stiffly, then he spoke in a dry, dispassionate tone saying that Asmund of Ambleside had weighty business to bring before the council. "Let him be heard by all men," he said. "Think well upon what he says and then signify whether you agree with him or not."

Side by side, Arnvid and Asmund walked up the mound and stood looking down on the crowd which like a rising wave flowed up a little closer. Arnvid suddenly felt drained of all emotion, like a gambler indifferent to the winning or losing of a small stake. Now that he saw, in perspective as it were, these few hundreds of men gathered to meet him he asked himself how it could profit either him or them if he became their king. How was so small a realm to be maintained, a hare among a pack of wolves? Yet as he looked at the stubborn, vindictive faces, the defiant blue eyes, he felt that there was a quality about these people that would make them more like a badger than a hare if surrounded by enemies. He knew the lines on which Asmund would appeal to them and at first he listened with impatience, thinking how little skillful words could effect, as in the case of that Welsh prince in Powys who carried his listeners with him on a high tide of passion. The growing ambition of the King of Scots, the savagery of his men, the indifference of Owen the Bald, the hatred and treachery Ethelred had shown toward both

Dane and Northman as compared with the friendliness of good King Edgar. Now was the time for them to strike a blow for themselves under a king of their own race. Now was the time for all Northmen to unite, from the Solway shore and the western mountains, from Westmorland, from Hougun and Lonsdale . . . He knew it all by heart. It left him cold, and seemingly it did not convince the crowd of listeners. They remained silent, or at most there was only a murmur of approval from Asmund's men. Peace with York, peace with King Sweyn who would soon be master of England, no more tax or service to Scot or Welshman . . . Now at last there was a roar of applause.

"Here is the man who shall be both a shield and a sword to this land, foe to none of you, friend to all, a champion well proved in deeds, Arnvid Torolfsson, grandson of King Leif, a just man and good. I ask you to crown him King!"

Now Asmund was taking him by the hand and leading him forward to the brink of the knoll amid a shouting and clashing of uplifted weapons that swept over the crowd from side to side like a sudden crash of thunder. Even the men round Orm seemed to be joining in as Arnvid stood there, a figure of manly beauty in splendid clothes, like a pillar of flame in the midst of that vast, somber heath bounded by blue hills. Self-distrust dropped from him; he felt gay and confident. Whatever fate had in store for him, this was a moment of triumph that would never lose its savor. He raised his arm and the clamor died away as though by magic. He smiled and said in a loud clear voice:

"Westmorings, Men of Hougun, all who have come to this council place, if you choose me as your king I swear to do all that a man can do to guard the land against its foes, to give justice to all, whether rich or poor, to honor your laws and customs, to give peace to priest and trader, to woman and child, even as my forefathers did. The land and its folk shall be my one care, to be cherished more than goods and gold, at the cost if need be of life itself."

The words came easily; they were largely what Asmund had instilled into him weeks ago and at the time he could hardly imagine that they would have much effect, but now spoken in an exalted mood, with seeming spontaneity, he saw that they struck exactly the right note. Again there was a shattering uproar that must surely signify overwhelming approval.

The old lawman came forward again, holding in his hands a plain circlet of gold. In a bleak, disillusioned voice he said to the seething mass of folk below: "Do you choose this man, Arnvid Torolfsson, as your king and lord?"

"We do!" came a great shout.

Well, that settles it, thought Arnvid. Now there were other matters to deal with. He must name Asmund as earl, he must form a retinue of young men, sons of the biggest landowners, and later on he must be wedded to Maria . . . He glanced at Asmund, wondering how he would bear himself now that his plan had come to fruition. But Asmund was gazing across the heath to northward at a solitary rider. He was a long way off, but Arnvid could just see that his right arm rose and fell incessantly as though he were flogging a tired horse. Then, with a start, he heard the old man say: "If there be any that would refuse kingship to Arnvid, let them speak now!"

At once there was a formidable shouting from where Orm stood. Orm himself pushed forward to the foot of the knoll and said defiantly: "I would put some questions to this man Arnvid, and it would be well if all we Westmorings hear what answer he can make to them."

Pale with rage, Asmund intervened. "It is too late for that! The folk have chosen; Arnvid is King!"

"I have as much right as you to speak and I claim to be heard!" shouted Orm in return.

"Speak, then," said the lawman dispassionately.

Orm came up beside Arnvid and stood fronting him, his hands thrust in his belt. He began in a voice that was calm and not discourteous.

"We have no quarrel with you, Arnvid Torolfsson, but we know who has persuaded you to come here and make this claim. We know, if you do not, that Asmund cares little either for you or Westmorland. What he seeks is power for himself and you are the weapon he would wield to fell his enemies and win goods and gold. Tell me, can you and Asmund, and such friends as he has here or in Hougun, hope to contend against the might of King Owen the Bald?"

"Aye, that we can, if you Westmorings stand in with us," answered Arnvid, and there was a shout of applause.

"And I say that if you called out every man, woman, and child in this land you would still be too weak to win against such odds."

"If it comes to war we can expect other help."

"Whence do you expect help?"

"There are Northmen in Cumberland and Lonsdale."

"I see none of them here. You have no pledge from them that they will be your men." A murmur came from the crowd. That shaft seemed to have gone home.

"There are also the Danes in York," said Arnvid.

"Never have we had aught but ill will from the rulers in York."

"Last year they gave me an army to lead into Westmorland. I might have won the land with fire and sword, but it was not so that I hoped to become king."

"Friends you may have in York, but they are not our friends and never will be." Again a murmur of assent, louder this time. "I say," continued Orm, "that without powerful help you cannot hold this land. You can only bring it to ruin."

"In old days there were kings here who held their own," said Arnvid quickly.

"Aye, there were kings who mostly died in battle. They only held the land by agreement with a Welsh king, or with a king in York, or with the King of England. I ask you, have you come to terms with Ethelred's earl in York?"

"No, but Audun the Stout is my friend."

"I say again, he is no friend to us. Have you come to terms with King Owen?"

"No."

"With the King of Scotland?"

"No."

"With King Ethelred himself?"

"Least of all with him."

"Outside Westmorland you can reckon on no help except for a few folk in Hougun?"

"There is King Sweyn."

Orm laughed. "King Sweyn! He is far away in Denmark. Do you know what manner of man he is? A viking whose only desire is to win gold and goods wherever he can and bear them away on his ships. Shall I tell you what will happen if you make yourself king? An army will come against you from King Owen and that soon. You think Asmund will stand by you when you have made him an earl? He will betray you and take your head to King Owen and at that price he, not you, will rule here in Westmorland."

Asmund stepped forward, his fists clenched in fury. "You lie, Orm!" he shouted. "You stand condemned out of your own mouth! You stand against the man who is chosen king by the folk!"

"You may have good reason to choose him. We do not."

"We shall teach you to choose him with the edges of our swords!"

"Take to your swords then, but they seemed blunt to me when I last saw them drawn on Anglesey."

"Hew at the traitors!" shouted Asmund to his men. He ran down the mound into the crowd which split abruptly as Orm went back to his own party. Everywhere weapons were raised aloft amid shout and countershout. A standard appeared in front of Asmund's booth and was swiftly borne forward. Only Arnvid and Kol the Old remained on the mound. The lawman shrugged his shoulders and put the golden circlet back in his tunic. For a moment Arnvid stared at the two hosts. Asmund's was much the larger and Orm was drawing back across a small stream, posting his men between two booths. The solitary rider appeared, jumped off his horse and ran up to Orm. They spoke together for a moment and Arnvid saw a grim smile on Orm's face. Heavy-hearted, he went down among Asmund's folk and drew his sword. A man handed him a heavy throwing spear and they surged forward across the stream, following the standard. Neither Arnvid nor Asmund were in the front rank when the crash came with

Orm's warriors, but Arnvid could see men falling on both sides and quickly trodden down in the press. He saw, too, Orm's three sons swinging their great axes to left and right with taunting shouts and a sudden rage gripped him. Frantically he tried to get forward and exchange blows with those young men, but he was wedged in among broad backs and frowsy heads, among red-faced landowners and sullen peasants. All at once the standard fell and all surged backward across the stream. There was a triumphant shout from Orm's men answered by a long unearthly howl out on the heath. It seemed to come from the other side of the knoll. Arnvid saw Asmund looking pale and desperate, saw him wave a bright sword and heard him shout: "Forward friends! Make an end of them!" Some gathered for a second charge, but most men kept looking over their shoulders. Then suddenly flowing round both sides of the knoll and over it came a horde of wild-looking men, bareheaded and barelegged, in brightly colored tunics, wearing no mail, but brandishing long knives and heavy axes. King Owen's men, thought Arnvid, Welshmen, but they looked much more savage and ferocious than any Welshmen he had seen. Asmund was beside him. "Picts from Galloway!" he said breathlessly. "I heard they might come. All is over. We must get to the horses if we can . . ."

The newcomers were taking them in the rear and now Orm's men came on, cleaving a path deep into the milling crowd. Here came Orm himself hewing dexterously with his sword, cutting down man after man. Arnvid turned upon him in a frenzy of rage and despair. He launched the spear with all his strength and saw it skim over Orm's shield, go through his mail shirt and stand fast like a stake driven into a mudbank. The helmeted head drooped, the old warrior fell forward on his face, and over his body stepped one of his sons, his eyes blazing with fury. The axe swept up and Arnvid turned and ran for dear life. For a moment he saw the Picts in front of him, hacking and stabbing. He swung aside and plunged into a knot of men. Here were wild-eyed horses with tossing manes and men scrambling onto them as best they could. He saw Asmund mounted and going off at a gallop, other riders streaming after him, a long trail of men running on foot. Someone held a horse for him and Arnvid threw himself on its back. He flogged the animal with the flat of his sword and went full tilt after Asmund, crashing through briars and sprays of blackthorn blossom, on and on until the land sloped down toward the Lune and he came up with Asmund and a score or so of men, now riding at a steady trot southward.

"Whither now?" said Arnvid bitterly.

"To Ambleside, where we can get fresh horses," answered Asmund, looking moodily straight before him.

"And then?"

"We shall be safest down in Hougun, well away from that hornets' nest in Westmorland."

Arnvid remembered that Maria would already be there. All had been planned for failure as well as for success, but what a failure it had been, when all seemed set for victory!

Asmund seemed to divine his thoughts. He said in a sullen voice: "All would have been well if we had finished with Orm last night. Then no one would have spoken against you at the council, and united we could have made short work of that band of Picts."

"I killed Orm, just before we all fled."

"You killed him! Then we must push on faster."

"Why so?"

"Because his sons will be following us. They will never rest until they have taken vengeance for Orm. I think you would not have an easy death at their hands."

"Nor you either."

Asmund looked back. Then he struck his horse hard with his heels. "They are on us already!" he said.

As they cantered away past the old fortress in the gorge of Lune, Arnvid could see a band of horsemen following them down the road, not far short of a hundred, perhaps. They shook off the pursuers in the high forest of Kentdale and reached Ambleside late at night with the horses more dead than alive. Asmund dared not stay more than an hour. Some of the men had turned off to their homes earlier in the day and he now rode on with only a dozen, all on fresh beasts.

"What will happen here?" said Arnvid as they clattered round the hall gable and down between the stout cow barn and the galleried lofts toward the lake side.

"They will burn it all," said Asmund indifferently.

"If I had a homestead such as this, I would fight for it."

"It may be no great pleasure, riding horses to death over forest and fell, but it is better than sitting in a hall and getting burned alive. It was the worst of luck that you killed Orm and left his sons living. I would have finished with all four of them if I had had my way. You may call yourself a champion, Arnvid; you looked a man fit to be a king when you stood on the mound, but the way you answered Orm's questions showed that you had no more wit than a child."

"I answered him truthfully," said Arnvid, beginning to feel rage and hate rising in him.

"You should give back lies for lies."

"I did not think they were lies, what he said about you and other matters."

"Bitter you are, friend, at the way things have fallen out, but we may recover ourselves yet."

"What is your plan?"

"We shall sail to Dublin. The ships are ready. There I shall have a welcome from King Sigtrygg Silkbeard. He will give us men and broad lands in Ireland. You shall still have Maria and my support. You may well be a king some day."

"I want no more support from you!"

"What will you do, then?"

"I will ride to Hauksborg and get my woman who is there."

"Get her if you will and bring her to Ireland. She may teach you some sense if I cannot. Where will you be without me, hunted like a deer from hill to hill and from wood to wood by Rolf Ormsson and his brothers? I will wait for you one day at the ships in Duddon Mouth, but one day only."

Arnvid said no more. They rode on in darkness till they came to the lake foot and could see the big hills black with forest against the graying sky. Here stood a cluster of farm buildings; they woke the people and demanded food. Then very soon they got back onto their tired and sweat-drenched horses.

"Here is the parting of the ways," said Asmund. "I will send one man with you to Hauksborg and he can guide you to Duddon Mouth. Do not dally with your mistress; there will be plenty of time for that on shipboard. Though Hauksborg is a strong place, Orm's sons will not take long to hack it open with their axes."

Arnvid did not answer. He saw Asmund and his following turn off to the right at a canter while he rode straight on with the single retainer. He kept to a walk or at most a slow trot. After a time the man said, "Should we not press on, master?"

"I ride at what pace I choose," said Arnvid sharply. He felt desperately tired, the more so because of the completeness of his failure at Hep and the sense that there was some truth in Asmund's stinging taunts. He was famished, too, for he had scarcely touched the food at the lake foot, tough maggoty smoked beef and hard oatbread. Day broke. Water flashed in the low sunshine, there was a mistiness of green buds over the thickets, the twigs that brushed against his face were cool with dew. Somewhere not far off he heard a cock crow. All was fresh and lovely, as on the mornings he had ridden off with Astrid. If it were not for the thought of her he would not have cared to live on as a fugitive eating other men's bread. What a snare was the quest for fame and power! But for Astrid he would almost rather have sat down by the wayside till Orm's sons came upon him and then died fighting. On one thing he was firmly resolved: he would never see Asmund again, nor would he show himself to Maria as a failure and listen to the excuses she might make for him. With Astrid he would be back where he was before—a homeless wanderer, but beside the woman who was surely his delight, though he had tried hard to forget her.

They came on a lean, ruthless-looking peasant felling an oak, and Arnvid thought that nearby might be a hut where there was something good to eat, at least a drink of warm milk. He got off his horse and went up to the man.

"A fair morning!" he said.

"A fair morning," said the peasant indifferently, not ceasing his blows at the tree.

Suddenly exasperated, Arnvid said haughtily, "You may not have heard who I am."

"Nay, and I don't want to hear either." The peasant dashed the sweat from his brow and gave Arnvid a shrewd glance.

"Yesterday I was chosen king at Hep."

"Well, king or no king, stand aside or I'll hew thy legs off."

The peasant swung his axe again and made the chips fly far and wide.

Arnvid, with a bitter smile, pulled up his horse's head from the grass and got back into the saddle. Another long hour through the woods and Asmund's man pointed across a marsh to a little conical hill topped with buildings. Arnvid recognized Hauksborg.

Chapter 19

THE SANDS

When arnvid entered the small, smoky hall in Hauksborg he gave a deep sigh of relief, for there on a bench before the fire sat Astrid, unmistakably the Astrid who had been his dear companion on land and water. There she was, looking as well or better than he had ever seen her, wearing the familiar wedding dress which also seemed to have been restored to something of its former beauty. How it came back to him, seeing her for the first time in that dress in the doomed hall at Kinver with the glow on her face, the sparkle in her eyes, though that was for Gunnar, not for him. Well, her face was glowing now, even if it were only a pale reflection from his own. He sat down on the bench beside her, tonguetied for the moment, forgetting that he came back to her a defeated man, a failure, thinking only that he would rather have her in his arms than that gold circlet on his head, the crown of Westmorland. He glanced round the hall; an elderly woman sat at a spinning wheel, a girl was stirring a pot on the fire, a cat stretched itself and arched its back. The men were out in the fields and woods, but Asmund's retainer would be summoning them to defend the ramparts against the sons of Orm. There was no safety here; he must get away with Astrid, though whither he did not know . . . Instinctively he put a hand on her shoulder. She laid down her knitting and said with a smile that had more of pity than of love: "How did it go at the council meeting? We heard that you and Asmund were to be there yesterday."

"I have not lost much time in coming back to you," he said with a laugh. "We failed."

"So I suppose." She looked thoughtfully at his fine clothes all mud-splashed and torn with briars.

"I should have been made King, but for a man, Orm Torkelsson, Asmund's enemy. He brought things to a fight and then King Owen's men came up and took us in the rear. I killed Orm and after that we all fled with his three sons after us. There was no standing against them. Asmund has gone to his ships, but it is my life they aim at. They should soon be here."

"It seems to be a custom of yours to kill some notable man and then have to flee for your life," she said not unkindly.

"This time I have no plan . . . I am so weary I can hardly keep my eyes open." His senses reeled in the warmth of the hall, his head fell forward. Quickly she got up and filled a horn with mead. "Drink this, Arnvid," she said. "This is no time for sleeping. Pull yourself together!"

Obediently he set the horn to his lips, but was asleep before he could swallow any of the liquor. She snatched the horn from him and slapped him hard on the cheek.

"Yes, Astrid?" he said dazedly.

"Drink this! Be a man! Do you want us both to be caught here and burned in?"

"Burned in? Yes, the sons of Orm. Are they here?" He emptied the horn at a draught, and sprang to his feet.

"Not yet, but they soon may be. You must get away, make some plan."

"I have no heart for anything unless you come with me."

Again she smiled pityingly. "Must you have me with you? I heard you were going to wed Maria, Asmund's daughter."

"The price of kingship. Now I need not pay it."

"Yet you would find safety on shipboard with Asmund."

"So he told me, but I never wish to see that man again. I left him and came to seek you."

"They say that when Earl Hakon fled before Olaf Trygvesson he fled to the house of his mistress."

"He did, and she hid him."

"I cannot hide you, this is not my house. You could not have come to a worse place. With the marsh all round no one can leave it without being seen. Is there time to get away? Are these men on your heels?"

"Plenty of folk have seen this scarlet tunic. They should not find it hard to track me hither."

"Folly not to have changed your clothes," she muttered.

"You need not tell me I am a fool—I know it. Come, let us go. Are you ready?"

"As ready as I was when I left Kinver."

"My horse is tired out; we may as well go on foot."

"Their horses will be tired too, but there are two good horses in the stable here."

"Well, let us have them, then."

They went out of the hall to the stable, the old woman

and the girl watching them in silence. "You speak as though you had no hope," said Astrid.

"Nor have I much," he said, wearily clapping a saddle on the back of one horse while she busied herself with the other. "It was foretold in Iceland that a woman would bring me to my end. My mother read it on the palm of my hand."

"I warned you I should bring you no luck."

"I don't care whether you bring me luck or ill luck as long as I have you!" he said violently. She looked at him and saw that his face was all red and puckered with rage, he foamed at the mouth, his hands shook and he dealt with the horse so roughly that it reared up.

He is like a Welshman, she thought, but then he is half Welsh. Maybe that is his undoing. Side by side they rode out through the gate that still stood wide-open. None of the menfolk was to be seen. Perhaps they had heard of peril approaching and had hidden in the forest . . . At headlong speed they went down the steep path and on to the causeway.

"There!" he said. "Look there!" as though it were her fault.

Not half a mile away on the edge of the marsh was a company of riders. Their horses seemed dead-tired and moved at little more than a walk. The men jumped off and started running.

"Our boat!" he said. "Is it still there at the quay?"

"Yes," she said, "but it is useless. The tide is out." She pointed past a rocky headland to brown sands stretching right across to the hills opposite. "If we ride hard we might get to Asmund before they can catch us on fresh horses."

"No! Not that!" he said, grinding his teeth.

"There is a way across the sands marked with poles, but the tide has turned, there are quicksands and deep channels, we may not reach the other side."

"Let us try!"

In a few moments they were riding down the beach, splashing through shallows, and then out on hard dry sand. Each had a whip and used it to such effect that the horses went like the wind, sometimes one ahead, sometimes the other. Here was a slanting weed-grown pole on the brink of a channel. Arnvid noticed that the water was flowing along it fast inland and that the sands ahead were full of rippling pools leading one into another. Even the sands that looked hard were now turning soggy. The horses' hoofs began to sink in deeper and their pace slackened no matter how hard they were driven with whip and heel. At the next channel they hung back till Arnvid pricked them both with his sword and then they went through with water up to their bellies. After this the sands seemed drier for a time, but soon little frothy wavelets came racing across them and then there was nothing but water ahead. At first it hardly reached the horses' fetlocks, but presently it was up to their knees. The creatures seemed to realize their peril; they struggled forward desperately without any urging from their riders. Now they were in up to their shoulders and their strength seemed to be giving out. A few more spasmodic efforts and they came to a standstill. The next pole rose only a few feet out of the swiftly flowing water and land was still half a mile away. Arnvid considered abandoning the horses and swimming ashore, but he caught sight of a floating log and from the speed with which it was moving he judged there must be a powerful current. Moreover the log was not drifting parallel to the shore but rather away from it. One might swim a long time without getting any nearer the land. Besides, Astrid could not swim.

"It looks as though we are going to drown," he said.

"Better than being burned alive," she answered.

"The danger was for me only. I need not have brought you to this pass, and yet I could not leave you behind."

"I should be pleased that you value me so highly," she said on a note of irony.

"But you are not pleased to die with me."

"No, I wish I could be."

"If you loved me it would be easier for you."

"Perhaps. I don't know," she said, looking blankly at the dancing waves. The horses were having to lift their heads above the water; they began to struggle again, but now they could hardly get their feet up out of the yielding sand. Arnvid looked around, considering the desperate idea of swimming with Astrid on his back. The log had disappeared, but now he saw something else; a boat making out from the shore. A man was rowing hard. At first he seemed to be heading away from them, but soon the current caught him and swept him nearer every minute. They watched, speechless, for a while, then Arnvid muttered half to himself: "That boat comes between us and death. What luck we two have when we are together!" Yes, he thought, lucky in everything except the thing that matters most: she does not love me as I do her.

The man drew alongside them and took them on board without comment as though it were a commonplace affair for him. The horses, relieved of their riders, started swimming after the boat. Arnvid kept hold of the bridles, and before very long they all stood on dry land. The fisherman, for so he was, and a Northman by the look of him, said little to Arnvid's thanks and the gift of several pieces of silver. He pulled his boat up the beach and was for leaving them to their own devices. Utterly dazed with exhaustion, Arnvid had sat down and immediately fallen asleep, but Astrid ran after the man and asked whether he could give them food and drink and a fire to dry their clothes.

"My hut is only a poor place for people such as you are," he said.

"It will not come amiss to a man in flight for his life."

"I guessed that the wind might blow in that quarter. There is seldom much luck in saving folk from the sea. Are men following him across the sands?"

"Most likely."

"He looks to me a doomed man."

"Doomed he is unless he can be well hidden."

"My hut is no good hiding place: all travelers across the sands go past the door."

"What would you do if you were in his shoes?"

"I would get a passage on a trader's ship. There is one sailing tomorrow from Lancaster quay, not three miles away."

Astrid ran back to Arnvid and woke him up. He protested with sudden petulance and she answered him with a sharp tongue. "Have you forgotten Orm's sons? They will be crossing the sands as soon as the tide falls. By then we should be well on our way and you will not get far, starving and soaked to the skin. Come to the fisherman's hut."

"Wherever we go we shall be followed," he said wearily. "I would sooner stay here and fight it out with them when they come."

"Have some sense! Why should you choose death now when you have escaped so often?"

"You despise me for running away time after time."

"I should despise you more if you had no heart to live."

"Why should you care what becomes of me, a failure at every turn?" he said sullenly.

"You did not fail when you got me away from Kinver. Be a man! There are more things to think of than how you appear in a woman's eyes."

He fell into a sudden rage. "I have made a fool of myself ever since I first set eyes on you!" he shouted.

"You let me go easily enough when you went off with Asmund. You need not drag me along with you now. I shall come to no great harm."

"A woman can always fall into some man's arms. I saw that when I found you with Cadogan ap Einion."

She reddened and flung out the words with an effort.

"You can have me when you like. What more do you want?"

"What more?" he asked, feeling rage ebb away and a throb of tenderness that was both pain and delight. There was so much more, as he knew from what Maria offered him; but Astrid did not and perhaps never would. He sighed and went off to catch the horses that were grazing unconcernedly on the wiry turf above high-water mark. The fisherman was waiting. He led them along a passage starred with primroses through oak and hazel scrub overwhelmed by rampant honeysuckle, and presently they came to a clearing with a cow and some goats and a small wattle hut. Sitting inside over food and drink, Arnvid listened to what the man had to say about the trader's ship at Lancaster. A chance to get clear of the country, what Asmund had offered him and he had refused, but he would not refuse now. The fisherman thought the trader would be sailing for Rouen to pick up a cargo of wine. The name meant nothing to Astrid, but Arnvid had heard it mentioned in York. The folk there were reckoned Northmen and they had a duke, a man called Richard the Good, who had not much land but what he had was as good or better than the best in England.

Astrid listened to what he had to say about it with obvious impatience. Why should he waste his time talking to her when the thing to do was to get away from this place as fast as possible? But for good or ill she had again become the center point of his life, something to be prized above all else. He had to consult her, tell her everything, not because she had a quick wit and could give him good advice, but because he was the slave of her pretty face and her young, healthy body, the body he had only once possessed in all the time that they had been together. Perhaps he would change if he had her continually, perhaps she would change also and become more of a woman as he might become more of a man . . .

Arnvid gave the fisherman a gold coin when they left the hut. He saw Astrid shrug her shoulders and he said gaily, "I need not be sparing of the gold Asmund gave me. These clothes I had from him. These are his horses. I have nothing that is mine save you and this sword."

"Much he staked on you," she said as they mounted and rode away.

"Gold and goods, bed and board, his daughter in marriage, but he would have been well repaid if we had won."

"Was it his fault or yours that you lost?"

"Mostly mine. I would not let him murder Orm the night before the council, and then I killed the man myself."

"But in fair fight?"

"Yes, but maybe fairness does not get a man far."

"If you seek power you will not often get it with clean hands."

"And if one seeks a woman?"

"That should be a simple matter. As the saying goes: choose your words well, make fair promises and stand by them."

"If I had sought you in that way, would things have been different between us?"

She looked annoyed and quickened her horse's pace with the whip.

"What could I promise you when we rode away from Kinver but toil and peril?" he said.

"What could I do but accept anything that gave me a chance of life?"

"And then you thought you could better yourself with that man Cadogan," he said bitterly.

"That always sticks in your throat! Did you not think you would better yourself with Asmund's daughter?"

"I never wanted the woman!" he burst out angrily.

"Yet you took what she offered, I dare say."

"What if I did?" He saw himself again with Maria on the crag above the old fortress. How was it that he had been able to enchant that girl while this one persisted in holding him at bay?"

"I suppose a plain girl is not likely to be very particular."

"Plain she might be, but she was not cold and hard as you are."

"It does not follow that I should be cold and hard to all men."

"It is only that you cannot find me to your liking!"

She frowned, wondering why it was that she felt critical of all he did. When he was gentle with her she was irritated, when he was violent she was contemptuous. But she was in his debt, he had saved her life—she did not forget that. She was mortified that she could not repay the debt in the way he wanted. It was love he kept demanding and she would give him only what a harlot might, with coldness turning to hate.

"You do not answer!" he cried, riding close alongside her.

"What answer is needed?" she said in sullen mockery.

He was caught in a spasm of rage like a tree in a gust of wind.

"I will teach you to despise me!" he shouted and struck her across the face with his whip. She did not flinch and said between clenched teeth: "It only needed that!"

He hit her again, and harder. He stared at the two red marks that sprang up from nose to ear with a little drop of blood where they crossed; then he suddenly threw his whip away and rode with his eyes on the track ahead. He had seen servants treated thus many a time, but never a free woman of good birth. He was aware of an unexpected pleasure coupled with shame and a foreboding of disaster. If he had struck Maria, little as he could imagine himself doing so, she would have been submissive, but perhaps Astrid would never forgive or forget this, any more than she would the killing of Cadogan in her arms. From him she would accept neither the sweet nor the bitter fruits of love, yet this only inflamed his passion to keep her for himself and never let her pass into the possession of another. He stared at her in smoldering fury and tenderness and all at once he resolved that he would not lie with her again till those marks were gone from her cheek.

In silence they rode down to the bank of a wide river and over a wooden bridge that led across to a quay with warehouses and a throng of men busy about a longship. On the hill above were ruined walls and within them fruit trees in blossom and a scattering of houses topped by the tall buildings of a monastery. This must be Lancaster, he thought, and that would be the trader's ship of which the fisherman had spoken. She looked all ready to sail and he urged his horse along the quay to where a thickset, shrewd-looking man stood watching a cask being rolled on board.

"Are you the master of this ship?" he asked.

"That I am," the man answered. "My name is Torbrand. What may be your business here?"

"I would seek a passage on your ship to Rouen, for myself and this woman."

Torbrand surveyed them both with an impassive glance.

"You do not look to be folk overburdened with luck," he said.

"All the same I am called Arnvid the Lucky."

"A Northman?"

"An Icelander. I have been in Westmorland and chanced to kill a notable man."

"So now you would try your fortune with Duke Richard?"

"That is my plan."

"You might do worse. I am not sailing further than Exeter, but there are always ships there crossing to Normandy. Can you pay for a passage with me?"

"There are these two horses."

"Those you will have to leave behind in any case if you go on shipboard."

Arnvid reflected that Saemund might have said the same, but clearly this Torbrand was a harder bargainer. He took out two gold coins from his pouch. Astrid was standing beside him seemingly uninterested in the talk, but now he sensed that she was feeling something like anger or disgust. He looked up sharply and saw Torbrand's eyes shifting from the heavy pouch to the beautiful woman with the scarred cheek. At once he thought: This man is reckoning up whether it might not be better to kill me and take all I have. Saemund had also looked at Astrid as though he wondered whether she would be left behind with the horses. And then he thought that a woman who had required that whipping might not appear to be much worth having. Anyhow, after a moment's hesitation Torbrand took the coins and they clasped hands on the bargain. Arnvid saw the horses led away toward a good homestead that stood behind the warehouses. He went onto the ship and saw it was loaded with wool and hides and iron bars. There was also plenty of good food for the voyage and he formed the opinion that Torbrand was a very wealthy man. Now that the bargain was struck he became pleasant-spoken and from the cheerful looks of his men Arnvid judged that he was trustworthy and a good master.

He took his place with Astrid beside him just below the steersman's platform. She might have refused to come, but she had come. Perhaps things would right themselves between them, he thought hopefully.

Now the ship was being pushed out and was beginning to glide down the river. The sail was run up, folk on shore waved and shouted farewell greetings. This was better than the escape from Gwynedd, thought Arnvid. The failure at Hep no longer rankled in his mind; all had gone well for him since he turned his back on Westmorland. There was only the way he had treated Astrid and after all that might not be such a bad thing—a women might have to learn something from a whip as a horse did. He remembered her two gold rings that lay at the bottom of his pouch. Now he got them out and handed them to her as a kind of peace offering. She took them and slid them up her arms without any thanks, turning very red when some of the men looking on began to laugh. Presently she got up and sat down again, looking angry and desperate like an animal in a cage. More laughter and more men crowded up to watch her.

"What's the matter, Astrid?" said Arnvid at last.

"They know if you do not," she said sulkily.

"Oh, that!" he said, catching some of the remarks. "Well, you must not mind there being no outhouse on a ship."

"I do mind. I have been decently brought up and I am not accustomed to having a lot of men staring at me when I have to do what I must."

He was pleased to think that from the very first she had shown no such squeamishness when alone with him.

"At sea it can't be helped," he said.

"I did not ask to come to sea."

"But you came. Is it not better to have me with you than to be left friendless among strangers?"

She did not answer and he felt angry and then after a while sorry for her. "Come," he said. "It's quite simple." He lifted her up on the gunwale, kept his arms around her so that she should not overbalance, and stood between her and the onlookers. He thought she might have given him a word of thanks, but she did not, and her wounded cheek did not invite the kiss he would like to have given her. Goodhumoredly Arnvid ignored a lot of laughter over the time Astrid had to spend on the gunwale, but when someone ventured on a more outrageously obscene remark he turned on the man with a clenched fist and the seaman backed away. After that he settled himself down against a bale of wool and in a moment he was deep in slumber.

Chapter 20

TORBRAND

THE VOYAGE TO THE SOUTH was cold and rough, but a strong northeaster swept the longship past Wales at high speed and with little incident except for the appearance of some vikings off Anglesey. The crew took their weapons and lined the gunwales, but Torbrand's adroit steering got them past without bloodshed.

For Arnvid this was perhaps the happiest time he had had since leaving Iceland. He felt no anxiety about the future and no regrets about the past. He had no enemy to fear and he was committed to no desperate scheme under the guidance of a dubious friend such as Asmund. Torbrand was good company and he offered plenty of strong drink. It was a delight to relax and sleep, lulled by the rhythmic plunge of the ship through the steep billows, and to wake seeing Astrid beside him, knitting in seeming contentment, for Torbrand had been able to supply her with needles and dyed wool. Though they said little to each other there was an enforced intimacy between them which for the moment was pure enjoyment, undisturbed by the sharp pricking of desire which he had felt riding beside her in dusky woods, sheathed in mail that forbade love-making, ever alert for a hostile face.

Astrid, once she had conquered seasickness and overcome such inhibitions as were due to an ingrained shyness and delicacy, accepted her conditions of life with nonchalance if not with pleasure. Torbrand and his men treated her with friendliness and respect. This she repaid by helping to prepare food, and those who ate it said they had never tasted anything better at sea. Sometimes she sat for hours watching Torbrand and Arnvid playing chess with quaintly carved pieces pegged into a board. Torbrand was a skillful player and almost always won, though Arnvid fought back stubbornly with desperate expedients. At last Torbrand challenged Astrid to play with him.

"I have never played in my life," she said.

"You will have learned the moves by now. Come, I will play you without my queen." He planted the board on a sack of corn between them and gave her the first move. Astrid shrugged her shoulders and put aside her knitting. Torbrand played quickly and confidently, Astrid with more deliberation. Before long Torbrand was mated. He smiled, not seeming to mind, and proposed that they should play with equal pieces. This time it was a long game, but in the end Astrid won.

"You let her win!" said Arnvid who had been looking on. "You made a fault in letting her take both your knights."

"Wise you are, friend, now that the battle is over," said Torbrand. "Once more, Astrid!"

This time Torbrand played very carefully, as Arnvid had to admit, but again Astrid mated him.

"Her head is better than yours!" said Torbrand gaily. "Are you called Arnvid the Lucky?"

"I was, in Iceland."

"I would say that your greatest stroke of luck was the winning of this woman who sits between us."

"Maybe that is true," said Arnvid shortly, turning very red.

Astrid had saved him in Gwynedd and again after they crossed the sands. But for her he would not be alive now and sitting at ease on this ship.

"It is untrue," said Astrid.

Torbrand looked at her searchingly. "If you say so, I can believe it. Luck turns," he said. She met his gaze steadily and said, "Not in the way you think."

Now Torbrand flushed and his face lit up like a smoldering fire caught by a draft when a door opens in a dark hall.

"A good chess player foresees much but seldom everything," he said. He put away the board and pieces in a chest and went to the steersman's platform. Arnvid watched with a frown. His pleasure in this voyage had suddenly lessened. The ship swung sharply and turned toward land. They stood up and could see pale sand hills and dark moors behind, and a fjord opening toward little green fields and round huts.

"What land is this?" said Arnvid.

"Torbrand said it was Cornwall."

"What sort of folk are they yonder?"

"Mostly Welshmen; at least they speak a kind of Welsh. Torbrand often does some trade with them on his way to Normandy."

"You have talked much with Torbrand?"

"Sometimes, when you lay asleep."

"I begin to think that man is not trustworthy, after all!"

"He has the mind of a chess player, always seeking for some advantage. Life is often like a game of chess, Arnvid."

"That I saw in Westmorland."

"It may also be so on this ship. I think you might be well-advised to go ashore here."

"I have little luck among Welshmen," he said gloomily. "No, I am set on faring to Duke Richard in Normandy."

Astrid picked up her knitting in silence.

Two days later they had rounded Penwith and were running before a blustery west wind. It was early morning: Arnvid was still asleep among the bales of wool, but Astrid stood by the gunwale, watching the big green waves that ran up to the plugged oarholes, the gulls swooping overhead, and the dark cliffs of Cornwall half-veiled in spray. Presently she was aware of Torbrand standing beside her.

"If this wind should hold we shall soon be in Exeter," he said genially.

"The wind has been lucky for you on this voyage," she said, without looking at him.

"Everything has been lucky so far. Was it not lucky for you that you reached Lancaster before we put to sea?"

"Otherwise Arnvid would most likely have fallen under the axes of the sons of Orm."

"And would you have grieved much?" he said in a low voice.

"Should I not be sorry to see death come to a man who had saved me from a burning hall?"

"Would you have chosen him otherwise?" said Torbrand shrewdly.

"That might depend on what other choice I had."

"For a woman that is straight-enough speaking, I would hardly say you look like a happy wife."

"I am no wife."

"I would have thought you too proud to be the mistress of a man you do not love and who mishandles you. When you came to Lancaster there were fresh whip marks on your cheek and I can see them yet."

"A horse must abide its master and I have often seen a horse get a hard blow for a small fault."

"A woman is not a horse and you are not like most women. It was a coward's work to strike you in that fashion."

"My tongue can be sharp enough to merit some punishment."

"I doubt it, Astrid. I would never lift my hand against you."

"Maybe not, for you are without passion and think only of what may advantage you most."

"You misjudge me. I have never seen a woman I desired more."

"My face is maybe beautiful, though marred at present. My body is well-shaped and healthy, though it would do with some washing," she said indifferently.

"That is not all . . ."

"But the main thing."

"No. Your wit matches mine; I would guess you are of good birth. I will make you my wife. I swear I will take you before a priest in the great church at Exeter; we shall be wedded and when we sail home you shall rule my household at Lancaster, and there is little there that you will find lacking for I am a rich man with many friends." He took her hand and she did not at once withdraw it.

She considered him for a moment; a handsome, formidable man, young—not more than thirty, fair and cleanly looking, a pure-bred Northman by the look of him, as different as possible from Arnvid with his dark, almost girlish beauty. This man seemed cold, shrewd, and ruthless, self-confident, little likely to fail in anything he undertook. His voice was pleasant enough, but his nose was too sharp and his teeth had a wolfish look when they showed through his beard. A man unswayed by passion and unbridled by honor . . . She could not imagine that many women would refuse an offer such as this, at such a time and in such circumstances, any more than they would have refused Cadogan ap Einion on that moor in Powys. But that was something violent, paralyzing, and inescapable, the leap of a wild creature upon its mate like a wave flinging itself on yielding sand and quivering shingle. This was something cold and deliberate, a well-considered bargain in which there was plenty of time to take account of all that was involved.

"What of Arnvid?" she said.

Torbrand threw a contemptuous glance at the sleeper a few yards away.

"What of him?" he said.

"He will fight for me."

"I can foil him in fight as easily as I can on the chessboard."

"I suppose you could kill him now if you chose."

He looked at her in surprise and uncertainty.

"I had not thought of that," he said slowly.

"You thought of it when you first saw me, and Arnvid taking gold out of a pouch."

He frowned and said after a pause, "The best of men have bad thoughts, but they do not act on them."

"But the fact is that if I become your wife it means Arnvid's death."

"Perhaps, if he is fool enough to challenge me."

"When is a man in love not a fool?"

"Does a lover slash his mistress with a whip?"

She laughed. "How little you know about love!"

He seemed to be baffled and walked away over the thwarts to the lookout in the prow. Astrid saw the men glance at him and then back at her. They jerked their thumbs toward Arnvid where he slept, winked at each other and laughed. She wondered to herself how far Torbrand would go to gain his ends and whether, in Arnvid's interest, it would be well to help or hinder him.

When they had rounded the Start of Devon the west wind veered to the north and soon died away. A warm sea fog lay over land and water and they rowed steadily northward along the coast, sometimes getting a glimpse of cliffs, gray at first, then red and topped with golden gorse. It was very early one morning that cliffs appeared on both sides of the ship and Torbrand said they were at the mouth of the Exe. The fog had thinned and the sun was rising redly above a swell of moorland. It gave promise of being a swelteringly hot day.

Suddenly a man gave a shout and pointed astern, and in a moment the oars were trailing in the water, everyone sprang up and left his task to gaze out from the steersman's platform or from the long curve of the gunwale. The fog was shredding away, they looked across the oily, glittering water and saw the sea behind them covered with ships, a great fleet making for the entrance to the Exe. Already they could hear the surge of oars and make out the upthrust dragon heads and their gilded collars flashing in the low sunshine.

"King Sweyn and the Danes!" said Torbrand, turning rather pale and gnawing at his mustache. Arnvid felt a chill come over him as he stood staring from the platform, spellbound by the sight of this mighty force—surely strong enough to conquer all England. As in a dream he heard Astrid say to him, "If those ships follow us to Exeter there will be no getting out again. You will have to give up your voyage to Rouen." Before he could answer, Torbrand was shouting to the crew: "Row, men! Row all you can. We must get to Exeter ahead of King Sweyn!"

Now they were pulling so that the oars bent like hazel shafts, churning up the placid water of Exe, driving the ship up the channel past hut and hall, herds of cattle and greening woods. As they watched they saw men already busy driving the beasts inland, and from a church tower came the monotonous tolling of a bell. Others besides them had seen ruin approaching.

Exhausted rowers let go the oars and fresh men took their places. Arnvid took his turn and pulled while sweat poured down into his eyes. Torbrand steered and kept on shouting encouragement. Astrid busied herself with handing out ale. Someone remarked that she was as calm and unhurried now as she had been when they sailed on empty seas, but another said: "She has something different to expect from Sweyn's men from what we have."

The estuary narrowed abruptly and again a mist hung over the water, but clear in the sunshine above it they could now see Exeter on its hill, a squalid congestion of thatched roofs confined by a vast and ancient-looking wall, and sprouting here and there a shapeless mass of ruined masonry and half a dozen somber church towers pointing like warning fingers to heaven. To Arnvid it looked like Lancaster over again on a greater scale. Here was the bridge over the river, the quay, and tied up beside it not one ship, but more like twenty.

"We shall have news to give in Exeter," said Arnvid, and then to his amazement Torbrand spoke to the crew and forbade them to say a word about the coming of the Danes. Arnvid looked at Astrid, who merely nodded, as though she had expected nothing else. The oars were taken aboard at last and Torbrand steered in between two stout ships heaped high with goods. The gangplank was put out and he walked ashore in a leisurely fashion, followed by Arnvid and Astrid and about half his men. It was obvious that no one here knew of anything amiss. Goods were being unloaded in no special hurry, and some ships were making ready to sail. Torbrand soon got into talk with other traders on the quay. A messenger ran up into the town and quickly came back with several more prosperous-looking men. Presently they all went on board the ship and began turning over the wool and iron. Voices rose high, but evidently bargains were being struck without much difficulty. They came ashore again and Arnvid heard Torbrand say to one of his men who knew Exeter well: "Go to Wulfstan's house just inside the North Gate and buy four pack horses and one good riding horse—no, two riding horses. Have them ready by the huts outside the gate as soon as possible and see that no one steals them. Here is a bag of silver." After that the company went into the town through a great double-arched gateway just above the quay, Arnvid and Astrid following close behind. Some of the traders went one way and some another, but Torbrand and one man, whom Arnvid thought might be the richest of the lot, went straight up a steep filthy street where there were many booths with goods for sale and smithies and eating houses and men plying their crafts with wood, leather, and pottery. On the top of the hill they came into an open space beside a big church, all new, with masons still busy at one end of it. Fronting the church were some broken columns and crumbling stone buildings partly reconstructed in wood. Torbrand's friend turned into one of these and they entered a long, dimly lighted room with a barrel vault. The floor was a great deal lower than the street outside, the walls seemed to have once been covered with painted plaster. Arnvid could make out part of the figure of a naked man holding a staff on which were entwined two serpents, but the others were more interested in the sight of a table loaded with food. They sat down at once to eat and he found he was very hungry and thirsty. Mead and strong ale were served out and he drank a good deal, growing more cheerful and talkative, till Astrid whispered to him to keep quiet. Someone might conclude from his speech that he was a Dane, and this was England, where King Ethelred had ordered all Danes to be killed.

"How does Torbrand manage?" he whispered back.

"He is speaking English, though it does not sound much like the English they speak here. Anyhow he manages to pass as an Englishman and that would be difficult for you. Keep your wits about you and don't drink any more of that mead."

But Arnvid had already drunk so much that he felt hopelessly sleepy. His head began to nod and presently it sank on the table. Now the other traders came in carrying bags and pouches. They drank for a few minutes, then went with

Torbrand to an inner room. Through the doorway she could see coins being counted and silver objects weighed on a scales. Torbrand was getting paid for his goods. She guessed that he would soon be out of Exeter, well before the arrival of King Sweyn, though news of the invasion must surely come very soon. How well he manages everything in his own interest! she said to herself. A clever man, much cleverer than Arnvid, but all the same I don't fancy him as a husband. If only she could keep out of his way . . . She said to a girl who was putting a dish of roast pork on the table: "I should like to wash myself. Can I have a basin and some water?"

The girl, who was being run off her feet attending to the guests, did not seem pleased, but she took Astrid up a staircase to an upper room and presently brought a bowl and a bucket of water. Astrid looked around. The door had no bolt and the room smelled badly to one who had lived for weeks in open air at sea. There were three beds in it made up with straw under dirty sheets. Sleeping on the ship had not been comfortable, but at least one had not been so plagued with vermin as one certainly would be here. She turned away from the beds with some disgust. At least one could relieve oneself without having to get up on the swaying gunwale under the eyes of a lot of men. . . . She carried the bowl onto an overhanging gallery and emptied it into the street below. Then she poured out water, took off all her clothes, and put her feet in the bowl. She ought to have asked for a cloth, but at least she could rub herself over with wet straw and rid herself of dirt and lice. She had not washed since she was at Hauksborg, and not often there, for water was short on the top of the hill. . . .

The door opened and Torbrand came into the room. She

felt very much annoyed at being disclosed to his eyes in this state, but before either of them could say anything they were aware of a growling murmur of voices outside the house and suddenly a jangling of bells began all over the town. To Astrid's quick ears the commotion sounded more like anger than panic. Torbrand only smiled. "The news has come at last," he said.

"Lucky for you it did not come sooner!"

"Yes, very lucky. I have sold all my goods. I have even sold the ship. I had to let things go cheap, but anyhow I have got paid."

"What is your plan?"

"I have bought some horses and I shall set off overland to Bideford where I know several traders. It should not be hard to get one of them to make a voyage with me to the north, particularly if King Sweyn is going over this part of England with fire and sword. There is a horse for you, by the way, so put on your clothes. I mean to be out of Exeter within an hour."

"And what if I refuse to go with you?"

"Why should you refuse? True, there is no time for us to be wedded here, but there is a priest in Bideford who will do as well."

"You know very well I am Arnvid's woman."

"So he is to stand between us, even though he is asleep as usual. By God! I can dispose of him easily enough."

"How will you do that?"

"I shall go to the King's Reeve, a man from Normandy called Hugh. Queen's Reeve, he should be called, for he came over with Queen Emma from Rouen and she got him appointed to Exeter. Well, I shall say to Hugh that a Dane has come into the town today, a man called Arnvid, who lately tried to raise a rebellion against Ethelred in Hougun and Westmorland. He is easy to recognize for he wears a scarlet tunic, and at the moment he is drunk in the house of Alfred the Trader . . ." His words were drowned by an outburst of shouts and curses in the street below. Torbrand went quickly into the loft gallery and Astrid looked over his shoulder. She saw a little man trying to get away from a gathering crowd that assailed him with sticks and knives. He ran this way and that, dodging some of the blows, but at last he went down and the crowd closed over him. There was a yell and then a shriek. Astrid turned back into the room feeling slightly sick.

"That fellow was a Dane, or at least they thought he was," said Torbrand.

"And that is how you would have Arnvid dealt with, the man who has been a guest on your ship for weeks past?"

"I would let him be if you would be reasonable, Astrid."

He was looking her over from head to foot, and whether it was the sight of her naked body or what he had just seen happen in the street, she sensed that he was losing his cold self-possession. He is clever and farsighted, she thought, but when it comes to lust and fear of death he is a man like other men.

Now he passed a finger over the scar on her cheek, he slid an arm around her and lifted her breasts. She shivered a little but remained calm.

"What better place can we find to play in than here?" he said.

"Here and now, with death around the corner?" she temporized.

"Yes. The Danes will not be at the gates for a good while yet."

"If I let you have your way will you swear to do nothing against Arnvid?"

"You cannot easily hinder me from having my way," he said with a cruel smile.

"I can call to the folk outside that a Dane is trying to rape me!" she said sharply. He changed color somewhat and looked doubtfully at her.

"Here and now," he said, "and I swear by Christ and by Thor that Arnvid shall not be harmed."

"A bargain is a bargain?"

"Yes. I never break my word over a bargain."

She hesitated, then said, "Very well."

At once he carried her to one of the beds and before long he had all that he wanted for the moment. She got up, flushed and humiliated, yet not altogether ill content. With trembling hands she began to put on her clothes. He sat on the bed watching her in silence.

At last he said, "Now will you ride with me to Bideford!"

"No!" she said decisively.

"You will stay in Exeter with this man Arnvid? What can he offer you compared to what I can?"

"Little enough, doubtless." She went out of the room and down the stairs and Torbrand followed. The vaulted hall was empty save for Arnvid asleep with his head on the table. Outside in the street there was now a formidable uproar which came faintly through the thick walls and heavy door.

"I can take you out by a back way. In a few minutes we can be at the North Gate where my men are waiting with the horses."

"I stay here," she said obstinately.

"For your own good I will tie you up, put a gag in your mouth, and carry you out of Exeter."

"You might not find that so easy as what you did upstairs!"

"I have six men within call."

She got to the other side of the table and laid her hand on Arnvid's shoulder.

"If you touch me," she said in a whisper, "I will wake him. I think he will kill you; he is skillful with his sword. I have seen him kill more than one man very quickly."

Torbrand looked at her for a moment, stroking his beard. Then he turned without a word and went out by the back door.

Chapter 21

THE SIEGE OF EXETER

IT WAS NOT LONG AFTER THIS that Arnvid opened his eyes and saw Astrid sitting opposite him across a table littered with bones and scraps of food. He was surprised not to feel the ship rocking beneath him; then his eyes took in the dim, vaulted hall and he remembered where he was. He looked again at Astrid who sat very still, with idle hands. There was no one else in the room.

"Have I been asleep long?" he asked.

"Long enough," she said.

"It was the hard rowing in the heat, the good food, the drink . . . What has become of Torbrand?"

"He has got paid for everything and gone off across country to a place called Bideford."

"I would like to have thanked him for all he did for us."

She smiled, but said nothing.

"I like to see you smile, Astrid," he said, resting his head on his hands.

"Not many people are smiling in Exeter today."

"Are the Danes here?" He got up abruptly.

"Not yet, but the town is getting ready for them. Folk have started looking about for Danes and killing them in the streets."

"I wish we could have got to Rouen."

"You will have to put Rouen out of your head for the present and make some fresh plan."

They fell silent as Alfred entered the room by the back way. He went to the street door to make sure that it was barred, then he turned on Arnvid with a hostile look.

"You came with Torbrand, but you have not left with him," he said. "What do you seek in Exeter?"

"A passage to Rouen," said Arnvid shortly.

"That you will have to forego. Did you see the Danish ships when you came up the river?"

"We did."

"I thought it was strange that Torbrand wanted to be off so quickly. Usually he stays a month here picking up bargains. Now he is safe with his silver and we are all in peril. He will not be so welcome when he shows his face here next time."

"Can you not get your goods into safety?"

"We have brought everything we can within the walls, of course, but the ships will be lost."

"Then the town is to be defended?"

"Of course the town will be defended, unless Hugh the Reeve loses heart. I dislike the man—a smooth-spoken foreigner! Sweyn has been here before; he harried far and wide over Devon, but he could not take Exeter."

"I would gladly take my place on the wall if there is to be fighting."

"I would sooner see you put outside the walls. By your speech I guess you are a Dane yourself."

"I am no Dane. I am an Icelander."

"An Icelander!" Alfred gave a contemptuous snort. "What about this woman?"

"She is from Worcestershire."

"How do I know that you are not telling me a lot of lies?"

"You can judge me when I fight against King Sweyn—and I can pay you for your hospitality." Arnvid took a gold coin from his pouch and threw it down carelessly on the table. He thought Astrid's eyes rested on him with something like approval. Alfred picked up the coin and looked at it.

"You can both stay in this house for the present," he said somewhat reluctantly, giving Arnvid a long measuring look as a master might do a new servant. Arnvid flushed in relief mixed with irritation. This man was maybe not quite so arrogant as Bermond and Edwin, but he seemed to have the Englishman's contempt for all foreigners.

"We have been to Hugh and settled how the townsmen are to divide up to guard the wall," he continued. "The folk from this part will take the southwestern angle up to the Bridge Gate. Come with me now and I shall show you your station."

"Can I have a mail shirt?"

"I can give you a shield; you have a sword and a helmet. That will have to do. There are not enough mail shirts to go round."

"Is my woman safe here?"

"She is as safe as any woman in Exeter, but if the worst comes to the worst she can go through with my wife and

daughters to a nunnery just behind the house. The nuns may
get raped; but that is the best we can do."

Arnvid glanced at Astrid who smiled and nodded. With a
light heart he followed Alfred out by the back way, across
a yard and so through a narrow stinking alley into the street.
They went down to the Bridge Gate where all was activity.
The tunnel-like archways were being blocked with carts and
barricades of timber, stone was being collected on the parapet
above, and bowmen sat about in groups eating and drinking.
Alfred led the way along the foot of the wall to the angle
which had been built up into a semicircular tower filled with
earth. They went up on top and looked out southward to
where several columns of smoke rose languidly in the still
evening air.

"The Danes have anchored off Topsham," said Alfred.
"They are plundering and burning as usual. We shall see
them here tomorrow."

Arnvid thought he had never looked on such a fair and
fertile land. There was forest along the hills to westward and
a bare crest of moorland caught the hazy glow of the sunset,
but on both sides of the water were miles of green pasture
and stripes of plowing, with many a cluster of mud-built
huts and tall thatched halls. A great deal might be destroyed,
but the fruitful earth would remain. Happy would those folk
be who could keep possession of it—the land and the great
town, packed with life like an ants' nest, house crowding on
house, gardens full of blossom, winding streets trodden into
thick black mud, all encircled by high walls of rust-colored
stone.

"These are good walls," remarked Arnvid. They seemed to

him in much better condition than those at York, breached
in many places and patched with palisades.

"They were repaired by King Athelstan, nearly eighty
years ago, when he fought against the Welshmen in Cornwall," said Alfred, "but walls are little use unless there be
tough folk to man them."

Arnvid thought of the swarming mass of townsfolk who
would line those parapets, eager to fight for home and goods,
for the treasures in the churches, for wives and children.
And then he thought of the men on the dragon ships, no less
resolute, and more practiced in war, greedy to win all they
could of the wealth that was heaped up in England.

It was late next morning when the bells of Exeter rang out
to announce the coming of the enemy and all the fighting
men hurried to their posts on the wall. Arnvid was on the
south face a little beyond the round bastion, where the wall
seemed rather lower than elsewhere and the moat in front
was more than half filled up with rubbish. On his way
through the streets a girl had given him a loaf of bread; she
had looked at him with shining eyes and he wondered
whether she saw him as a great champion or merely a handsome young man. The men on the wall only saw him as a
foreigner. They scowled and avoided speaking to him as he
sat by the parapet, eating the bread with assumed nonchalance, but struggling against the heavy beating of his heart
which always started at the approach of danger.

A growling shout ran along the wall. The Danes were in
sight. Here they came, a great mass of men bristling with
weapons, with helmeted heads flashing in the sunshine,
flowing blindly and inexorably over hill and hollow, breaking through fences, treading down the crops. A few riders

galloped ahead and then swung away as they came within
bowshot of the walls. The host split into two, one portion
making for the South Gate, the other bearing round toward
the Bridge Gate. There followed a long pause, then suddenly
a growing hum of voices was broken by a loud blast on a
horn. At once a ferocious shouting started among the Danes,
answered by a jarring uproar from the defenders. Looking
along the wall, Arnvid could see a rush being made at the
South Gate. The Danes seemed to have a tree trunk mounted
on wheels to use as a battering ram, but the approach was
steep and the air was thick with arrows. It did not look as
though much was going to be accomplished in that quarter,
and soon everyone's attention was diverted toward the Bridge
Gate. From where he stood Arnvid could only see the rear
of the archways across the roofs of the town, men swarming
like bees upon the parapet and more and more streaming
along the wall to join them. Smoke was pouring up from outside the gate, soon followed by leaping red flames, and
amongst the shouts and countershouts he could hear the
hissing and crackling of the fire. There was a tang of tar in
the air. Evidently the Danes were trying to burn down the
gates. Someone said that they were getting thatch from the
huts and warehouses on the quay. But there was more than
this: half-screened by the smoke a determined assault was
being made with scaling ladders on either side of the gateway. Against a background of flame Arnvid could see weapons
rising and falling, men surging from point to point. Triumphant yells announced that some Danes had got a footing on
the parapet. Then they were pushed off again by weight of
numbers.

Of all the defenders on Arnvid's section of the wall, he

was the only man remaining at his post. All the others had gone up to get a better view from the corner bastion or had actually joined in the hand-to-hand fight near the gate. Buckets of water had by now somewhat dampened the fire, but the uproar of the assault was increasing every moment. It struck Arnvid that he might be charged with cowardice if he stayed on here where nothing was happening. Had he not better go to the gate where every man might count at the crisis of the fight? He had not yet drawn his sword, but he picked up a stout spear that someone had left behind and considered dropping down the earthbank behind the wall and cutting across the angle of the town to the gateway. First, however, he took a good look out over the moat, beyond which was a grove of pollard willows with long sprays of silky foliage.

He looked, and for a moment his heart almost stopped beating. Out from among the knobbly trunks came two groups of men, each with a long ladder. They seemed to be picked men, all in helmets and ring mail. Behind them rode a big evil-looking man on a black horse. He had a long forked beard, thick fair hair hung down to his broad shoulders, he was mailed from neck to foot and carried a brightly painted shield. Beside him was another formidable-looking man with a standard. In a moment the two ladders were planted against the wall and men began to scramble up. One ladder was longer than the other and reached a good bit above the parapet. Arnvid got hold of it and dragged it sideways with all his strength till suddenly it slid away and fell with a crash, spilling the men out into the moat and breaking in two. Then he rushed to the other ladder and made frantic efforts to dislodge it with the spear, but the weight of men on it made it impossible for him to stir it either outward or sideways. The leading climber was already trying to step off onto the wall when Arnvid thrust the spear in his face and he fell backward, knocking the next man off the ladder. A third man came up immediately. He swung a heavy axe in both hands, but he had no hold on the ladder. He failed to parry Arnvid's spear thrust and went backward like the others. Up came a fourth man with sword and shield and got a footing on the wall. After that Arnvid did not remember much of what happened. He lost his spear somehow, but he managed to grab his shield and tug out his sword. For a moment there were two Danes on the parapet, but one he pushed off, getting a stunning blow on the helmet from an axe. He sprang to and fro, mechanically using one trick of swordsmanship after another—the tricks he had so often practiced with Gunnar. Sometimes a blow seemed to go home. Blood splashed in his face, he stumbled over a fallen man, gave ground before two others, closed with them and killed them both, but still more came swarming up the ladder. Despair gripped him, he panted for breath, thinking he must have taken half a dozen wounds though as yet he could feel none, but still his sword whirled, clashed and bit. . . . Suddenly there were other men fighting beside him. He recognized Alfred, and then there were no Danes left alive on the parapet and no more were coming up the ladder. He looked down and saw the man on the black horse shaking his fist and shouting at his warriors. Arrows slanted past and he felt a sharp pain in one ear before he could cover himself with his shield. He sat down and felt himself all over. A bruise here, a scratch there, the ripped ear was the worst wound he had got. Alfred came by and threw him a glance.

"I will not deny that you are a good swordsman," he said grudgingly.

After that the attacks slackened. No harm had been done at the South Gate; the doors of the Bridge Gate had been burned through, but the Danes had failed to dislodge the barricade within. They prowled around the whole circuit of the walls, exchanging a few bowshots with the defenders, but toward evening they had withdrawn to a camping place on the south side of the town. There they began to slaughter sheep and cattle and make up cooking fires. There was also feasting and drinking in Exeter and many men predicted that next day would see the Danes moving on elsewhere.

Arnvid and Astrid sat at meat that night with Alfred and his people. No one spoke to them, but they were treated with marked respect, doubtless as a result of Arnvid's prowess on the wall. Personally he thought that the town would have been taken if he had not delayed the stormers till help came, and perhaps others thought so too, though they did not say so. He was for once well-satisfied with himself, though now that he came to think of it he felt no special ill will toward the Danes. Indeed he felt more akin to them than he did to these gruff and haughty Englishmen. It had been his misfortune to have to draw his sword against Welshmen and Westmorings—folk with whom he would gladly have been on good terms. He might have felt it his duty to fight the Danes, for they had helped to fell his father in the great sea fight when he stood by King Olaf Trygvesson. Still, unlike most Northmen, he had never been much obsessed by a desire for vengeance—but was Astrid like that? Was she perhaps biding her time to pay him back for those blows with the whip?

Gloomily he recalled the story of Sigrid, widow of the Swedish king, whom Olaf Trygvesson had courted and then struck in the face with his glove because she would not become a Christian. And so Sigrid had married King Sweyn and egged him on to kill Olaf. King Sweyn had failed, but Earl Erik, the Northman, had succeeded and so paid off the score he owed Olaf for the death of his father. And now Sweyn was in England seeking vengeance for the killing of his sister on Saint Brice's Day. There was no getting out of it. A man was dishonored if he did not take vengeance for an injury, no matter what the cost might be to himself or others. True, the Christian priests frowned on the idea of vengeance, though few Christians followed their precepts. They talked about God's vengeance in a world to come, the everlasting fire, and so forth. It came back to him how he had debated this with Sigfrith and Gunnar as they rowed up the river to York, and he had decided that he could never become a Christian. Yet he perceived now that at heart he was not a good pagan. The code on which he had been brought up in Iceland was in the main sound common sense, but when it enjoined vengeance as an honorable obligation he felt instinctively that it was evil. And so he was a lone and friendless man, wandering uneasily between two opposed faiths and helplessly in love with a woman who despised him. . . . All his self-satisfaction ebbed away. He drank and drank, but the strong mead did not cheer him, and his head began to ache. It still seemed to sing from that blow he had got on the helmet. He turned to Astrid and in a low voice repeated the old verse:

"The pine tree withers on the dry hill
Without shelter of bark or needles:
So also the man whom no one loves;
How shall he live long?"

"You are drunk," she said. "Have a care what you say; the folk are listening to you."

"Let them listen!" The blood rushed to his face. He began to boil with rage. "I saved Exeter today, but what I did was useless, for King Sweyn will take it tomorrow or the next day. Nothing that I do avails anything!"

He started up and threw his drinking horn across the hall. The others glanced at him without much concern. Alfred said contemptuously: "Our mead seems to be too strong for this Icelander. Buttermilk will be what he is accustomed to."

"You are behaving like a fool!" said Astrid sharply.

"I am a fool to fight in other men's quarrels! I am a fool to be enchanted by a cold, heartless woman!" he muttered in a thick voice and staggered out of the room. Outside in the street he was sick and soon felt clearer in his head. Yes, doubtless he had been behaving like a fool, but what did it matter? What did anything matter? A full moon was shining on the town and he was aware of the great church towering above him. A dim glow showed in the tall narrow windows toward the eastern end. He saw a door standing open and went inside. His glance traveled past pillars and arches to a man standing far away in the radiance of many candles. He was chanting words that Arnvid did not understand and suddenly there was a response from rows of other men standing nearby—priests—he could see their shaven heads, and then he realized that in the darkness about him hundreds of men were kneeling in silence, listening to the strong spells put out by the priests and maybe praying that they might escape the everlasting fire. It would be better, he thought, that they should pray lest those red flames that had burned above the Bridge Gate should be spread all over the town, licking up timber and thatch in one huge blaze. Perhaps that was what they were doing, and the priests were working their magic against King Sweyn. For a moment he felt a superstitious dread of this tall building and its mighty arches, the fruit of almost incredible skill and labor, of that priest holding aloft a cup in the candlelight, of the stern voices all speaking in accord with such assurance and finality. Then he told himself that it was all make-believe, that the people were being cheated. There was nowhere any power to protect them except in their own right arms. It was no more significant than when a man shouted at a cliff and had his words flung back to him by the lifeless rock.

He strode out of the church, but in the doorway a priest or monk plucked at his sleeve, saying: "Turn back and pray that God may forgive you your sins."

"I have no sins for which I need forgiveness," said Arnvid defiantly.

"No man is without sin, but through the blood of Jesus Christ his sin may be washed away."

"I do not think anything can be made clean with blood."

"Not by the blood of common men, but by the blood of our Lord, the Lamb of God, that was shed for our deliverance."

"What power can there be in a dead man hanging on a cross?" said Arnvid in a tone of ferocious mockery.

"I see you are a heathen and a blasphemer. Your words

will be held against you on the day of judgment and you will
burn in hell."

"You will not frighten me with your everlasting fire!"
said Arnvid with a laugh. Roughly he shook off the fingers
that clutched his arm more and more tightly, and lurched
away down the street.

Ridiculous to suppose there could be anything in what
the man said. The monstrous injustice of it! And yet, what
if it were true? Was God necessarily a just and merciful
master any more than a king might be? What justice would
any man expect from King Sweyn?

Gloom settled on him and not for the first time he wished
he had never come to England. Wealth, easy living, the rich
earth, the vast trees, the towns swarming with folk—he did
not belong here and now he was weary of it all. Had he not
been far happier riding with Gunnar over the mountains of
Iceland with no care save to ward off some unneighborly act
of Grim Hareksson? Gunnar and Grim, they carried his
thoughts to that house at Kirkwall. Such places had been
strange to him then, but now he was more experienced.
There must be many such in Exeter, he thought. Good
company, food and drink, pleasure with girls . . . Here was
an open door and candlelight, but no chanting of spells by
shaven priests; here was laughter and someone roaring out
a song. He went in and saw men drinking at a long table,
some of them with girls sitting on their knees. The singer
recognized him as the champion who had fought so well on
the wall. There were shouts of welcome, a place was made for
him, he drank and let himself be carried away on a spate of
friendly or boastful talk. When a man said that his speech
was hard to understand and asked him where he came from,

he said "Worcestershire," and no one seemed to think much the worse of him for that. A girl slipped in beside him—she was dark and pretty and modest in her bearing. Confidently he put an arm around her and let her drink from his mug of ale.

"Birds of a feather," said a man opposite.

"What does he mean?" said Arnvid to the girl.

"He means that your hair and eyes are the same color as mine," she said in a whisper.

"There is something else in which we are alike," he whispered back. "You too speak Norse."

"Yes. It is well that no one but me has noticed what tongue you speak."

"Why so?"

"A man came in here last night; he spoke English, but that man opposite knew he was a Northman and he killed him, here at the table. The mark of the blood is not yet washed out. They killed all the Danes here on Saint Brice's Day and they say that Northmen are as bad or worse."

"And do you think so too?"

"I am not English."

"I did not think you were. Are you Welsh?"

"No, I am Irish. I was brought up in the house of a Northman, but he sold me to a trader who took me to a place called Bristol where I was made a harlot."

"Would that man try to kill me if he knew I was a North-man?"

"Yes, he would. His wife was carried off by vikings from Norway."

Arnvid looked at the man across the table, a thick-necked,

squinting fellow, who was now very drunk and beginning to quarrel with his neighbor.

"Vengeance," said Arnvid, half to himself.

"Yes. Men are always thinking about that, but it does them no good. All the girls here hate that man—he is so rough and cruel."

The pair had now come to blows and men were trying to separate them.

"Let us go somewhere else," said Arnvid.

She got up at once and led him through a passage to a room where there was a bed behind a curtain.

"Here you are safe," she said.

"Why should I be safe with you? Surely you have no cause to love Northmen?"

"Maybe not, but I think you are a kind man and a great champion." She sat down on the bed.

"You might not think that if you knew me better."

"No man is without faults, but I would guess that you have fewer than most men."

"No man is without sin . . ." he recalled the words he had heard in the church doorway, but now, instead of the febrile clutch of his arm there was the gentle pressure of a girl's hand, drawing him down beside her. Presently they lay quietly caressing one another and talking of many things, and he was happier than he had been for a long time, till suddenly they were silent and passion swept them together as some placid stream in a narrow valley comes inevitably to a rock edge and bursts into foam and tumult. Then he grew sad again, for he thought that it would never be quite like this with Astrid.

Next morning there was disappointment in Exeter, for the

Danes showed no signs of abandoning the siege. True, watchers on the church towers could see smoke rising here and there in the countryside showing that raiders had gone out to do what mischief they could, but the Danish camp was still packed with men and before long a noise of hewing and hammering could be heard from the town walls. A square timber tower began to rise with surprising speed, hung on three faces with raw oxhides. By afternoon it was pushed forward on wheels nearer to the Bridge Gate and it was obvious that the upper stories would considerably over-top the wall. Alfred said that a gangway would be let down to make the attack and the top would be crowded with archers, but he was confident that the fate of the tower and its inmates would be settled by a few buckets of burning tar. He went to a council held in the Reeve's Hall and came back almost speechless with rage. Hugh the Reeve and the leading churchmen had decided that their best course would be to surrender the town on terms. Arnvid said little. Privately he thought that the defense would not long be able to cope with such a resolute and resourceful enemy and unlike the infuriated Alfred he shrank from the thought of what would happen if the town were taken by storm. Astrid merely shrugged her shoulders. She had not forgotten Saint Brice's Day and was little concerned that retribution should fall on Exeter.

That evening two abbots went out to the Danish camp and soon returned with the news that King Sweyn would spare the town if he received a payment in gold and silver and jewelry to the value of five thousand pounds. The men of God looked glum, thinking of how much would have to be collected from the church treasuries; the traders protested angrily, but Hugh the Reeve, a timid man and newly wedded, gave the word for surrender.

Next morning the Bridge Gate was cleared of all obstructions and the Danish host poured into the town. Up the steep street came first a band of truculent-looking warriors, picked champions all in ring mail and heavily armed with swords and axes; then, riding a black horse, King Sweyn himself, looking neither right nor left, and with a malignant scowl on his bloated face, but evidently swelling with pride and satisfaction. Then the standard bearer holding aloft a pole with a small silken emblem of a raven; then, filling the street from side to side, a throng of the King's bodyguard, followed endlessly by chieftains with their retinues, the general levy of peasants and freeholders, fisherfolk and craftsmen, looking greedily at empty booths and barred doors, a gruff-voiced, sour-smelling multitude, chanting from time to time some boastful alliterative couplets.

In the town there was silence; no bells clanged from the towers, and most Englishmen remained in their houses. However, in the open space before the great church Hugh the Reeve and a few of the leading churchmen and traders gathered to greet King Sweyn and bid him and his men such hospitality as the town could provide. A feast was to be held in the Reeve's Hall on the top of the hill in the northeast corner of the walls and hopes were expressed that the army would deal peaceably with the townsmen and abstain from plunder and rape. In return a good proportion of the ransom would be handed over at once . . .

King Sweyn sat on horseback listening impassively to these appeals or smiling contemptuously as he thought of how these folk, who had defied him so successfully several years ago, were now adequately humbled, thinking too how lightly his men would heed any pledges that he chose to give. His gaze wandered from the agreeable and subservient Hugh and the downcast faces of the abbots to a sprinkling of townsfolk standing back against the houses. He saw a man in a scarlet tunic standing with folded arms and regarding him steadfastly, a darkly handsome man with a careless, defiant air about him.

"Who is that man dressed in scarlet, with a helmet on his head?" said the King. "He looks little like an Englishman."

There was a silence, then Alfred, standing sullenly beside Hugh the Reeve, said: "He is an Icelander."

"I marked him in the fight. Few men defended the wall better than he did. Come here, Icelander!"

Arnvid stepped forward.

"What is your name?" asked King Sweyn.

"I am Arnvid Torolfsson. My father fought against you on Olaf Trygvesson's ship, the *Long Serpent*," said Arnvid boldly.

"I could do with some fighters of that breed. What call have you to fight for Ethelred the Reedless?"

"None. But I am a guest in Exeter and a guest bears arms beside the man that gives him food and drink."

"Food and drink and good pay you can have in my service. Will you be one of my bodyguard, Arnvid?"

This was the first time he had been offered something by a king, thought Arnvid. Surely he would be a fool to refuse; though it stuck in his throat somewhat that it should be King Sweyn, a false and pitiless man and his father's enemy.

"Gladly I will fight for you and help you to win England," he said, after a moment's hesitation.

"Well spoken," said the King, and gathered up his reins as though to ride on, but at that moment a big fair-haired, brutal-looking man thrust himself forward from among the bodyguard.

"If that be Arnvid Torolfsson," he said, "I ask leave to challenge him to fight here and now."

"Who is this fellow?" said Arnvid in a contemptuous voice, though he grew pale and his heart started to beat wildly.

"You need not pretend you have forgotten Grim Hareksson!" said the other tauntingly. "Fast you fled from Iceland before me, but I have caught up with you now."

King Sweyn looked amused. "Touchy folk are you Icelanders where honor is concerned," he said. "I want no ill will between any of my bodyguard, so it will be best for you to settle your differences right away. Make a ring, men, and let us see them fight it out."

"I am ready, except that I lack a shield," said Arnvid, trying to suppress a trembling of lips and knees. Anyhow it was luck that Grim wore no mail. Doubtless he had left it in the camp, like so many of Sweyn's men, oppressed by the sweltering heat of Devon.

"Let it be sword to sword without shields," said King Sweyn.

Indifferently Grim unslung his shield from his neck and tossed it away. They stood in a tightly packed ring which included the scowling faces of a few townsmen. Close above them Astrid looked down from the gallery of Alfred's house. Measuringly she considered the two men who were now stripping to the waist. Grim seemed to her by far the stronger and tougher; he reminded her of Tord, the man she had wedded and been freed from on Saint Brice's Day.

If he killed Arnvid, she would be freed again from a man she could not love, and yet for all that there was a bond between them that she would hate to see broken by Arnvid's death. I cannot give him what he wants, yet without me he is lost, she thought. A rudderless ship, a house without a hearth . . . Perhaps she needed him as much as he did her. What other protector had she? Tord was dead, Cadogan was dead, she had sent away Torbrand. It was not so good to be a lone woman in Exeter among all these lustful warriors.

Now the fight began and she watched spellbound while Grim rained heavy blows at Arnvid, who parried them adroitly enough, but lost ground foot by foot, pale and desperate, while the Danes began to shout encouragement to their champion and offered heavy wagers for his success. There was a louder shout when a blow seemed to get home and a trickle of blood showed on Arnvid's left shoulder. Astrid had a sickening feeling that he had lost heart, that in a moment he would drop his sword and run in among the spectators, he would be disgraced forever and killed ignominiously like a sheep that rushes for shelter into the flock.

Suddenly she shouted in a high, angry voice: "Stand up to him, Arnvid! Hew him down!"

She saw his face change, his eyes glitter with rage. His sword seemed to spring to life: it whirled and whistled about Grim, who gave back in turn, confused and out of breath. He set his teeth and dealt a tremendous backhanded blow at Arnvid's head, but the head ducked, Arnvid's sword shot forward in a lunge and went through Grim's hairy chest nearly to the hilt. Arnvid tugged it out and hewed at his tottering opponent. The stroke fell on his neck, the same stroke that had killed Cadogan ap Einion, and this time the head fell clear amid a great spout of blood.

There was a roar of hearty if somewhat reluctant applause and immediately a lot of talk broke out.

"I thought Grim had him, but I was wrong," said a man, ruefully handing over a silver arm ring.

"Grim was too confident; the other fellow led him on and then caught him off his guard."

"A good swordsman I call him. I have seldom seen a better."

"He would soon have been a dead man if that woman had not egged him on."

"Now see that you serve me as well as Grim did," said King Sweyn to Arnvid, as he turned his horse to ride away.

Chapter 22

THE HARRYING OF WESSEX

By July the danish host had advanced into the heart of Wessex, moving slowly, fanning out from sea to sea, burning and pillaging. Resistance flamed up here and there. Sometimes a band of exasperated peasants made a futile defense of their homes or sallied from the woods shouting defiance and letting fly a few arrows. But nothing was organized— the big landowners deserted their levies and fled eastward, the might of England was crippled for lack of a leader. Arnvid could not understand why Sweyn hung back over this plundering instead of pushing forward and dealing a decisive blow at Ethelred which might give him the kingdom. His Danish comrades told him that it was easier for wasps to eat out a ripe plum than to pick it from the tree. Ethelred sat in London and that was the strongest of cities; more than once it had been besieged in vain. Moreover it was unwise to move too far from the ships and perhaps get cut off from them. Already there were rumors of a force coming from Mercia to aid the West Saxons . . .

One morning Arnvid and a few others had climbed a steep round hill and sat themselves down on the top of one of the enormous grassy ramparts that encircled the crest, keeping a lookout over the countryside. The bodyguard were encamped in a village at the foot of the hill, making merry with food and drink and a flock of women they had rounded up. At first Arnvid had been surprised and disgusted by the eagerness with which English girls welcomed the rough wooing of Danish warriors fresh from slaughter and burnings-in. He soon perceived that women here were shrewd enough to waste little sentiment on the losing side. Instinctively they gave themselves to the victors. It was much the same with Astrid. To begin with she had been cold and reluctant, unmoved by his tenderness, doubtful about his showing as a man; but after his prowess on the wall at Exeter and the duel with Grim Hareksson her manner to him had changed. Loving she was not, but it became a matter of course to her that they should live together as man and wife while the army stayed in the town, and when it marched away with Arnvid in the ranks of the bodyguard, she went willingly enough into the nunnery, there to await his return.

And what then? Arnvid asked himself. He might sail with the bodyguard to Denmark, to return to England summer after summer till the land was so devastated that it would no longer be worth coming to, or till it took Sweyn for King as the lesser of two evils. This sort of life was well enough for a time, for a proved champion in an invading host—the cheerful companionship of men who might be greedy for wealth but were in the main good-natured and easygoing, the spice of adventure, the ever-changing scene in hot summer weather, going knee-deep through yellowing corn, camping under the spreading branches of huge oaks, songs and sports, now and then a clash of weapons and an easy victory, or lying with a willing girl in the cool dusk among abandoned haycocks or deep in lush greenery among the pennons of foxglove and the creamy plumes of meadowsweet. Still it was not a way of life that would content him for long. More and more he felt the desire for a home and land of his own, and there were times when he thought the greatest happiness for him would be to sail back with Astrid to Iceland.

Since the plundering of Glastonbury the bodyguard had moved eastward through marshy country, but now the ground rose before them, covered as far as the eye could reach by the great forest of Selwood. This bare hill on which they sat was the first of many hills smothered under broad crowns of oak, an old frontier between Englishman and Welshman, where there was every chance of an unwary army being ambushed and overwhelmed. But beyond the woods were famous monasteries, rich towns and cities. The march was to go on in search of yet more booty . . .

A man came leisurely up the hill from the camp; he greeted the watchers on the rampart.

"Any sign of the Englishmen?"

"None," said Arnvid, "except that out north we can see peasants busy carting hay."

"King Sweyn orders that we set out on better work than burning haystacks. The bodyguard are to march southward through yonder woods to a great abbey; Sherborne the place is called. We should be there in a few hours."

Arnvid thought of the church in Exeter where a monk had spoken to him so threateningly. He had no great liking for the plunder of Christian shrines. What if that man was

right, that they were affronting a power that could destroy
them body and soul?

His companions leaped up in high spirits. A fresh haul of
gold and silver would mean more for every man when it
came to sharing out, but Arnvid went down heavyhearted
through the elder scrub, with its fading sprays of bitter white
blossom, to take his place in the long column of fighting men
now getting on horseback. It was a burning-hot day, windstill, with ivory clouds rising into fantastic towers and
toppling pinnacles along the northern horizon, but to southward was a darkening haze. As they rode across the field
beyond the village, the loose dry hay began to lift here and
there and suddenly it whirled up into a fleecy column that
shredded out and drifted away over the woods ahead.

"Odin points out the way for us to fall on the Christfolk,"
said a man, but the cheerful talk died down and the rising
gloom ahead seemed to be reflected on many a sunburned
face. In they went through man-tall bracken, among the shining rods of hazel and the sprouting butts of felled trees—into
the high forest. Here and there a gnarled oak trunk caught
the sunlight, but soon there was only blackness ahead along
winding corridors of moist stagnant air full of dancing midges.
Uphill they went and down into swampy glades, scrambling
over rotten stems half-buried in black ooze, wrenching their
way through monstrous brambles, treading down pale orchids
and bog asphodel. The darkness grew more intense and now
a gusty wind blew at their backs as they came out among
brakes of fireweed onto a heath sweeping up to another wall
of forest. There, along the crest of the ridge, could be seen
a long line of men, and at once they raised a wavering shout
and made a clatter of weapons on shields. From somewhere

not far off came a peal of bells, *ding, dang, dong.* The Danes
got off their horses and went forward in line through the
dusky heather, following King Sweyn's standard bearer. They
were halfway up the slope when the inky sky split suddenly
in a white glare and instantly came a deafening racket of
thunder that went growling and booming away, now near,
now far. A few big drops of rain fell in a breathless silence.
The Danes halted. Another flash and a still louder roar of
thunder. They began to give back. There was a muttering:

"This is a magic storm!"

"Whitechrist is angry!"

"We shall have no luck in going against Sherborne!"

Suddenly King Sweyn came riding through the disordered
ranks of warriors.

"What are you afraid of, men?" he shouted. "The sun
shone on us when we took Glastonbury: what if it rains when
we take Sherborne? Forward and hew the Englishmen!" He
spurred his horse and galloped up the hill. A gleam of sunshine flashed on his uplifted sword, and the bodyguard rushed
after him brandishing their weapons and setting up a horrid
yell. Arnvid was in the center of the line. He saw the English
on the right standing firm and presently meeting blow with
blow, but falling back in the center, while on the left their
men shredded away in full flight. Only a solitary warrior
stood his ground: for a moment Arnvid saw his fair hair and
laughing face against the darkness of the sky and thought,
There at least is one brave man. He ran on among his comrades. A standard confronted them, but it was quickly thrown
down and trodden underfoot, and then they saw only the
backs of Englishmen running to the shelter of the woods.
The fighting, such as it was, had only lasted a few minutes

and now they were pressing on, over the crest of the hill and down scrubby slopes into a wide valley full of corn and hay. In the midst of it was a little town clustered round some tall buildings whence came the melancholy sound of bells. Sherborne was theirs to do with what they would.

Toward evening, when most of the town was burning and the monastery had been stripped of its treasures, Arnvid was sitting on a bench outside the abbey gateway eating some food he had taken from a house before it was set on fire. A warrior he knew well came by among some who had been in the church. He was in high good humor, displaying a jeweled crucifix, and with his arm round the waist of a pretty girl, who seemed to accept her lot passively enough, though she still looked scared and miserable.

"Haven't you been in to take your pick?" he inquired.

Arnvid shook his head. He was not yet so hardened by war as to take any pleasure in rape.

"It has been a lucky day for us," went on the other. "Only six men killed in the fight, and we have gained a man in return.

"How so?"

"There was one man who did not take to his heels; he was out there furthest to the left and he came over to us, saying he had long wanted to fight for King Sweyn. He has just been before the King and it seems he is no Englishman but an Icelander. The King knew him, he had seen him in Denmark, and straightway he gave him leave to join the bodyguard. See, here he comes along the street."

"I know him too," said Arnvid. "He is my foster brother."

"Why, then it should be a happy meeting for both of you," said the warrior. He had let go of the girl, but when she tried to slip away he caught her again, saying good-humoredly, "She is a bit wild at present, but I shall soon tame her."

Arnvid gazed at the familiar figure of Gunnar coming along through the smoke of burning houses and glancing with complete indifference at some very ugly sights. Gunnar, whom he thought must surely have gone to his death returning recklessly to that woman at Chaddesley—but here he was, unharmed, self-confident as ever, as fine-looking a champion as any in King Sweyn's army, his foster brother, his dear companion . . .

Arnvid sprang up and went out to meet him. "Welcome Gunnar!" he cried joyfully. "I had hardly expected to see you alive again."

"Nor I you, Arnvid," said Gunnar, looking him over measuringly. His voice had the old ironic detachment, but his face lit up in a way that Arnvid had seldom seen before and at once Arnvid realized that however envious or hostile he might have felt at one time there was a bond between them that could hardly be broken except by death. It was the same feeling that he had about Astrid, the one key that could turn the lock in him. There he felt the glow of passion that was unchanged, no matter what other woman came into his arms, and here was the sense of admiration and comradeship aroused in him by no other man.

They sat down on the bench side by side, shared out the food, and began to talk, while the smoke drifted about them from the burning town and warriors thronged past piling up their loot in the market square.

Gunnar said presently, "You have done well for yourself to win a place among Sweyn's bodyguard. Now you have fame and wealth, and this may be the beginning of many good things to follow."

"All the same it is not what I would have chosen," said Arnvid.

"It was ever hard for you to find anything that brought you content. What more do you desire?"

"It may seem folly to you," said Arnvid, reddening, "but far more than fame and wealth I prize a woman whom I took from Steintor's hall when it was on fire, Astrid the bride of Tord Otkelsson, who was killed there by the Englishmen."

"Now I come to think of it, there was a girl there. So you got her away? She must have been grateful to you."

"Maybe, but she does not love me, at least not in the way that I do her. I took her to Wales and then oversea to a land called Hougun. I tried to get myself made King in Westmorland and failed. I had to fly and I got away to Exeter and helped to defend the town against King Sweyn, and then when the place was taken King Sweyn picked me out to be one of his bodyguard. There in Exeter I came face to face with Grim Hareksson. He challenged me and I killed him. I left Astrid in Exeter and came on with the army, and here I am in Sherborne."

"I should not grieve about the love of a woman if I had done as much as that," said Gunnar, smiling. "That will be news for them in Iceland that you have killed Grim. What plan have you now?"

"I had thought of taking Astrid to Iceland. I might be able to buy a good farm somewhere on Breidi Fjord."

"England is a better land than Iceland, foster brother! I doubt whether I shall ever go back there."

"A better land, aye, but only for those who can get a hold on it," said Arnvid gloomily.

"What I have done you may also do."

Arnvid reflected that so far he had only talked about himself. Gunnar must have something to tell him. How was it that he was here at all?

"What happened when you rode back to Chaddesley?" he asked.

"I was with Thyra that night and next morning when Edwin came back in a great hurry I killed him with very little trouble. After that I wedded Thyra and now I am the master of Chaddesley. I live in a fine hall, I hunt in the forest, I sit in council with the peasants."

"They accept you as master?"

"Why not? It is Thyra's manor and I am her husband. Edwin was hated by everyone. He was a hard and cruel man."

"And how do you bear yourself to these English?"

"I laugh and joke with the men, but I see that I am not cheated. The women like me all right. There should be some children of mine when I get back to Chaddesley."

"You are going back?"

"Certainly I am, when Sweyn has shared out the booty from this summer's work."

"Folk will know that you fight against Ethelred."

"I doubt it. Some levies were raised to come here into Wessex, but you saw how they fled this afternoon up on the heath. We shall not see much more of them. If my men get home they will not know how I have spent my time, nor will they greatly care. The Mercians have no very friendly feeling for West Saxons."

"It seems that the whole country crumbles under Ethelred."

"I have no doubt that Sweyn will get it in the end, and that will suit me well enough."

"And Thyra, does she bear you a child?"

"Not as yet, so far as I know."

"Is she faithful to you?"

Gunnar's face changed somewhat. "Why do you ask that?" he said.

"She betrayed her first husband very readily."

"Is this Astrid faithful to you?"

"She seems to be, but I do not know and that is a grief to me," said Arnvid.

Gunnar slapped him on the shoulder. "Forget her, and let us find what pleasure and profit we can from this harrying of Wessex! Then you shall go back with me to winter in Worcestershire."

"With Astrid?"

"By all means. Bring her or any other woman you fancy."

Arnvid thought what a joyful prospect this would be but for one thing. Would not Gunnar outshine him with Astrid as he had already done in that brief moment in Steintor's hall? He had felt at a disadvantage even with Torbrand, who was far less of a figure to captivate a woman than Gunnar was. Still Gunnar had his Thyra, and was he still so much the better man of them that he had appeared in Iceland, in Orkney, and York? Gunnar had not stood on the wall at Exeter fighting singlehanded against a swarm of King Sweyn's champions, nor had he felled Grim Hareksson. No, it was not in warlike prowess that he, Arnvid, stood at a disadvantage in a woman's eyes. It was in something that went deeper than that, some diffidence, some unsureness of aim, some sensitiveness to things that most men reckoned of no account: the dusk of early morning with the chorus of bird song in the woods, the clear light of evening, the lengthening shadows, the splendor in the west that seemed a reminder of God's majesty to a wicked world, the awe that oppressed him when he looked up at those high, dim arches in the great church at Exeter . . .

Abruptly he said: "Have you become a Christian, Gunnar?"

"Aye," said Gunnar easily, "living at peace in England it is best to be a Christian like other folk."

"You believe what the priests say about heaven for holy men and hell-fire for sinners?"

Gunnar did not answer at once. Then he said, "To be a Christian the main thing is to believe that Whitechrist was the Son of God, a good man with magic power. I can believe that, even as King Olaf Trygvesson did, and what was right for such a great warrior is right enough for me."

"But you believe that men who hold to other gods and who sin against the code of the Christians will be cast into a burning pit?" persisted Arnvid.

"Some will only burn for a time, it seems."

"Only the best of them. Most men such as we see here will burn forever." Arnvid made a gesture toward men dragging women through the abbey gateway and others going into the church with torches. Gunnar merely shrugged his shoulders and was silent.

"But what justice is there in such a doom?" burst out Arnvid. "That is what I ask myself. An evildoer may have to abide punishment in this world or the next, but who could condemn a man to punishment such as that?"

"Men seldom stint punishment when they have the power to inflict it. What is King Sweyn doing in England but taking vengeance, so far as he can, for the killing of his sister on Saint Brice's Day? And God, they say, is all-powerful, so His vengeance may well be heavier than any man's."

"How can you take pleasure in the life you lead if you are to pass into eternal fire?"

"A brave man is not so easily frightened by what priests may tell him. We cannot be sure that they tell us the truth, even if they know it themselves. They talk much about hell-fire when they would have men make gifts to the church—it was not long before I noticed that. Moreover they tell us that Whitechrist is merciful and much may be forgiven men who repent when they come to their end. When we come to the end of this life we go in a great company to the next, if indeed there be anything beyond the grave, and I doubt whether I shall fare worse than most men."

"You may be content to believe what you say, but I could never be," said Arnvid bitterly.

"Do you believe in the power of Odin and Thor, and Valhalla for the champions in fight?"

"I would sooner believe in that, I think, though I doubt whether I should be welcome in Valhalla," said Arnvid with the ghost of a smile.

"One must stand for one faith or the other. In olden times the old gods seemed to men to have power, but now maybe that power is wasted away, as the poets told us it would be. Nowadays, and here in England, I judge that it is better to be a Christian."

"Then why are you with Sweyn and not with Ethelred?"

"I seek fame and wealth, foster brother, as most Christians

do, for that matter. I shall not bear arms against priests nor lay my hands on treasure in a church, though I hear that Christian kings in Ireland have often done so; and whether you put your trust in Whitechrist or in Thor I see no reason why you and I should not always be good comrades. Here and now we can have joy together, whatever may come to us in the end."

"Thought is the enemy of joy," said Arnvid, half to himself, but it seemed to him that the joy of being with Gunnar was an easy and comfortable thing, very different from the joy of being with Astrid, which was both pain and delight.

Chapter 23

OVER BRENDON HILL

THE DANISH HOST gathered itself together and passed eastward through Selwood into a country of fertile valleys between chalk downs. Shaftesbury and Wilton were taken without difficulty, but there was fighting at Sarum, where the town was girdled by a formidable earthwork. However, it fell at the first assault and Arnvid and Gunnar were among the foremost who got in over the palisade. Harvest had now started and King Sweyn's soldiers began to clamor for a return to their own country. Some urged the King to winter in England with his bodyguard, saying that Ethelred would not dare to attack them, but most men thought the English were not so cowed as all that and that it would be best to get the booty safely to Denmark. The King agreed and by slow stages, devastating yet more of Dorset and Somerset, the host returned to Exeter. There the booty was divided according to the King's pleasure and no man was ill content with his share. Then the ships were made ready in haste to take advantage of a strong west wind. Arnvid and Gunnar asked leave to stay in England. Sweyn said he could ill spare such good champions and offered them land in Denmark, but Gunnar persisted and promised that both of them would take their places among the bodyguard when King Sweyn's standard appeared in Mercia. The King was not pleased, but in the end he gave them both leave. Already Gunnar had set about converting their shares of booty into two gold arm rings and two well-filled bags of silver coins, and now he bought cheaply enough three horses that the Danes were leaving behind. His plan was to ride across country to some harbor on the Somerset coast where a small vessel might be found to take them up the Severn into Worcestershire. Meanwhile Arnvid hurried off to fetch Astrid from the nunnery. She smiled to see his eager face at the door; it was pleasant enough to see a man again after all these weeks among grave-faced nuns, listening to the continual chanting of prayers or to the discontented whispering of the novices. They went out together into the streets where there was an angry hum. Most of the Danes had marched away to the ships and it was only the fear of reprisals, of having the town set on fire, that hindered the English from falling upon those that were still within the walls. She answered a few hasty questions as they hurried along, avoiding groups of scowling men and shrill-voiced women. "I am well," she said. "I am with child. See, I have made myself new clothes."

"Gunnar is waiting for us with horses by the North Gate," he said. "The sooner we are out of Exeter the better."

"Gunnar?"

"My foster brother. We have been together in Sweyn's

bodyguard. Now we are going to Worcestershire, to Chaddesley."

"What has he to do with Chaddesley?"

"He has killed Edwin and wedded Thyra."

Arnvid could not guess what she thought about this. At that moment they came on Gunnar with his three horses and they made haste to mount.

"Down with the Danes! Kill them! Skin them alive!" shouted someone in the crowd, but daunted by the look of the two mail-clad warriors no one barred their way as they clattered under the arch and out into the open fields. They pushed on fast, but once they were out of sight of the red walls and slender towers of Exeter and were following the loops of the river below hanging woods they rode more leisurely and began to talk.

"Did no Danes come to molest the nunnery?" asked Arnvid.

"We used to hear them roaring in the streets," said Astrid. "The nuns took no notice, but some of the townswomen who had come in for shelter, they began to shriek and hide in corners, and one or two were mad to get out to the Danes. Only once there was a hammering on the gate. The mother superior and some of the oldest and plainest sisters went out and showed themselves, chanting a prayer and the Danes soon went away."

"They would not have gone so quickly if they had seen you in the gateway," said Gunnar, laughing.

Astrid reddened a little and looked pleased, while Gunnar eyed her with frank admiration. It occurred to Arnvid that he had never made that sort of remark to Astrid and he was nettled to think how unpracticed he was in saying the sort of thing women liked to hear or in catching the light mood

[263]

that put them at ease with men. Perhaps he was too serious, too gentle and tentative, until he was roused to passion, and then, maybe, he was too rough . . . He was nettled, too, to see how Gunnar took the lead in everything, picking the best way, taking no risks in difficult places and quickening the pace when the going was good, while Astrid, who used to depend on his judgment, now followed Gunnar without the least hesitation. Gradually he fell silent, and as the track was narrow he dropped behind, letting Astrid and Gunnar ride side by side, obviously to their mutual satisfaction. He was not much perturbed by this, thinking that Astrid carried his child and that Gunnar had his own woman waiting for him at Chaddesley. Still for him this ride had little of the pleasure and excitement that he had found riding in desperate peril with Astrid to Wales.

Late in the day they passed the little burned-out town of Bampton and came at nightfall to a solitary inn below the Brendon Hills. Nothing here showed any sign of war: there was a field of shocked corn and friendly blue smoke rose from the long low building against a mounting wall of gorse and heather. They had food with them, but Gunnar thought it would be safe enough to go in, drink, and rest till morning. "We are two English thanes going home after fighting the pagans," he said with a grin.

"Our speech may betray us," said Arnvid, who now had an impulse to oppose any plan made by Gunnar.

"I can manage tolerably well in the speech of Mercia," said Gunnar.

"And I can help you out," put in Astrid.

"As for you, foster brother, silence might be the best thing and you do not find that difficult."

"Folly he talks who is never silent," flung back Arnvid, but Gunnar only nodded good-humoredly. They got off and went to the door. The folk inside seemed friendly when they heard who they were and got the news that the Danes were gone from England. The horses were turned into a green meadow and places were found at a long table where sat a few travelers who had goods they hoped to sell in Exeter. There was not much to eat, but plenty of mead for those who could pay for it. The three of them had not been there long before half a dozen rough, dirty-looking men came in, tenants under the freeman who held Bampton.

"Free mead!" they shouted jokingly.

"Why so?" said the innkeeper.

"Because Devon is free of the Danes. The news has just come from Exeter."

"These folk have come from Exeter and they are paying for their drink."

The innkeeper pointed to Gunnar and Arnvid.

"Free drink, I say!" shouted one man. "Our houses are burned and for months we have had nothing but a sup of milk or water. You may get your house burned if you do not heed us!"

"Aye. Free drink for all!" shouted the rest.

Grudgingly, but making the best of it, the innkeeper put a small tub of mead on the table and each man made haste to dip a mug in it. For a few minutes they gulped the strong liquor thirstily, then they all began to talk at once, but in such a slurred speech that Arnvid could make little of it. A great black-bearded man was sitting next to Astrid. He leaned up against her, plying her with questions which at first she answered in a cool, curt voice; then she remained silent. Soon the fellow had his arm around her waist and pressed a kiss on her averted cheek. The other men roared with laughter, but Arnvid sprang up and began to tug out his sword. Astrid threw a swift look at Gunnar, who sat opposite. He stood up and pushed Arnvid down onto the bench, saying heartily, "We are all friends here and it is no great fault to kiss a pretty girl!" He dipped his mug in the mead and raised it aloft toward the black-bearded man.

"Drink with me, friend!" he shouted. "Let us drink to all the rosy-cheeked girls in Devon and may we get to bed with a good many of them!" They emptied their mugs and immediately Gunnar filled his afresh.

"Now let us drink death and damnation to King Sweyn!"

"I drink in the hope that we have seen the last of him," said one of the traders.

"I would say that you are right, friend. The man is a coward at heart. The road to London lay open, but he turned back and now he has sailed for Denmark with his tail between his legs."

The black-bearded man had loosed his hold on Astrid. He drank again and said thickly, "Were you in battle with King Sweyn?"

"That I was, before Sherborne. I never saw such a faint-hearted host. There was a peal of thunder and they all turned to fly. If we had had more men we could have chased them to the sea."

"But Sherborne was taken, was it not?" said someone.

"It would never have been taken if the men of Dorset had been the warriors that the men of Devon are."

"It is not men we lack, but leaders," said an older man. "When Alfred the Good was King it was a different story. He gathered the West Saxon men under his standard and taught the Danes a lesson that they did not forget for a hundred years."

"Leaders or no leaders, we can match the Danes, man for man. We can more than match them. This friend of mine here fought on the wall at Exeter and killed a dozen pagans singlehanded."

All looked at Arnvid with respect.

"How many Danes did you kill, friend?" said Gunnar to the black-bearded man.

"I killed one when he was lowering the bell from Bampton Church!"

"What were you doing in the belfry?" said the innkeeper, with a malicious grin.

"Why, I was hiding in the belfry, but I stepped out and threw the Dane down and I would have thrown down any more that came up, but they didn't dare."

"What did you do when the Danes came to your house?"

"I hid in the hay. The devils tried to set it on fire, but it wouldn't burn."

"Like as not," said another man. "I never knew you to get your hay in dry."

"It was as good hay as yours!" Blackbeard banged his mug on the table.

"Whatever my hay was like, I hid my wife and daughter in it and so saved them from getting raped as yours were."

Everyone began to laugh except Blackbeard, who scraped up another mug of mead, drank it off, muttered, "Women come to no harm," and then suddenly fell asleep with his head on the table. Gunnar, Arnvid, and Astrid got up and made their way out. The innkeeper followed and showed them a loft where they could sleep.

"You handled that well, Gunnar," said Astrid.

"We could have fought them, no doubt, but it was simpler to fool them. English peasants are easily fooled," he said with a laugh. "That kiss you got was not worth a lot of bloodshed."

They stood under the low cobwebbed beams of the loft, Arnvid holding a rushlight. He wondered what Gunnar would have done had he been with Astrid on that heath in Powys. Surely he was not like the drunken peasant who did not care what happened to his woman? And then it was manly to answer an injury with blood. If you loved a woman you could not bear another man to touch her—and yet how often had he felt during that march through Wessex that bloodshed was a senseless thing, if not a wicked thing as the Christians professed to think? All those lives lost, all that work of man's hands destroyed, because King Sweyn's sister had been killed ... He was confused and unhappy, wishing he had some sure guide to conduct. At one time he thought he had only to copy Gunnar, but now he felt more and more that he and Gunnar were poles apart, even as Geirfin had said that they were. He would never have Gunnar's aptitude for finding the easy or sensible way out of every situation. Suddenly he realized that Astrid and Gunnar were exchanging a long look: their faces expressed surprise and a sort of consternation, a flash of understanding quickly cloaked, but presently, quite naturally, Astrid came and lay down beside him and Gunnar went to sleep on the other side of the loft.

Next morning they rode on, up through the dewy brakes of Brendon onto the broad crest of the hills. For a long way ahead the land rose and fell in low waves covered by a uniform mat of heather. Not a soul was in sight; there was only the keen, fierce scent drawn out by the sunshine and the blaze of purple under the blue sky; but Gunnar thought they should push forward as fast as possible and get clear of Wessex before someone recognized them for what they were. The horses were in poor form after the heavy work they had done all summer. Gunnar and Astrid rode them hard, but Arnvid could not bring himself to treat a horse like a tool, to drive it as one drove a plowshare through the sods till it fell to pieces. Again he dropped behind and watched the pair ahead. They rode side by side and so close together that Astrid had to take her hazel switch in her left hand. All their movements seemed to be instinctively in accord; their heads turned simultaneously to glance at a hovering hawk, from time to time they jerked the reins and struck their horses at the same moment and in the same way, from time to time they both turned in the saddle and impatiently beckoned him on. Slowly he realized that this was more exasperating to him than when Astrid was kissed by the peasant or when she lay in the arms of Cadogan ap Einion, for he could do nothing about it—or could he? Like the look that passed between the two in the loft, it might mean everything or nothing. Either all was well or his life lay in ruins. The sunshine and the smell of the heather seemed to sharpen his passion for the woman so that everything about her, the fair hair caught by the wind, the glimpse of her cheek, all the curves of her body, the harsh movements of hand and heel, gave him a raging pleasure that suddenly boiled over into murderous jealousy. He got his horse into a gallop and as he thundered in pursuit he thought of what her face might reveal when he came up with her—

[269]

the welcoming smile he had seen at the nunnery gate, or the sullen distaste when he had helped her up on the gunwale of Torbrand's ship. Now he was only a few yards behind; but here the hill dropped before him into space which was filled with a prospect so startling in its grandeur and significance that instinctively he drew rein and gazed for a few moments. Astrid had taken no notice of his approach: she and Gunnar glanced briefly at what lay ahead and then urged their horses on tight rein over the brink, leaning back and gripping hard, their eyes watchful of the ground that fell away like the roof of a house.

Down there, flanked by hills to left and right, was a low, tangled country of fields, woods, and marshes and beyond it a wide expanse of sea, ruffled by the wind, darkened here and there by cloud shadows; and beyond the sea was another land full of dim hills, pale in watery sunshine, ashen gray in showers of rain. That, he knew, must be Wales, his mother's land. Again he felt a longing for it, as he had done when he crossed Offa's Dyke with Astrid in the snow, but now he no longer had any hope of making a home there. His thoughts returned to Astrid and Gunnar. There they were, already far down the hill, entering the fringe of the ascending woods. His mind clouded with anger and dismay. What was he going to do? What could he say that might arrest the infatuation that was surely springing up between them? He thought of the night in the loft. He had slept heavily and Astrid lay beside him when he woke, but had she been across to Gunnar while he slept, as that woman at Kirkwall had changed partners during the night? Full of rage he gathered up the reins and gave his horse a shower of blows with his hazel switch. The surprised animal set off down the hill, but

very soon stumbled over a gorse bush and turned a somer-
sault. Arnvid was thrown clear; he got up at once and remounted. He did not seem to be hurt, but his ears sang and
everything looked misty. He rode slowly, wondering why he
had been in such a hurry; then seeing Gunnar and Astrid
waiting for him in a ferny glade he remembered, but now
he felt no anger, only a dull bewilderment.

They stared at him in a puzzled way as he came down to
them and Gunnar said, "Why, foster brother, what is amiss?"

Everything, thought Arnvid, but he only said: "I had a
fall coming down the hill." He looked at Astrid, but her face
did not change, showing neither sympathy nor aversion.

Gunnar said anxiously, "Have you broken any bones?"

"Not that I know of."

"You can keep in the saddle?"

"I suppose so."

"The sea is not far away now. By evening we should be
afloat making up toward the Severn."

"The Severn," Arnvid said as they moved on. His mind
was clearer now. "It was beside the Severn that we had our
first night together, Astrid."

"It was a very chilly night," she said.

"Even for lovers?" said Gunnar.

"We weren't lovers," she said. "Arnvid used to sleep in a
coat of mail. He was always expecting an Englishman behind
the next bush."

Gunnar laughed. "I remember that coat. It must have
meant little comfort or joy for either of you. I wouldn't have
worn a thing like that. Did it save you from any thrust in the
belly, Arnvid?"

"So far as I remember it never had to turn either thrust

or blow and I forget now where I parted with it, maybe at Ambleside in Westmorland."

"You had a girl there, I hear. Most likely she cured you of wearing that mail coat," said Gunnar jokingly.

Arnvid did not answer. He thought: If I had made love to her at once she would have been content; she would not have hardened herself against me. Even if she had not wanted love-making at first she soon would have wanted it if I had been Gunnar. And then he thought: He could take her away from me now if he liked, but from the way he talks he has no such intention, whatever Astrid may think about it. I was a fool to imagine that I could not trust Gunnar. He looked at Astrid, wishing to think she was equally trust-worthy. Their eyes met and she smiled. He was reassured; the dizziness had passed off and so had that torment of jealousy. All was well, and yet a suspicion haunted him that Astrid's smile was only an echo of Gunnar's laughing face, that she was so attuned to him that all her actions reflected his, much as two birds will swoop and wheel together in the air with elaborate precision actuated by the same impulse.

Late in the afternoon they reached the little harbor of Watchet. The Danes had been here and there were not many people about, for some had fled across the sea to Wales. How-ever, there were two or three fishing boats by the quay and Gunnar had no difficulty in hiring one with a show of silver. Two men agreed to take them up the Severn; they said it would not be difficult to reach Tewkesbury. After that it would be hard work against the current. Gunnar sold the three horses for a small sum and bought more food. They went aboard and ran up the sail. Arnvid sat at the rudder with Astrid, the two men were amidships, ready to row if

need be, Gunnar lay in the prow keeping a lookout. The
wind freshened with heavy rain. All that night Arnvid sat
side by side with Astrid under one cloak. Sometimes one
slept, sometimes the other. Sometimes his hand strayed over
her body. She made no response, but neither did she resist
him in any way, and he was reasonably content.

They were three days on the water, for progress was slow,
with much hard rowing when they got into the loops of Severn, but Tewkesbury was reached at last. Gunnar paid off
the boatmen and they went ashore in a land that had seen
no fighting for generations. So far all had gone according to
plan. They ate and slept, they secured some well-fed horses,
and when they set out northward through the forest of Hore-
well, Gunnar's mood of gaiety had spread to both Astrid and
Arnvid. It was a warm evening in August with the sun going
down behind the rough humpy hills across Severn, when
they came in sight of Chaddesley; the high gabled hall, the
little timber church, the long line of peasant cots, backed by
the dark mass of Pyperwood. The hay was in stack, the
meadows dotted with cattle and sheep, the corn was all set
up and casting shadows across the long strips of plowing.

"Well, foster brother, would you change this for Iceland?"
exclaimed Gunnar.

Arnvid looked thoughtfully at what lay before them. Nine
months had passed since he rode away from Chaddesley, neither expecting nor wishing to see it again. It had seemed a
secret sort of place, steeped in treachery and lust, where
guests had to beware of being murdered in their beds and
where women betrayed their husbands. All was dark and
still in those great woods that lay about it on every side.
Here was nothing of the harsh freedom of Iceland with the

blustering wind coming from the sea and the sight of the towering fells patched with snow.

"Maybe I have seen too many places like this go up in smoke," he said. "I would sooner be in Iceland."

"And what do you say, Astrid?"

"In this land I was born and bred. Here I will stay," she said decisively.

"You were glad enough to get away from it on Saint Brice's Day," said Arnvid bitterly.

Chapter 24

FLIGHT FROM CHADDESLEY

THEY RODE ACROSS THE FIELD and into the village street. At once the people came to their doors, stared, and burst into excited talk.

"The lord has come back!"

"He is alive after all!"

"He has come back with that dark stranger who was here before."

"They have a woman with them."

"Now what will happen?"

"Nothing good!"

"Nay, things will right themselves now the lord is back . . ."

The gray-bearded steward came out into the street. He bowed before Gunnar and Gunnar greeted him in friendly fashion, but became a trifle impatient when the steward spoke at length about the success of the hay harvest, a sickness among the swine, and the progress of the dispute with the lord of Harvington about the forest boundary.

"The lady Thyra is well?" interrupted Gunnar.

"The lady Thyra is very well." The steward dropped his gaze and stroked his beard. "As I was saying, the Harvington folk have felled the boundary mark, the old oak with three trunks—"

"Look!" said Astrid suddenly. She pointed toward the hall.

There, through the gate, went a man on a horse at full gallop. For a few moments they saw him careering across the field, knocking over some of the corn shocks, then he was lost to sight.

"Who is that man?" said Gunnar sharply.

"That will be Aldred, the son of the Lord of Broughton," said the steward with an attempt at nonchalance.

"He seems little anxious to meet with us," remarked Arnvid.

Without another word Gunnar urged his horse hard and they all three clattered up to the hall. A servant was about to shut the gate in their faces, but Gunnar burst through, leaped from the saddle and caught the man by the collar.

"Do you know who I am?" he said menacingly.

"I do, lord!" answered the servant, turning deadly pale.

"Then tell me no lies! Was that Aldred of Broughton who has just ridden away?"

"Aye, lord. Aye, that was Aldred," stuttered the man.

"Did he know I was come back?"

"The steward's son ran into the hall a little while ago with a message. I do not know what it was."

"You know very well!" Gunnar shook him so that his teeth rattled. "How long has Aldred been here?"

"Two weeks; maybe three weeks."

"Where has he been sleeping? No lies, or you will hang from the hall gable within the hour!"

"He slept in the hall . . . in the locked bed with the lady Thyra."

Gunnar slung the man away.

"The other bird has not yet flown!" Arnvid pointed to a man holding a saddled horse by the hall door.

"Why not let her go?" said Astrid.

Gunnar had turned red as blood and foam gathered at the corners of his mouth. He looked at Astrid and suddenly he was calm again.

"There may be more in this than meets the eye," he said.

"How so?" said Arnvid. "Guilt is plain enough for anyone to see."

"He was not taking the way to Broughton," said Astrid.

"Your wits are sharp," muttered Gunnar, as he strode toward the hall. They went in and saw Thyra standing there in a group of girls. She had a whip in her hand and one girl was fastening a spur to the heel of her shoe. On seeing Gunnar they all ran into a corner like a flock of sheep, but Thyra did not move. Gunnar halted in front of her.

"Did you think I was dead, Thyra?" he said, with his hands gripping his belt as though to hinder them from laying hold of her.

"I had no reason to think you were dead, but now I have very good reason to think that you soon will be," she said in a hard, steady voice.

"What has Aldred been telling you? Answer me!" He shot out an arm and took her by the hair.

"I am not afraid to answer. You and Aldred were together in the army before Sherborne. Is that true?"

"True it is. He fled and I did not."

"He was wounded and got to Shaftesbury, where the monks cared for him. He lay there in the abbey and saw you in King Sweyn's bodyguard when the Danes came in. Is that also true, that you went out to fight for Ethelred and turned over to fight for Sweyn?"

"True enough."

"Then what do you expect, coming back here?"

"I did not expect to find another man in your bed."

"A doomed husband is no use to me."

"Nor have I any use for a harlot." He let her go and stepped back. "Ride your way! Catch up with your lover if you can; he has got a long start."

"He rides to the earl in Worcester. Men will be sent to take you and put you to death. You may be King Sweyn's warrior, but King Sweyn is not here to protect you in the heart of Mercia."

"Do your worst, both of you, and now be off! I hope never to see you again." Gunnar sat down at the board; Arnvid and Astrid sat themselves beside him. They watched Thyra stand irresolute for a moment; then she stepped out into the sunshine and they soon heard her horse thudding across the yard and out at the gateway.

"Get us food and drink, the best you have!" shouted Gunnar to a growing crowd of servants that stood in a corner.

They ate in silence and then Gunnar sent the servants out of the hall. There was a vat of mead into which they dipped their drinking cups. Arnvid drank a good deal; the other two only moderately. They leaned back in comfort and began to talk.

"It does not look as though I could offer you bed and

board at Chaddesley," said Gunnar. His gaze wandered over the hall taking in the great oak pillars that upheld the dusky roof, the carved doors of the cupboard beds, the big chests, smooth with age, the woven hangings along the wall, the weapons and painted shields, the well-wrought dishes and cups, one of them silver. "A lot to lose, both indoors and out," he said, half to himself. "Still one cannot take all this with one to the grave, nor have I a son who might have joy of it when I am gone."

"You only won this and held it by a woman's favor, and a bad woman at that," said Arnvid.

"Easy it is to be wise after the event, foster brother! I will not deny that I made a bad choice and that my plans have gone amiss. Nor have yours prospered overwell." He looked thoughtfully from Arnvid to Astrid. "Now we have to begin afresh."

Arnvid said rather thickly, "At least we have won some fame and wealth, which was what we set out to do, and Astrid carries my child."

Gunnar saw a frown on Astrid's face. She stared at the table and remained silent. Arnvid went on drinking.

"There is nothing for it," said Gunnar. "We must get away from here and that soon."

"I see no hurry. It will be a day or so before Aldred gets back here with men from Worcester. Drink, Gunnar! Things might be worse, and anyhow this mead is as good as any I have tasted."

"It will not help us to make a good plan."

"Where will you go now?" Astrid looked at Gunnar.

"There is Wales," he said.

"I cannot show my face in Wales again," said Arnvid gloomily. "Nor in Westmorland."

"There is Audun in York," said Astrid.

"He could hardly shelter us if Ethelred's messengers follow us to York. The Danes there are yet a long way from taking Sweyn's side. All I can think of is that we seek King Sigtrygg Silkbeard in Dublin." Gunnar traced a pattern in the mead spilled on the table.

"There I should find Asmund, and I have no wish to seek his company!" said Arnvid angrily.

"It might be a gain for you if you wedded his daughter," said Gunnar with a provocative smile. "All was agreed, was it not?"

"What do I want with Asmund's daughter!" shouted Arnvid. He looked at Astrid, but she did not raise her eyes.

Gunnar shrugged his shoulders. "I do not greatly favor Dublin," he said. "From what I heard last King Sigtrygg's power in Ireland grows less and less. Still, maybe we cannot do better. If we can get to Chester ahead of our enemies a ship would take us to Dublin."

"There is Iceland."

"Ships to Iceland are few and far between. Besides Astrid has no wish to go to Iceland."

"She will go where I say!" shouted Arnvid, who was now rather drunk.

"It would be better if I stayed here," said Astrid. "A woman heavy with child will not easily win through to Chester, riding hard as you will have to."

"True," said Gunnar, "but we cannot stay here and defend Chaddesley against all who come."

Arnvid's head was beginning to drop on the table. Presently he rolled himself in his cloak and lay down on a bench. In a few minutes he was asleep. The little oil lamp flickered and went out; there was only the dying glow of the fire and no sound except for Arnvid's snoring and the hooting of an owl on the hall roof.

"Things have come to a difficult pass," said Gunnar, after a long silence.

"It is hard that you should be shorn all at once of house and land, of wife and home." As though impelled by some irresistible force, Astrid lifted her hand and smoothed down the bushy fair hair on his head. He looked at her with a deep flush.

"I am well rid of the wife," he said, "but there is more than that."

"What more?"

"There is you to think about."

"It is far better that I should take my chance here."

"Have you no will to live with Arnvid?" he said after a long pause.

"I have never wished to be his."

"Yet he is a fine figure of a man, and a good man, too."

"It is my misfortune that I could never find any love for him."

"Why not?"

"Maybe he is too gentle and to trusting for the world in which we have to live. He is never sure of himself except when he falls into a rage and he is never content unless things are exactly as he wants them, and so he will never be content with me."

"Does it make no difference that you are going to bear his child?"

She was silent for a moment, then she said shortly, "It is not his child."

"Not his child! Whose, then?"

"Torbrand's, the Northman who brought us in his ship to Exeter. He was mad to have me. The townsfolk were killing any Danes they could find and Torbrand and Arnvid passed as Englishmen, but Torbrand was going to betray Arnvid, who was asleep, drunk as he is now, unless I gave in to him . . . So he had his way with me and Arnvid did not know."

"He will have to know sometime."

"Yes."

"And then what is going to happen?"

"He will be angry, of course, but he will not let me go."

"No, not if he knows why you did it."

Suddenly she spoke passionately, as he had never heard her speak before.

"I owe him my life, but surely I have paid my debt to him by now! It is unbearable that I should live with him any longer!"

"You might go further and fare worse, Astrid."

"Is that your last word?"

"Nay, if you came to me we should both be happy; we fit together like hand in glove."

"You felt that when we rode over Brendon together?"

"Then and many times since."

"I thought it might be so when first I saw you, in Steintor's hall."

"And I wish now that I had stayed with Arnvid and not turned back to Chaddesley and Thyra. Still, it might have made no difference."

"How so?"

"I think it was fated that you should come between Arnvid and me," he said somberly. "What is to happen if neither of us will give you up?"

"What happens when both Sweyn and Ethelred desire to have England? The weaker will have to give way."

"Sweyn and Ethelred are not foster brothers, men who have trusted each other all their lives."

"Then what you feel for me does not outweigh what you feel for Arnvid?"

"You are the one woman I have seen that I would choose to live with till parted by death."

"Did you not think so of Thyra?"

"Thyra? I thought well of her to start with, and then she brought me Chaddesley, and I had never seen a place I liked as much."

"There is little I can bring you . . . except love."

"From you I desire nothing more than that."

"Then have it if you will!"

"Aye, but can I let my bond with Arnvid be broken by a sword stroke?"

"It would come to that?"

"Surely it would in the end."

"Does my mood count for nothing with him? Would it not be more manly for him to let me go?"

"He would think it more manly to fight for you."

"Even against you?"

"Have you not seen into his heart, Astrid? It would take very little to turn his love for me into hate, but not his love for you."

"He is jealous of you."

"He has little reason to be. He has done more daring things than I have."

"Jealousy pricks him on like a spur. He longs to prove himself bolder than you are, but in his heart he knows you are his better."

"It is a great misfortune for both of us."

"Then go your ways and leave me alone!" she said angrily.

"Nay, that is just what we cannot do."

There was a long silence, then she said, "Do you believe that after we are dead we meet again with those we have loved?"

"You are a Christian, as I am, but what we are told to believe and what we believe in our hearts may be two different things," he answered, taking a sip of mead. His sense of gloom and foreboding lightened to faint amusement.

"It is true I am baptized," she said, "but I have never paid much heed to what the priest said, nor did my father, Steintor, for that matter."

"So far as I can make out, we are most of us doomed to hell, and it may not be easy to recognize our friends among the flames, nor would it be much pleasure to us if we did."

"I think it is a wicked judgment that we should burn in fire when we go hence!"

"That is what Arnvid thinks. He cannot believe it and so he will not let himself be baptized. Still, that will not protect him if it be true."

"But you are not afraid to think it true?"

"Who am I to say what the truth is? Many good and wise men think it true, else why should they give up land and gold, rear these great buildings to the glory of God, forego the clasp of flesh and the joy of children?"

"All for fear of the fire?"

"That is what it comes to. And they pray to Whitechrist who may mediate between them and a cruel God and so relieve them of some of the torment. What can bridle men except fear or love?"

"But if there be nothing beyond the grave, then they have given up the good things of this life in vain."

He rested his chin in his hands and stared at the dying fire. At last he said: "If dead be dead, as seems to me most likely, then the Christians are all deceived, even as our forebears were in their thoughts of Valhalla."

"Then while we live it is only plain sense to take what happiness we can."

"Whether Christian or pagan, there is little happiness unless we be of good fame with those about us and those who are to come; unless we be proud enough to hold back from things that bring us shame and dishonor."

"And that is how you guide your life, Gunnar?"

"It has not been hard for me to do that till now."

"We get no further in this talk," she said wearily, and took his hand in hers. For a long time they sat in silence, side by side, then suddenly there was a sharp knocking on the hall door.

Gunnar got up quickly and took down the bolt. He opened the door a little way and looked out. A man stood there in the darkness. When Gunnar asked who he was he answered, "I am Alfgar, lord. I slipped out of the village to warn you that Aldred is back with near on a hundred men, all armed. They are going to surround the hall and kill both you and your friend, the dark man who came hither with you."

"What grounds have they for killing me?" said Gunnar with a chuckle.

"They say that you fought for Sweyn down in Wessex. I know naught about that, but you are my lord and I have had nothing but good at your hands. I think there is still time for you to get away before they make a ring around the buildings."

"The horses, where are they?"

"The steward had them put in the further hay meadow."

"Then we must go on foot. Get back to the village, Alfgar, before harm comes to you."

"Shall I not stand by you if it comes to a fight?"

"No, friend. It would be useless." Gunnar turned back into the hall and found Astrid close beside him.

"We must go, and at once," he said. "No time to get the horses, no time even to put on a coat of mail."

"I heard what the man said. I am ready."

"Let us wake Arnvid."

"I have awakened him."

Arnvid was sitting up on the bench, still dazed with sleep.

"Buckle on your sword and come. Our foemen are upon us!" said Gunnar sharply. He reached up the wall and took down a long-shafted axe, the gift of Earl Erik, that had stayed in its place all the time he had been away. They went silently out at the door and listened for a moment. There came a murmur of voices from the direction of the village, a creaking from a fence not far off as though men were climbing over it.

"Our only chance is northward," whispered Gunnar. He led the way with a quick noiseless stride, pulled open a hurdle and went out into a field thick-set with ghostly looking shocks of corn. Before long they scrambled over another fence and now there were dark shapes about them, hard-nibbled thorns and gorse, clumps of briar and bramble. Some shouting broke out for a moment down by the hall, then all was silent again.

"We shall be followed," said Gunnar. "They will reckon on our going this way and getting clear before the ring closed on us."

Ahead in the darkness showed the deeper blackness of the forest. Now bracken brushed against their knees and old misshapen trees arched above them.

"There is a path here if I can but keep to it," said Gunnar. "Thyra was right when she warned us that we could not win our way through Pyperwood to Kinver, but I know more about it now. Let us keep close together, I first, then Astrid, then you, Arnvid." Gunnar probed ahead with the shaft of his axe, the other two followed, shielding their faces against the hazel branches. It was hard going through the forest, but in the gray of morning they came to open ground thick with heather, in the midst of which was an old grave mound. Here and there stood rowans, their branches dark and bending under their load of scarlet fruit, magic trees that averted evil spirits, yet to Arnvid they had an ominous look as though presaging blood.

"I know this place: I had hoped that we had got far beyond this," said Gunnar ruefully. He looked at Astrid, standing pale and listless under the drooping trees, and said: "Here it would be well to rest awhile." They drew back into the cover of the woods, but Gunnar lay where he had a sight of the open ground. Arnvid was gloomy and short-tempered, harping back on how it would have been better to go southward and take ship to Rouen. "It was against my judgment to return to that cursed place, Chaddesley, and I laughed to myself when Astrid said she felt safe there. Safe, among these murderous Englishmen!"

"You talked then of Iceland," said Gunnar.

"Iceland! I doubt whether I shall ever see that land again. Here am I stuck in these great woods like a fly in a spider's web!"

"You would not be much safer in Iceland now that you have killed Grim Hareksson. They are revengeful folk over there."

"Every blow I strike turns back against myself!"

"You might think less of yourself and more of Astrid who is in worse plight than you."

"What is amiss with Astrid?" said Arnvid angrily.

"A woman heavy with child should not be going on foot through Pyperwood."

"Whose fault is it that she is here?" Arnvid's voice rose on a note of fury.

"Be silent!" said Gunnar sharply. "Here come men onto the heath."

He crouched low, staring through the stems of the bracken. Presently he said, "They have gone on northward. We had best turn westward for a time." Astrid rose slowly to her feet and followed the two men who were plunging ahead into the darkness of the forest. It was not so bad in the carpet of yellowing bracken under the big oaks, but in time the old trees grew fewer and the wood closed up in dense undergrowth full of half-dead hawthorns that caught their clothes and tore their hands and faces. The day wore on with a drizzle of rain in the air. They came out into fields where peasants were busy carting corn. Arnvid wanted to make for a farm and buy food, but Gunnar said it was too risky to reveal their presence hereabouts. He kept out of sight of peasants whenever they showed themselves; as for food he said cheerfully that there were plenty of blackberries and plenty of oats to chew when they skirted the edge of a cornfield.

After a while they came to a river across which rose high banks of wood with here and there the red stain of a sandstone cliff. Further back was a bare hill crest.

"Do you know that hill, Astrid?" asked Gunnar.

"I do; it is the Edge of Kinver," she answered. "Near here is the place where I was born and like enough where I shall come to die."

They looked at her questioningly. She had sunk down on the ground and her face was twisted with pain.

"Safer we shall be across the river," said Gunnar.

They found a lonely place and plunged in carrying Astrid between them. The water came to their armpits, but they got through to the other side and began to climb up through the woods. At the top Astrid said she could go no further. She lay down and was soon delivered of a stillborn child.

"This is the worst of misfortunes!" exclaimed Arnvid. He could not bear to look on, but sat apart, his head in his hands. Gunnar did what he could for Astrid.

"I have seen this sort of thing happen before," he said.

"Will she die?" asked Arnvid, looking up, green in the face.

"In time she should be all right, but rest and shelter she should have at once. We must take a chance."

With his axe he cut down and trimmed some saplings and made a sort of litter which they could carry, one in front and one behind. Astrid lay with closed eyes, but when they brought the litter she raised herself on one arm.

"Cheer up, man!" said Gunnar roughly to Arnvid. "A long face will get us nowhere."

"It is not such a small matter, to lose one's firstborn," muttered Arnvid.

"It was not your child, but Torbrand's," said Astrid in a hard, contemptuous voice.

"Torbrand! You let that hound take you! I might have guessed. All along you would have any man rather than me!" He sprang forward with a clenched fist.

"Hold your hand, foster brother!" said Gunnar warningly. "You owe more to Astrid than you know or care to know."

"I have done with her! Do what you like with the bitch!" shouted Arnvid. A gleam of triumph flashed across Astrid's drawn face. Gunnar looked from one to the other. His face also lightened somewhat, then he said to himself: A man's rage is often only a measure of his love. . . . "Help me to lift her up," he said curtly.

"I shall not touch her!"

"Be a man, Arnvid!"

"If you help me, I can manage," said Astrid to Gunnar.

Soon she was on the litter and then, shamefacedly, Arnvid took up one end. Gunnar went first. He steered the way toward a line of sandstone crags where there was a slight haze of smoke.

"There is a nest of outlaws here," he said. "Folk hold that they are some sort of Welshmen, but whether that be true or not they are thieves who come far afield for their booty. They have been at Chaddesley and the steward blamed them for the loss of two heifers in milk. I had some thought of coming to root them out, but now I am glad I did not."

Where the crags began, half a dozen villainous-looking men sprang out of the undergrowth. They made a ring round the litter, drawing knives and raising axes aloft. Their teeth gleamed wolflike through their dirty beards.

Gunnar did not set down the litter, he merely looked at the men with a shade of amusement and said, "Hail friends! We come seeking shelter and can pay you for it. We are outlaws as much as you are."

"What can you pay?" said a man in broken English.

Gunnar and Arnvid lowered their burden to the ground. The men glanced briefly at Astrid, then clustered around the two warriors. Gunnar took a handful of small silver from a pouch.

"This should buy us food and warmth," he said casually. "The woman must be well looked to; she is very sick."

One of the men took the silver and drew apart with the others. They argued together for a few minutes, but Gunnar and Arnvid could make nothing of their speech.

"They may think their best plan is to kill us and take all we have," remarked Gunnar. "Let us be ready with our swords if the worse comes to the worst."

Presently the men were back. They looked narrowly at the two and the weapons they carried, then they smiled and said they would be welcome to such rough fare as they had to offer. Two of them took up the litter and Gunnar and Arnvid walked behind it up a steep path by the foot of the cliffs. Here was a row of caves cut deep into the soft rock and before them on a ledge of filthy ground were groups of women and children, an old man or two, and pigs rooting

in the dungheaps, and snarling dogs, and some woebegone-
looking poultry sheltering from the rain which now came
down heavily. The caves, however, seemed to be roomy and
dry. A fire burned in one and the smoke went up a flue and
out on the cliff face higher up. The folk were inquisitive but
friendly, and here the three wanderers housed in reasonable
comfort.

One day, when Astrid had taken a turn for the better, the
men came in a body to Gunnar—there were now twenty
or more of them. Their leader said, "There is a party of
well-armed folk riding down to the river. Most likely they
are coming here to search for you."

"Likely enough," said Gunnar. "What are you going to
do?"

"We shall all hide in the forest till they are gone. The
women can stay here; they will come to no great harm. But
your woman we can hide under a heap of kindling at the
back of the cave, if you think she cannot be moved."

Gunnar said that it might be best to do so, but that he
and Arnvid would stay nearby. He proposed that they should
conceal themselves in a small cave well up on the cliff face
which could only be reached by a rope from above. Here
no one could get at them, but they could jump down to defend Astrid should she be discovered.

"You are two men of spirit," conceded the outlaw. He
went on the cliff top and helped them down into the cave,
but he did not offer to accompany them. Before long the
riders were dismounting in front of the cave mouths. Gunnar and Arnvid got a brief glimpse of them: there were fifteen and one of them Gunnar recognized as Aldred himself.
From where they lay, flat on the cave floor, they could hear

him putting gruff questions to the women, who answered plausibly enough that two men and a woman had arrived a few days ago, had stayed a night and then gone on westward. By now they might be across the Severn and making towards Powys. The caves were searched without result. No one seemed to notice the little opening higher up, hidden as it was by some bushes that grew out of a crevice in the rock. Soon the riders were making off again in a dispirited fashion, all but two who had started molesting a young girl. They were in the cave in which Astrid lay and after a while they chanced to find her under the sticks. She called out loudly and at once Gunnar and Arnvid slung themselves out and dropped onto the ledge below. With drawn swords they rushed into the cave. Arnvid got in first and killed both men before either they or Gunnar could strike a blow. They had Astrid between them and were on the point of dragging her out. Arnvid was red in the face and shaking with rage. He had saved her, he had been in time again, as he was outside Steintor's hall and on that heath in Powys, but the thought still stung him that he had failed to cut down Torbrand. He turned away sullenly and sat down outside the cave, surrounded by a circle of admiring women and children.

Gunnar sheathed his sword and turned to Astrid.

"You see he still loves you!" he said in a low voice, resigned yet humorous.

"His passion begins to rage again now that I am no longer with child," she said gloomily.

"It is a sickness that afflicts most men, as I know from myself."

His face softened and shone for a moment, like a landscape

bathed in sunshine after rain. She flushed deeply and said in a whisper, "What are we to do?"

"Time will show," he said. "Meanwhile we must deal with these dead men so that their comrades do not find them if they come back." He dragged out the two bodies and told women to wash the floor of the cave. A pool of blood gathered outside, but that was soon licked up by the pigs and dogs. Gunnar gave the clothes and weapons to the women to hide, knowing that the outlaws would be glad of them, but the horses he said he would keep. He led them away deep into the forest, hobbled them and put the saddles and bridles in a hollow tree. When he returned, the outlaws were back again and loud in praise of what had been done. The two bodies had been dumped in the river and all looked as it had been, when four riders came up to the caves asking about the missing men.

"They turned homeward," said an old woman. "They thought there was little point in searching further among these woods and hills." The riders seemed to be of the same opinion. They went off with black looks and curses, kicking their tired horses into a canter.

Chapter 25

LOVE AND DEATH

A WEEK LATER they set out again, Astrid riding one horse
and Gunnar and Arnvid taking turns to ride the other. At
first they kept away from dwelling places, but when they
found that no one in these parts seemed to have heard of the
hue and cry raised by Aldred, they grew more confident and
overnighted with any peasant who would take them in. Even
so the riding was too much for Astrid. She was ill again by
the time they crossed the Watling Street, that hard, raised
ribbon of turf that here went dead straight east and west as
far as the eye could reach. Now, however, they were among
friendlier folk and they stayed ten days in the hall of a hospitable Danish settler midway between the forested hills of
Cannock and the high blue bow of the Wrekin.

While Astrid was well looked after in the women's bower,
Arnvid and Gunnar disputed as to where they should make
for. Chester was near, but now Arnvid had a fancy that they
would be perfectly safe in York There was more chance of

finding a ship for Iceland there, or at least an Orkney ship, and if there were no ships sailing north they could very well winter with Audun.

They were standing outside the hall looking moodily at a wide level landscape full of autumn-tinted trees; outwardly they were calm, but now each had a sharp edge to his temper.

"Audun had little profit from wintering us a year ago," said Gunnar. "We failed against the Westmorings and our mission to Otkel achieved nothing. I have no mind to go back and ask him for bed and board this winter."

"It was you that turned back from the quest for Otkel, not I," said Arnvid provocatively.

"Nothing could have saved him. We were too late."

"Because you dallied at Chaddesley, and much good it did you in the end!"

"When a piece of good luck comes his way a man is a fool not to make something of it. Something I had, though I lost it making a bid for more. You, too, had luck in finding Astrid, but you have little joy of her now."

"Whose fault is that but yours?" Arnvid's voice grew hoarse with rage.

"That is a dangerous thing to say, Arnvid."

"It is true!"

"I have never made love to Astrid."

"I have never known you backward in making love if you fancied a woman."

"Up to now I have never laid a hand on her."

"Perhaps, while she was with child and while she was sick, but what is going to happen now?"

"That is for Astrid to say. No man has much pleasure

with an unwilling woman: a lump of ice is little comfort in bed."

"I say again, but for you we could be happy together. What woman would prefer me to you if she could choose? It is maybe only in my birth that I have any advantage of you—"

"My mother was honorably wedded and she was not a Welsh servant girl!" interrupted Gunnar. Now his voice rose uncontrollably and a red mist floated before his eyes, but suddenly he was calm again. He said, "We do ill to wrangle together, foster brother! I have stood by you all my life and I thought that you could trust me."

"I have learned to trust no man further than I can see him," said Arnvid bitterly.

"At least will you listen to the advice I would give you?"

"I can listen."

"I would say that you should go to Dublin, seek out that man, Asmund, and wed his daughter. It seems she is of good birth and she loves you. There you might surely find happiness and honor."

"And what would you do then?"

"I would wed Astrid and take her to Iceland, if she be willing."

"A good bargain for you and a bad one for me! That is only to be expected when a man offers advice to another. Would you have been content to exchange your hall at Chaddesley for an outlaw's cave? Asmund's daughter is no better than that in comparison to Astrid, and as for Asmund, he had no thought but to use me for his own ends. Never will I put myself in his hands again: a scoundrel if ever there was one!"

Gunnar shrugged his shoulders. "If that plan is not to your liking maybe you have a plan of your own?"

"It is the same as yours."

"Iceland with Astrid—but what if she be not willing? In our country the law lets a woman separate from her husband if she cannot agree with him. Moreover it will be death for you if you return to Iceland. Harek will see to that. Then Geirfin and his sons will seek to avenge you and they will be killed likewise. Your plan is bad in every way, for yourself and others."

Arnvid had a feeling that this was sound sense, and yet he felt that there was another side to it, something that Gunnar did not uncover. He wanted Astrid and Astrid wanted him: that was what lay behind the friendly words, the good advice. Was it possible for him to give up the woman on whom he had set his heart, with whom he had shared all these perils and intimacies, who was now so much a part of his life that without her all his future seemed blank and meaningless? Yet how could he hold her if she were determined to leave him for Gunnar? And then he thought: She was ready to betray me with Cadogan, and she did betray me with Torbrand. Do I mean so little to her that she could let that man have her, that crafty, smooth-tongued fellow who thought of nothing but keeping himself out of harm's way? When did it happen, in Exeter, or even on the ship, perhaps? How blind I was, thinking I could trust her!

Mechanically he followed Gunnar back into the hall. There sat Astrid on a bench, her head bowed, her hands on her lap. She glanced up and he thought how pale she looked and how the beauty had drained out of her face. He saw how her glance slid past him and fastened on Gunnar smolderingly, as a hungry man will look at meat that is denied him. Abruptly he went out again, full of rage and despair. He walked through the yard vaguely aware of cheerful voices and an irregular thudding of flails coming from one of the buildings. All was peace and content here; how different from the ruin and misery he had seen in Wessex. And then he thought of how he and Gunnar had helped in that bad work. Perhaps God had resolved to punish them and so Gunnar had lost Chaddesley and he had lost Astrid, the two most precious possessions that they had won in England. He laughed bitterly. God must surely have weightier business on hand, even as Ethelred and his earls could hardly concern themselves much with taking vengeance on two men out of the thousands who had plundered and killed down there in the south. And yet the priests said that God's eye rested on every man and that none would escape judgment, in this life or hereafter. Here he stood in health and strength, but already feeling the smart of God's anger and soon perhaps to burn in the eternal fire. His heart began to beat heavily, a clammy sweat seemed to be breaking out on his body. Yes, what if it were true, all that the Christians believed? Gunnar was a Christian and he did not seem to be much concerned about it; as for Astrid, he doubted whether she ever gave it a thought. They had their own pattern of life, their own standards, and never seemed to be in doubt about good or evil. They pursued their own aims, steadfast and unafraid. Perhaps they relied on the mediation of Whitechrist in the day of doom. There, out of the darkness of terror, appeared a gleam of hope. At least the priests and monks might be saved; in those great buildings that resounded with the chanting of magic spells, it might be possible to shelter from the wrath of God. Supposing he let himself be baptized and joined some community of monks—would he not feel happier or at least more secure? Even if it were only an illusion, it might be a shield against despair and dread. With this thought in his mind he said nothing when Gunnar announced that evening that he was resolved to ride to Chester, as offering the best chance of getting out of England with the least hardship for Astrid. He had bought a pony for her to ride and he and Arnvid would have the two horses. They could do the journey comfortably in three days.

It was a dull, rainy evening when they came in sight of the red walls of Chester rising above a wide river on which were moored a few ships. Far to the west, outlined against a streak of yellow sky, were the dark hills of Gwynedd, and the chilly wind that met them had a tang of the sea. Gunnar and Astrid's faces were alight with excitement, as though they stood on the threshold of a new and joyful life, but Arnvid sat on his horse listless and withdrawn, aware only of a bell clanging drearily in the town, the bell of the great monastery of Saint Werburgh. There was an inn near the waterside where they got food and sleeping quarters easily enough, for at this season there were few traders going and coming. Gunnar lost no time in making his way to the quay, while Arnvid turned in the opposite direction toward the town.

Some seamen stood about in groups looking meditatively at the ships. Gunnar went up to the first man he met and said casually, "Tell me, friend, who is the master of that stout ship yonder?"

"Sigfrith he is called," said the man, "an Icelander. He and his men are aboard, waiting for a wind to carry them to the north. By the look of the weather they should be able to sail tomorrow."

"The best of luck!" muttered Gunnar to himself. He hailed the ship and Sigfrith stood up on the steersman's platform. He recognized Gunnar and greeted him warmly. A gangplank was put out and Sigfrith came on shore. After they had each given some news of what had passed since they were together in York, Gunnar asked whether there was room for two or three folk to make the passage to Iceland. Sigfrith said that he was not heavily laden and that there was plenty of room. They might as well come aboard now, for it looked as though the wind would soon shift to the south and let them get away. Gunnar hesitated; then he said he had business to to see to first and that he would come to the quay in the morning.

He went back toward the inn and soon saw a cloaked woman coming toward him, ignoring some bantering remarks from the seamen standing around. His heart gave a leap of pleasure to recognize Astrid.

"I could not keep away," she said breathlessly. "I was afraid that Arnvid would come back and find me alone and that there would be hard words spoken between us."

"Perhaps he will not come back. I do not know what he has in mind, but he no longer has any joy in our company."

"No, nor I in his, but I think he is in a mood to do something both desperate and foolish. Let us walk together along the shore, Gunnar. What news have you got among these seafolk?"

"The best news. Here is Sigfrith, an Icelander who brought Arnvid and me in his ship to York. Now he will take us to Iceland, if you be willing."

"It is all the same to me where we go, so long as we are together and apart from Arnvid."

Gunnar stroked his beard. He said: "It was Arnvid's idea to go to Iceland, but maybe I have persuaded him against it."

"If he wishes to sail with Sigfrith we must go elsewhere," she said decisively.

"Aye, well, we can think about that when we know what he decides."

"We must decide for ourselves, Gunnar. Is your heart set on having me to wife, come what may?"

"You know it is; yet I am grieved about Arnvid."

"The time has come for us to think about ourselves."

He laughed. "I think of little else when I see you."

"Then do you notice that we are alone now, and may not be alone again for a long time to come, for I suppose it may be many weeks' sail to Iceland?" She took his hand and turned toward a ruin that stood up just above the tidemark. It seemed to be some sort of tower built of large squared stones. The upper part had been thrown down, but below was an opening into darkness. They looked in and saw bales of cloth and sacks of corn stored under a vaulted roof. A man carrying a sack on his back pushed past them and let it fall within.

"Whose goods are these, friend?" asked Gunnar.

"They are bought by a lord in Gwynedd. I have to keep watch over them till a boat comes to fetch them tomorrow," the man answered, straightening himself up and looking curiously at the handsome warrior and the bright-eyed woman.

"A dull task is yours. Here is something that will buy you ale in the town and meanwhile we two shall keep watch." Gunnar gave the man a silver coin.

"Ha ha! Ho ho!" laughed the man, going off in high good humor.

They watched his figure growing smaller and smaller as it lurched away along the strand. Dusk had fallen, there was no sound save the gentle lap of water on the shore with the incoming tide, the occasional cry of a gull, and the faint tolling of a bell in the distant tower of Saint Werburgh. They went into the vault.

"Now we can end what has tormented us this long while," she said.

"Where there's a will there's a way," he conceded. They began to laugh softly together.

*　　*　　*

It was late when Arnvid came out of the monastery and went down the straight wide street to the watergate. Light showed in the doorways of the timber houses, but here and there were patches of darkness; heaps of slimy rubble overgrown with nettles and shapeless lumps of ruin clasped in ivy, relics of the forgotten city of Roman times. He drew his cloak about him and stumbled on unseeingly, eager yet dreading to find Astrid and Gunnar at the inn, as a hungry man is daunted by an aching tooth. He was coming to bid them farewell, and love still contended with hate for mastery in his mind. They could do what they liked. Tomorrow he would enter the monastery and accept the instruction which would prepare him for baptism. After that would follow a long period of trial as to whether he could fit himself to become a monk. He might be set to labor on the farm or to help the builders who were at work on the church. It was hardly an agreeable prospect, and yet, as in Exeter, he had that sense of awe when he heard the chanting in the great dusky church and further a feeling of being sheltered from all the perils and perplexities of the world without. Illusion, perhaps, but had he not been happier when he had the illusion that Astrid was his and his only? Instinctively a man wanted to know the truth, yet it might be better for him to be sheltered from it. He was both attracted and repelled by the monks with their calm assurance of power, their searching yet not unkindly scrutiny. They had pressed him to stay in the monastery, but after a moment's thought, he had refused, saying he would come again next morning.

He entered the low, smoky hall of the inn and immediately saw Astrid and Gunnar sitting side by side. He saw a look of proud contentment on their faces and a knife seemed to turn in his heart. Then he saw a change come over them, a sudden gravity and watchfulness. He sat down opposite without a word, and when a servant brought him a wooden mug of ale he left it untasted.

"Where have you been, foster brother?" asked Gunnar in a kindly tone, yet Arnvid thought there was a hollow ring in his voice as though it cloaked some deceit.

"To the monastery up in the town," he said shortly.

"Are you turning Christian?"

"Perhaps."

"Afraid of retribution for what we did in Wessex?"

"Retribution has fallen on me already." He looked at Astrid and suddenly he dashed the mug of ale away with his fist.

She got up composedly and said she was going to bed in the loft. He half-sprang up to go with her and then sat down heavily again.

"Sigfrith is here," said Gunnar when Astrid had climbed up the ladder. "He will take us to Iceland, he sails tomorrow if the wind be favorable."

"You mean that you and Astrid will go with him?"

"Aye, but he will take you too, if you be set on it."

"I have done with you both. Go where you will!" said Arnvid roughly.

"You are for the monastery, then?" Gunnar stared at him with a mixture of relief and concern.

"I aim to become a monk. What is there left for me to live for? Everything to which I set my hand and my heart turns against me."

"It is true that Astrid and I have become lovers," said Gunnar gravely. "There was nothing that we could do against it."

"It was to be expected! Naturally a woman who could give herself to a man like Torbrand would not hesitate long to give herself to you." Arnvid clenched his fists so that the knuckles went white.

"You do her wrong, Arnvid! If she had not let Torbrand have her you would not be here now—you would have been dead long since. Willing she was not, but it was the best she could do for you."

"What is that you say? How could it advantage me to be betrayed so shamelessly?"

"Torbrand found she was true to you and he wanted you out of the way. It was only at the price of her body that she hindered him from handing you over to the townsfolk in Exeter as a Dane."

Arnvid sat motionless for a minute. Then he said hoarsely, "Why did you not tell me this before?"

Gunnar flushed darkly, but was silent.

"I will tell you why it was," said Arnvid in gathering rage. "You wanted to poison my thoughts about Astrid, letting me suppose she was no better than a common harlot, so that I might stand aside and leave her to you!"

"I had to let the tide run the way it was going . . ."

"Between you it was planned to tell me that was Torbrand's child, in the hope it would turn my love into hate. Maybe it was my child after all!"

Gunnar shrugged his shoulders. "It might be easier for you to part from Astrid if you hated her—so I thought at the time —yet hate is an ugly thing, Arnvid, and unmanly between man and woman. I did not want it to drive you into being a monk, so I had to tell you the truth. Come, man, there are scores of women as fair as Astrid who would have you as a lover and gladly bear you children. Do not be deceived by those monks who say that flesh is sinful and doomed to burn in fire."

"I brought Astrid alive out of the killing on Saint Brice's Day, she was my dear companion, I want no other woman but her!"

"Even now, when she is mine?"

"Even now. I cannot help it." Arnvid stared morosely at the hacked table between them, littered with bones and gristle.

"You know what this means?" Gunnar got up and stood there, gloomy-faced, with folded arms.

"Aye. Life is out for one of us. There is no other way." Slowly Arnvid rose to his feet. "I see now what my mother read in my hand, when we sat together on the turf outside Harek's house."

"Is any woman worth the shedding of blood between us two? I ask you that, Arnvid."

"If Astrid be not worth it, will you give her up?"

"No. It is too late for that."

"Then fight for her! It rests on you if blood is to be shed. This is all your doing, and now we shall see which of us is the better man!"

"That has ever been in your mind, Arnvid, ever since I can remember anything on Geirfin's land. Well, so be it," said Gunnar defiantly.

They both unsheathed their swords, flung off their cloaks and stepped out onto the floor. Gunnar kicked the logs together on the fire to give a better light and the innkeeper, who had been watching from the end of the room, came running up.

"We want no swordplay here!" he cried threateningly.

"Take yourself off or you will get a taste of the sword yourself!" shouted Arnvid.

The innkeeper went back, slowly and truculently, into a corner and his servants gathered round him.

"Let the bloodthirsty Danes fight it out! A good thing if we could be rid of them both, beastly pagans that they are!" said one man.

The foster brothers stared at each other in the flickering light, they swung their swords and quickly Arnvid dealt a series of sweeping blows, backhand and forehand, but Gunnar parried each as a chess player who knows his opponent's mind and foils his moves, one after another.

"I wage a silver penny on the fair man!" called out an onlooker, but no one answered him.

"Put up your sword and be reasonable, foster brother!" said Gunnar, stepping back.

"This has got to be settled, one way or the other!" Arnvid clenched his teeth and suddenly a frenzy came over him as it had done when he turned on Grim Hareksson. His sword whistled, light as a hazel wand in his grasp, he cut and thrust, now high, now low, he felt an extraordinary sense of power, of certainty that victory was his.

"He fights like a Welshman, but it won't last," said someone.

Gunnar's expression changed, not to fear but rather to dismay. He knew all these tricks of swordsmanship—they had tried them out together long ago by the Breidi Fjord—but he found it harder and harder to ward off this frantic assault. Now he struck back, desperately, with point and edge, but Arnvid countered everything in a flash. He touched Gunnar on the forehead; it was little more than a scratch, but the blood came trickling down and Gunnar gave back another step. Neither man saw Astrid come swiftly down the ladder. Now she stood behind Arnvid, who came on with a rush.

"Take that, and that!" he shouted. Gunnar parried with difficulty, half-blinded by the blood that ran into his eyes.

"You shall not kill him!" screamed Astrid in an agonized voice and forced down Arnvid's sword arm. Gunnar's blade shot out at the same moment and ran deep into Arnvid's breast. Mechanically he drew it out and blood spurted across the room. There was a great shout from the onlookers. Astrid let go and stood away with blazing eyes as Arnvid dropped his sword, tottered for a moment and then fell forward. Gunnar caught him in his arms and dragged him to a bench. He pressed his hand to the wound, he smoothed back the dark, matted locks from the clammy forehead, his face twitched and tears ran down his cheeks mixed with blood. Presently he stood up.

"Is he dead?" asked Astrid in a toneless voice.

"Aye," answered Gunnar somberly.

"It is better so."

"Maybe so. His life was broken and he had little will to live. But it should not have been I who brought him to his end."

"It was my doing, not yours." She took a dishcloth from the table and deftly bound up his forehead.

"What shall I say about this in Iceland?" he muttered to himself.

"Tell the truth and few will blame you," she said.

The innkeeper came forward, followed by his servants. "Now fellows!" he said, "dig a grave and let us get this dead man out of sight." He slid a foot in a pool of blood and said: "The place looks like a butcher's shop."

The servants laid hold of the body, but Gunnar waved them off. He said: "I shall carry him now, as I did many a time when we were boys together."

Torches were brought out and a grave was soon dug in the soft earth of the riverbank. Gunnar closed the dead man's eyes, he stopped up his ears, mouth and nostrils and laid him in the grave with his sword beside him. Next morning he wrenched out a long block of dressed sandstone from the quayside and taking his axe he scratched deeply in runic letters: GUNNAR RAISED THIS STONE TO ARNVID. After some thought he added a small cross in a circle. Astrid looked on, saying nothing. Then between them they rolled the stone up the bank and set it upright in earth at the head of the grave.

After that their eyes brightened a little, they turned away from a group of silent onlookers, lifted their faces to the breeze from the south, and walked hand in hand toward Sigfrith's ship, where men were chanting a song as they hauled up the anchor.

"Life is sweet," she said.

"Sweet enough, Astrid, but it is over for Arnvid. What is there for him?"

"When life is done there is only the remembrance of a man's deeds, his wisdom and folly, and his love," she answered.